TANDEM

Ambridge Summer

Lilian could not help thinking yet again how unlike his father Nelson Gabriel was. There was no trace of Walter's idiosyncratic speech or rough edges in Nelson. He looked both successful and self-satisfied.

'Tell me about the Brigadier's estate,' he said. 'What's the local interest?'

'Ralph Bellamy is after it,' she blurted out.

'That figures,' he retorted, with a trace of a sneer. 'Ralph has always fancied stepping into the Brigadier's shoes, though he might find them a few sizes too large. Is he after the Dower House as well?'

'Especially that.'

'Whatever for? It's far too big for a single person, unless he's thinking of maintaining some of the best traditions of the old randy county set.'

'He's asked me to marry him,' Lilian volunteered, simply.

'Are you going to accept?'

'I don't know,' she answered honestly. 'I really don't know, Nelson.'

Another novel of the Archers of Ambridge in Tandem

SPRING AT BROOKFIELD Brian Hayles

Ambridge Summer

Keith Miles

TANDEM

First published in Great Britain by
Allan Wingate (Publishers) Ltd in 1975

Published by Tandem Publishing Ltd, 1975

Tandem Books are published by Tandem Publishing Ltd
14 Gloucester Road, London SW7
A Howard & Wyndham Company

Printed in Great Britain by litho by The Anchor Press Ltd
and bound by Wm. Brendon & Son Ltd
both of Tiptree, Essex

Chapter One

The habit of command leaves its mark upon a man. It had given the figure on the chestnut hunter that thrust of his jaw and that upward tilt of his head. It had given him that military straightness of spine and that dark, arrogant authority in his eye. It had also endowed him with a voice which, after all these years, could still sound like the report of a pistol.

'Out of the way!'

The placards remained defiantly aloft. They crowded closer to him and were waved more vigorously.

'Stand aside, I say!' Another pistol shot.

The horse backed up and whinnied as if enjoying the display. Its rider did not share its opinion of the various slogans which were being thrust up at him. 'Get back!'

A tall man with a beard and a thin, intelligent face stepped forward. He seemed older than most of the demonstrators. He spoke calmly. 'We're here to register our protest against blood sports.'

'Protest be damned!'

The old man glared down at the demonstrators with unconcealed contempt. They were calling his world in question. His whole life-style was being challenged by these nondescripts. It was an indignity he could suffer no longer. He dug his heels sharply and his horse made a path between the placards and trotted off towards the public house on the other side of the green. Some yelled abuse after him but he was deaf to their taunts.

Demonstrators apart, the scene outside the Bull at Ambridge on that fine April afternoon would have graced a picture postcard. Colours blended superbly. Red or black coats, white breeches, gold buttons, black hats and boots, horses and dogs of varying hues, green grass, and the glistening hunting horns were all framed by the half-timbered beauty of the public house itself. The scene spoke of tradition and country life and social distinction. According to the imperious character on the chestnut, it spoke exclusively of England.

Followers of the Ambridge foxhounds had been gathering together in this same way for countless generations. The placid Hereford bull, who creaked gently to and fro on the inn-sign, had gazed on similar scenes for centuries. He had grown used to that strange mixture of serenity and excitement which distinguishes the preliminaries of the hunt. From his privileged position, the bull had looked down on elegance and alertness and horsemanship. There was no suggestion in what he saw of the cruelty and fear and panic which were proclaimed on the placards at the far side of the green.

'Damned impudence!'

The man on the chestnut caught sight of the demonstrators again.

'What's that, Brigadier?'

He had been joined by a big, powerful man on a grey.

'That!' indicated the Brigadier with a jerk of his head.

His companion laughed and told him not to bother about the protest. One had to consider it as an inevitable part of the hunting scene. People protested against everything these days. For some of them protest was a way of life. It was best to ignore their antics.

'Rubbish!'

The force of the Brigadier's exclamation won him an instant audience. Several conversations were abandoned in mid-phrase. Riders moved in nearer so that they could pay attention to the Brigadier's words. It was not often that the Joint-Masters of the Hunt engaged in open argument. For though the man on the grey had not meant to provoke a row, he now found himself firmly in the middle of one.

'That's as good as agreeing with them!'

'Not at all, Brigadier.'

'Don't talk nonsense!'

'They have a right to protest, if they so wish.'

'Not in my book.'

'Everyone is entitled to his own point of view.'

'Do you call *that* a point of view?' Murder danced in the Brigadier's eyes and his voice took on a lower register. As far as he was concerned, the demonstration was a symptom of all that was wrong with English society. It showed lack of respect. It interfered in personal liberty. It was a sinister political presence. It was a shameful comment on the poverty of some people's lives that they had nothing better to do on an April afternoon.

'Hear, hear!'

The Brigadier's tirade drew many admiring grunts from those around him, though some of the youngest riders merely giggled. The old man concluded his speech by leaning forward in the saddle and speaking directly at his companion. 'I don't care for your attitudes, Bellamy.'

Then he moved abruptly away and began talking to some riders who were waiting near the old village pump.

Ralph looked after the Brigadier, at once annoyed and worried. He was very annoyed at the dressing-down in public which he had just been given and which, for a number of reasons, he had had to take on the chin; but his worry was far greater than his annoyance. He could not fathom out why the Brigadier should speak to him, of all people, like that. Relations between the Joint-Masters had always been very cordial. The Brigadier had always had a rather trenchant way of expressing himself, but Ralph could not recall a time when the older man had aimed so much personal venom at him. Could the Brigadier's strange behaviour be explained by his ill-health?

Observing him carefully, Ralph grew even more concerned. Though he was sitting bolt upright in the saddle and exchanging pleasantries with those around him, the Brigadier was clearly far from well. There was a pinched look in his face, a whiteness, a hint of controlled pain. Ralph chose his moment and then eased the grey up alongside the chestnut.

'Ah, there you are, Bellamy!'

The Brigadier smiled warmly and seemed to have forgotten his fierce words only minutes earlier.

'Splendid turn-out.'

'Yes, Brigadier.'

'And they say hunting is a dying sport. Nonsense!'

'I couldn't agree more.'

'A man needs an invigorating pastime and there's nothing like an afternoon's hunting to set the blood racing. Do you know what that damn fool of a doctor tried to make me do? Put my feet up! Yes – he claims that I ought to take no strenuous exercise at all. As if I could bear to miss a day like this!'

Inwardly, Ralph endorsed the doctor's opinion, knowing that a fox-hunt was a rigorous test for the fittest horseman. The old man read his thoughts and let his temper flare up again.

'What are you staring at, man?'

'To be perfectly honest –'

Ralph's perfect honesty was checked by the other's stern gaze. It was pointless to argue with the Brigadier. Hunting was second nature to him. Nobody could persuade him to give it up. The subject was changed tactfully.

'That rain last night might favour us, Brigadier.'

'Yes. Moisture does wonders for scenting conditions.'

'It could make the going soft in places.'

'Good. We'll have a few mud-bathers.'

The Brigadier's laugh was infectious. Even Ralph joined in. He voiced majority opinion about the Brigadier.

'I'm glad you managed to get here, anyway.'

'Last meet of the season. Had to get here.' The smile vanished. 'You don't think I'd let you be cock of the walk, do you?'

'Well, no . . .'

'I'm not done yet, Bellamy. Take fair warning.'

'About what?' asked Ralph, genuinely baffled.

'You know quite well,' asserted the other. Then, louder, he added, 'Besides, I owe it to the village to get back at a time like this. Ambridge needs to see its squire once in a while.'

'Yes, of course.'

Even though the Brigadier had lived away from the village for some time, and even though he had handed over the running of his Ambridge estate to his niece, he was still looked upon as the nearest thing to the local squire. The Brigadier's place in the village hierarchy was acknowledged by all. Ralph Bellamy was the first to recognise this. In his heart, he was also the first to envy it.

'Hurrah!'

A cheer was set up and Ralph was grateful for the interruption. A plump, efficient-looking woman of middle years had come out of the Bull with a large tray. It was a signal that things were starting to happen. Sensing that they would soon be in the field, the horses pricked up their ears. Beneath the arches made by their legs, the hounds jostled together even more energetically. Riders and well-wishers alike shared the increased excitement. The Brigadier, exuding his customary goodwill once again, was the first to take the stirrup cup.

'Thank you, Mrs Archer.'

'Good hunting, Brigadier!' Peggy Archer's sympathies were with the hunted rather than the hunter, but she had her job to do. As owner and licensee of the Bull, she knew that her personal views were irrelevant at a time like this. A hunt was excellent business.

Ralph Bellamy did not enjoy the stirrup cup. He was too busy brooding about the Brigadier, and had to admit to a surge of resentment against him. It was not that he envied the Brigadier his Ambridge estate. Ralph was himself one of the biggest landowners in the county, and he could give the older man more than twenty years. No, what rankled with him was the social status which the Brigadier enjoyed, the unforced superiority which he had over everyone else and which was reflected in the deferential smiles and agreeing nods of those around him. Now in his middle forties, Ralph was a comparatively rich man. He was a progressive farmer, a shrewd businessman and a natural leader. Yet he remained in the shadow of Brigadier Winstanley. Whenever the latter chose to return to the village, Ralph was reminded very forcefully of this fact.

'Good luck, Mr Bellamy!'

'Mm? . . . oh, thank you.' Ralph managed a smile for Peggy Archer who had come to collect his glass. She looked towards the Brigadier.

'Doesn't look well, does he?'

'I'm afraid he doesn't.'

'Someone ought to keep an eye on him.'

Peggy moved off about her work and left Ralph to ponder. He found that he had elected himself to watch over the Brigadier. There were others in the Hunt with whom he would have preferred to ride – one, in particular – but Ralph felt it was his duty to stay close to his colleague. The grey horse took up its position once more beside the chestnut hunter.

'Quick – look at this, lads!'

'Blimey!'

The workmen on the building site in Manorfield Close caught their first glimpse of the Hunt. They had come from Borchester, the county town. Foxhunting was a complete novelty to them. As the Hunt moved steadily up the main street, the workmen watched with a mixture of awe and derision. The huntsman led the group, and the hounds padded happily along with him. They had got the scent of the chase in their nostrils now and their tails were active. The whippers-in trotted at the heels of the hounds. Ralph Bellamy and the Brigadier were at the head of the procession that followed.

'Stand aside!'

The Brigadier lashed out with his riding crop as a placard

was brandished close to him. Some of the other riders responded to the demonstrators with similar impatience. But most, like Ralph, viewed the protest with good-natured amusement. It was only a brief interruption, after all. Horses run faster than demonstrators.

'Afternoon.'

Ralph nodded to the tall, bearded man who had organised the protest. The latter replied with a wry smile. They had known and respected each other for years. On almost any topic they could chat easily and pleasantly. Foxhunting was the one exception. It put them in opposing camps. The man stood there with quiet dignity, holding his placard. Ralph did not agree with the sentiments behind 'Blood Sports are Organised Torture' but he admired his friend for having the courage of his convictions.

'The old grey mare she ain't what she used to be. . . .'

On the building site, the workmen broke into song. Their refrain was clearly aimed at Ralph's mount. He tipped his hat in acknowledgement. The men laughed and mimed his gesture to each other.

The Hunt moved on and was soon in open country. The last of the demonstrators gave up chasing the horses and turned back towards the green. Onlookers returned to the Bull, their houses or their places of work. In the distance the hunting horn sounded and the last echoes of a bygone age faded away.

Ambridge was no longer a traditional English village at any time in the last few hundred years, going through established rituals. It was a place that belonged unmistakably to the twentieth century. The cottages still had their period charm, the green remained unspoiled, and the church was as fine an example of Norman architecture as it always had been. But the television aerials on the thatched roofs, the new building going on, and the busy garage at the edge of the village testified to the fact that Ambridge was no anachronism. While the Hunt might take some people back into the past, the village was rooted securely in the present.

Such thoughts were far from the mind of Brigadier Winstanley, who was cantering across a field with Ralph Bellamy alongside him.

'Don't crowd me, man!'

'What's that, Brigadier?'

'Stop trying to nurse-maid me!'

Ralph allowed the Brigadier to pull some lengths ahead but he was determined to keep in touch. He had a responsibility to look after the old man, however testy the latter might be. Ralph glanced over his shoulder, but the person for whom he was looking was nowhere to be seen. When he turned back again, Ralph was surprised how far ahead the Brigadier had now gone. The grey had to increase its speed.

The hounds put up a dog fox near the Forest of Am and the hunt was really under way. The fox headed due east, in the direction of Felpersham, with hounds and hunters in frantic and noisy pursuit. Unable to shake off the hounds, the fox doubled back in a wide circle and made for the Forest. There it found all its earths well-stopped and was forced to strike out across open country again. The hounds picked up its line which took it south across the Bellamy estate. Scenting conditions favoured the pursuers and they began to make ground on their quarry.

Twenty minutes of hectic riding had spread the horses out over a distance of a quarter of a mile. Some of the more inexperienced had already come to grief. The most ardent jumpers were not disappointed. Hedge, fence and ditch confronted them at regular intervals. A four-foot stone wall posed special problems and claimed a few victims. A wide brook accounted for three more of the riders. Skill had to be matched with courage at the jumps. Indecision was fatal. Few of the followers of the Ambridge foxhounds actually caught sight of the hounds. Fewer still saw the fox itself. Yet they raced along nevertheless, finding the exhilaration and danger of the chase its own reward.

The Brigadier was riding with the dash of a man half his age. He seemed to have shed his infirmities completely. Ralph had no time to assess the damage which was being done to his land by the Hunt. He was too busy marvelling at the way the chestnut was taken over the most formidable obstacles. The Brigadier set a fine example of fearless riding. He pounded after the baying hounds with a kind of controlled recklessness.

'That's it, Mr Bellamy!'

'Go it. You can catch him!'

From a neighbouring field, two of Ralph's farmworkers shouted encouragement to their employer. Ralph chose his line carefully as a hedge hurtled towards him. The grey went safely over and continued to chase after the Brigadier.

The fox was now tiring and the hounds were beginning to close in. As a last desperate resort, the fox attempted to confuse his pursuers by trotting upstream for a while when he next came to water. The device bought him precious minutes in which to take his bearings. But he was out of luck. No cover offered itself and the hounds picked up his line again. He was driven up a hill towards a thick hedge. In sheer panic, he tried to dive through a gap in the hedge and found himself on a road. The coach driver could not avoid him. When the hounds arrived, they found the remains of their quarry flattened into an absurd profile on the road. It was a kill, but hardly in the best tradition of foxhunting.

'Pig-sticking, Brigadier?'

'Yes. My grandfather swore it was the only test of horsemanship to compare with foxhunting.'

'Very possibly.'

Ralph and the Brigadier were heading back towards the village at a leisurely pace. They had had a full afternoon's sport. After the frustration of losing the first fox to the motor vehicle, the hounds had quickly put up another animal from the covert. There had followed a thrilling chase for over half an hour, at the end of which the fox was run triumphantly to ground. A third fox had provided further sport though it had finally shaken off its pursuers in a wood.

Brigadier Winstanley felt well pleased with the day, though Ralph observed the definite signs of fatigue in his face.

'Of course, there's always stag-hunting.'

'Never tried it.'

'You should, Bellamy. Ireland. County Meath. That's the place for it. Do you know, the ditches there are so deep . . .'

The Brigadier rambled amusingly through the pages of his Hunting Memoirs and, though he had heard all the anecdotes many times, Ralph did not stop him. He was glad that his companion had enjoyed the Hunt but was anxious again because the colour had drained out of the old man's face and his voice had grown wearier.

'Give me your fox every time. Grand animal!'

'And usually too clever by half for a pack of hounds.'

'That's the whole point, man! That's what these blessed banner-carriers can't understand. They think we're just sadists who chase the damn animal so that we can hurt it.'

'Some people imagine that we're just trying to put down a countryside pest.'

'Exactly! Instead, we're sportsmen who have been lucky enough to find a worthy adversary. What is it Surtees says . . . um, the fox should be hunted like a gentleman!'

'And he was this afternoon.'

'To be sure, to be sure.'

The Brigadier became silent, even morose, and Ralph wanted to ask him if he was all right until a glare from the old man vetoed this idea. He waited and hoped that the Brigadier was not as ill as he now seemed to be. For over a quarter of an hour not a single word was spoken.

'There!' announced the old man, as if waking from a dream.

Ralph examined the five-barred gate ahead of them with misgivings.

'We've done enough jumping for one day.'

'It's a challenge, Bellamy. That gate demands to be jumped.'

'Another day,' suggested Ralph. 'The horses are tired.

Besides, the ground is too soft and treacherous.'

'Call yourself a horseman?'

No matter what arguments he advanced, Ralph found the other proof against them. Ralph's protests were having the same effect on him as the protests of the demonstrators earlier in the afternoon. They simply hardened the Brigadier's resolve and invited his ire.

'Stop trying to mollycoddle me!'

'There's a gap in the hedge further along.'

'For amateurs. Now – you jump first.'

Ralph was brought up with a jolt. The Brigadier was not only insisting on tackling a difficult jump himself. He was seeing the whole thing in competitive terms. It was almost as if the long period of silence had been a deliberate rest, a summoning up of his strength for this final test. Ralph was uneasy at the idea of being pitted against the old man for no apparent purpose. Why did the Brigadier want them to compete?

'Very well. I'll show you how it's done.'

'But there's no point,' urged Ralph.

'There's every point.'

The chestnut was made to turn round and trot back twenty yards or so, giving the Brigadier a good long run at the gate. Ralph lifted an arm to halt the Brigadier. The response he got was hardly what he expected.

'That girl. From the Bull. Too young for you.'

It was an odd remark, all the more so for being barked out like a command. Ralph was quite bemused for a moment. Thoughts which had been swimming around in his own mind had been put into words by someone else. The experience was unnerving. How had the Brigadier guessed? Did Ralph wear his heart so openly on his sleeve? What was more to the point – was the Brigadier right?

'Come on, boy!'

When Ralph jerked himself out of his reverie it was too late. The chestnut and its rider were almost upon the gate, and tragedy was at hand. A soundless cry formed on Ralph's lips. The horse gallantly attempted the gate, lost its purchase on the muddy ground, connected awkwardly and solidly with wood, and hurled its rider sideways. The Brigadier's head struck the gatepost with a thud, and he lay quite motionless. The horse recovered its legs and looked about it rather balefully. Ralph dismounted and rushed to see if he could do anything. The Brigadier was beyond help.

The announcement of the death of Brigadier Rowland Winstanley caused sorrow and regret throughout the village of Ambridge. Older residents, who had known him from the time when he had bought the Lawson-Hope estate and settled in the area, spoke about his warmth and his gift of enthusiasm. Others talked about his distinguished army career, revealed to the village for the first time in the generous obituaries carried by the newspapers. Some drew comfort from the fact that the Brigadier must have died happily. Foxhunting was his first love. There could be no more fitting way for a man like that to go. All agreed that the Brigadier would be sorely missed in the village. Whatever his faults, and however infrequently he had visited Ambridge of late, the Brigadier was much loved and respected. With his death an important value passed out of the community.

Nobody was more aware of this than Ralph Bellamy. As the Brigadier lay dying in hospital, Ralph was a prey to a series of conflicting emotions. Guilt, remorse, helplessness, fear and anger tracked him down with the relentlessness of a pack of hounds. There seemed to be hope of escape for Ralph, no possibility of survival. Then the news came from the hospital. The Brigadier had died without regaining consciousness. Suddenly Ralph knew what he had to do to shake off the thoughts which were biting at his heels.

He went straight to his stables, saddled the grey and rode out across his estate. In the gathering dusk he found what he was looking for and addressed himself to his task. His legs spoke sharply to the horse and they galloped towards their objective. Ralph waited for the crucial moment then threw himself up and forward. The grey rose magisterially. It rapped something with its hooves but held its balance. Horse and rider landed safely and pulled up to a halt. Behind them stood a five-barred gate.

Ralph Bellamy had jumped the first necessary hurdle in his bid to take the place of the Brigadier.

Chapter Two

As soon as she saw it, lying there on the mat, her heart sank. For some minutes she was quite unable to move or think, and then a voice from upstairs released her from her paralysis.

'Are you down there, Poll Doll?'

'Coming,' she muttered to herself.

Polly Perks bent down and picked up the crumpled brown envelope with its familiar handwriting, and the guilt stirred within her. On impulse she decided that she would tear the letter up, and not allow it to hurt her in this way.

Her husband's voice made her pause long enough to change her mind, and she slipped the letter into the pocket of her housecoat.

'I'm just getting the milk!' she called.

Unlocking the door, she opened it to retrieve the two pint bottles on the step, and then closed it again, leaning against it. She began to wonder what she should do and found her thoughts getting more and more confused. The voice shouted down the stairs for the third time of asking, and it now brought a headless body with it.

'Where are you, love?'

'Just coming.'

'Watch this, then. Ready?'

Sid Perks was trying to force his head through the neck of his working shirt without undoing the top buttons. Normally, she would have chided him and warned him that he could sew on any dislodged buttons himself. But this was no longer a normal morning and Polly hardly noticed his performance.

'And here he comes – wait for it, please – the latest of the emergent nations to emerge – Sidney Perks!'

The curly head popped out of the shirt on cue and the button remained intact. Sid grinned broadly at his triumph. He licked his index finger and marked up a score on an imaginary blackboard. Polly did not oblige with her usual indulgent smile at his clowning, and he felt cheated. He pulled his collection of funny faces at her, but still gained no response. He ruffled his hair, hunched his shoulders and bent double so that his loose cuffs trailed on the ground. His ape routine never failed.

'I'll get the breakfast,' said Polly, climbing the stairs and walking past him.

She loved Sid very much but there were times when his playfulness and eternal grin could be very irksome.

'Uh, any mail, Poll?'

He followed her into the living room above the shop, tucking his shirt into the top of his trousers.

'No,' she replied, busying herself in the small kitchen.

'Funny. Could have sworn I heard the letter-box.'

'It must have been the wind.'

'But I never suffer from it,' quipped Sid, supplying a laugh to his own joke. 'Ah, well, not to worry,' he added, philosophically. 'That fifty thousand quid which some rich uncle is dying to leave me will probably come in tomorrow's post. How would you fancy that, then? Being married to a man of means?'

But Polly was not in a conversational mood. She prepared the food, served it, then sat brooding. Sid fell back on his impersonation of a parrot.

'Pretty Polly. Pretty Polly.'

An involuntary smile flitted across her face. She tried to pull herself together, take a more positive attitude towards the day.

'Are you still working at Mrs Turvey's?' she asked.

'Yes. Worse luck. Honest – the old dear's taste in wallpaper. Diabolical. I have to hang it with my eyes shut.'

Sid's work as an interior decorator was the latest in a long line of things which had somehow not fulfilled their initial promise. Polly was troubled by his inability to find a job which really satisfied him. It was not that Sid was unhappy. Far from it. His cheerful readiness to undertake each new job was what worried Polly most. It led him into all kinds of blind alleys. The letter in her pocket brought these anxieties into focus and prompted the next remark.

'Sid, why don't we leave Ambridge?'

'Leave?' he gasped.

'You might get a proper job somewhere else.'

Even as he spoke the words, Polly knew that they carried no conviction. Sid assured her that he already had a proper job. He pointed out that she had always hated the idea of moving to a town. He reminded her how much she enjoyed running the Village Stores.

It was all true. Polly liked the life in Ambridge immensely. She loved its slower pace, its gossip, its many eccentricities. To let anything frighten her away would be a mistake. Besides, where could they run?

'Wonder who'll buy it?' mused Sid, spooning sugar into his tea.

'What?'

Polly was miles away. Sid added a new impersonation to his repertoire, achieving instant effect as an alarm clock.

'Brrrrring! Awake now? Good. I was talking about the Brigadier's estate.'

It was less than a month since the fatal accident at the five-barred gate and Lady Isobel, shocked by the death of her uncle, and having no reason to maintain the Ambridge connection, had decided to auction off the property which she had inherited. The Dower House, one of the most imposing houses in the district, was to be sold along with a thousand acres of farming land.

News of the auction had sparked off great speculation in the village, with the tenant farmers on the estate particularly anxious to know who their new landlord would be. Rumours of all kinds were rife and Polly had been as interested as anyone to discuss them.

'If *I* was to take the Dower House in hand . . .' boasted Sid.

'I don't want to hear about – '

'Listen, will you! Be educated.'

He conducted her through each room, decorating it and filling it with furnishings and fitttings. In his freewheeling fantasy, Sid was as much the local squire as the Brigadier had been, and he was determined that he and Polly would set the tone for the whole county.

'What about that, then?' he concluded. 'I'd keep you in a style to which you were not accustomed.'

'Have you seen the time, Mr Dower House?'

'Yes, it's only . . . Stone me!'

The erstwhile squire leapt out of his chair, downed the remains of his tea in one fearsome gulp, grabbed his overalls, kissed Polly and charged out. Mrs Turvey was a strict timekeeper who made no allowances for potential owners of the Brigadier's estate.

Polly herself had no leisure to sit and think, and it was nearly nine by the time she had dressed and cleared away. She was soon serving the wide variety of items which the Village Stores carried. She took orders for groceries, sold toys, magazines and nylon tights, and obliged Peggy Archer with some hair lotion and some cough mixture. Polly was even able to accomodate the boys who came in for a fishing net, a puncture outfit and a packet of chewing gum. It was almost lunchtime before she could turn her attention to the letter. She retrieved it from where she had placed it beneath the counter and examined the spidery scrawl on the envelope once again. She opened it and read it with an air of defeat. It said exactly what she had expected. Word for word.

The postman, whose early morning delivery had caused quiet anguish for Polly Perks, had been kinder to Ralph Bellamy. Amongst a large mail which found its way to the Bellamy house was a communication which Ralph had been awaiting for days. He had read it avidly. He had taken out his Ordnance Survey map and pored over it with renewed interest. He had spent over an hour at his desk, making calculations, consulting documents, finalising details. Then he had made several long telephone calls, speaking to his broker, his bank manager and his solicitor with especial urgency.

Weeks of immobility and suppressed hope had suddenly given way to a frenzy of activity. When his mind was made up on something, Ralph could move with speed and assurance. As he lunched alone, he picked up the brochure again and flipped through it. Two phrases caught his eye. The first was in brackets and was below the announcement that the property was For Sale by Auction in May. Ralph was going to investigate all the potentialities of 'unless previously sold'.

As soon as he thought about the Dower House, Ralph heard those last words of the Brigadier's again. Was he too old for her? They were separated by all of twenty years. Many people might consider that an impossible gap. Did she? Ralph got up from the table and walked to the mirror above the fireplace. He appraised himself critically. Though broad and big-boned, he carried no excess weight. He had always taken pains to keep relatively fit. His hair might be thinning slightly and the lines in his face were getting more pronounced, but he still had much to recommend him. Many women found him attractive, no question about that. Was she among them? Could the Brigadier's verdict be wrong?

Ralph went back to the brochure, which had been rushed out by the estate agents at such short notice. The second phrase which had haunted him now captured his attention once more. It made his desire to buy the Dower House even greater. For the first time in all his life Ralph Bellamy wanted an Ideal Family Residence. At all costs.

'Might be late tonight, Poll Doll.'

'What's that, Sid?'

'You're not listening,' complained her husband through a mouthful of custard tart. 'Tonight. Darts match at the Bull. Might be late.'

'Oh yes . . .' murmured Polly, picking at her own lunch.

'Look, are you sure you're okay?'

'Quite sure.'

Polly was evasive. Under pressure from Sid, she conceded that she felt tired. He urged her to rest that afternoon, which was half-day closing. Polly shook her head.

'Then get out somewhere, love,' he suggested. 'Blow the cobwebs away.'

'I've got to see Mum.'

'Better you than me,' he chuckled.

'Sid . . .' she warned.

'*After* you've done your weekly penance at your mum's, I meant. Go out. Nip over to the Dower House, maybe. See if it's what we really want.'

Polly looked across at Sid with a mixture of fondness and sadness. She hated having to deceive him in this way, but she had no choice. Sid must never know. It was the one thing which was guaranteed to remove the grin from his face.

'Well, back to the grindstone,' he sighed.

'Is Mrs Turvey pleased with what you've done?'

'I should blooming well hope so. There's real skill in hanging a wallpaper you daren't even look at . . . still, I must be off.'

He kissed her on the cheek and went off down the stairs. His voice sailed up from below.

'Don't forget what I said. Take yourself out. Why not dig that old bike of yours out of its mothballs? Just the weather.'

The slammed door confirmed his departure.

As she did the washing up, Polly found herself preoccupied by the letter. It must not take over her life so completely. When she finished her jobs, she found some writing paper and scribbled a few lines on it before slipping her reply into an envelope. She had a bath, changed her dress and went out into the sunshine. Once she had dropped her letter into the post box immediately outside the shop, she felt relieved. At least she had taken some action.

'Have another cup, Polly.'

'No thanks, Mum. I really don't – '

'There's plenty here,' said Mrs Mead, pouring more tea into both cups. 'Help yourself to sugar, dear.'

Polly's mother was a small, red-faced, bustling woman who found it very difficult to relax for more than a few minutes. Even as they were talking, she was on the move, plumping cushions, crossing to peep at the golden hamster in the cage by the window, generally tidying up the small living room in her bungalow. When Polly tried to take her leave, the other looked quite offended.

'But you've only just arrived.'

'I know, Mum, but – '

'Try one of these,' she urged, whisking the lid off a cake tin. 'I made them special. They're your favourites.'

Mrs Mead belonged to that generation of mothers who feel that they have failed in their duty if their children are not constantly having food thrust at them. To oblige her mother, Polly took one of the cakes and nibbled at it without relish. The older woman went over to the cage.

'Benjy loves them, too, don't you, Benjy?' she said, crumbling a cake and feeding it through the bars. 'Yes, I wasn't going to forget you, Benjy.'

The hamster's nose twitched by way of appreciation and it made short work of the new rations.

Polly's regular Thursday afternoon visits meant a great deal to her mother, and she did not want to upset her by leaving; but the uneasiness which she had felt all morning was stronger than ever, and it was visible in her face.

'Everything all right?' asked her mother, solicitously.

'Of course.'

'Nothing . . . troubling you, is there?'

'Nothing in particular,' she lied.

'Is it Sid?' questioned her mother, sharply.

Polly shook her head. Mrs Mead lowered her voice and accentuated its soft Somerset tones.

'You look a bit off colour, that's all. . . . You haven't got anything to tell me, have you?'

'No, Mum!'

Polly regretted the firmness with which she spoke, as her mother's face crumpled a little.

'Give us time, Mum. You know what they say about a watched pot.'

Her mother nodded, smiled, fed another section of cake through the bars of Benjy's cage, and chatted about the weather. Eventually, Polly was able to get away. She felt sorry for her mother, living all alone as she did and taking a rather restrained part in village life. But it was impossible to stay too long with Mrs Mead. The feelings of guilt which had stirred in Polly earlier on were beginning to overwhelm her in that room.

Polly returned to the shop, walked around to the rear of the premises, and rescued an old bicycle from beneath a tarpaulin. Once the tyres had been pumped up, the handlebars straightened and the seat cleaned, the machine looked quite inviting. Polly was soon pedalling through the village. She rode out into the country with no destination in mind. Simply to enjoy the fresh air and the sense of freedom was enough. It was only when she had to swerve to avoid a tractor near Grange Farm that she realised where she was going. Whether by accident or design, Polly was on the road which led to the Brigadier's estate near Heydon Berrow.

She had often seen the Dower House in passing but she had never really stopped to look at it properly. Now her curiosity was aroused and she began to pedal faster, getting up some speed to climb the steep hill which was ahead of her. From the top of this hill she had her first view of the house and she understood why it was so much admired, and why it had set Sid's imagination racing.

The Dower House was a large, striking building which stood in a couple of acres of garden. Polly knew enough about architecture to identify it as early Georgian, though she could place no date on it. As she rolled down the hill with the wind in her face, she wished that she was with someone who could explain all the features of the house to her, some expert like John Tregorran who could help her to appreciate the place in the way it obviously deserved.

Braking to a halt near the drive gates, she parked her bicycle against the fence, then saw that she was not the only visitor. Further along the drive, holding the reins of the horse from which she had just dismounted, was an attractive girl in her early twenties. The girl took off her riding hat and ran a hand through her long, fair hair as she gazed up at the house. The horse began to crop the grass.

Polly was about to hail the girl when the sound of a car horn made her start back from the gateway. A Range Rover turned slowly into the drive with Ralph Bellamy at the wheel. He raised a hand to thank Polly, adjusted the pipe in his mouth, and then drove on. She now found herself witness to a rather puzzling scene, which was enacted in mime because they were out of earshot.

The Range Rover screeched to a stop near the fair-haired girl and Ralph jumped out quickly and greeted her. In reply to whatever question he was asking, she pointed towards the house. He seemed to be suggesting that she went with him, but the girl shook her head and laughed. She pointed to the horse, put on her hard hat again, then mounted the animal in one easy move. Ralph patted the horse in order to detain her, then repeated the invitation with a gesture towards the house.

Polly felt that she was intruding on a private moment, but somehow she could not look away. What surprised her was the man's obvious nervousness. Though impressed by what Ralph was, she had always thought him rather cold and unapproachable; yet here he was looking very embarrassed by the girl's refusal and starting after her with some annoyance as she began to trot away.

At this point, he saw Polly at the gateway and realised that she had been watching all the time. It made him move smartly towards the car, jump in and drive off. The horse, meanwhile, made its way steadily towards Polly and its rider seemed to have treated the whole incident as something of a joke.

'Hello, Polly. Fancy a tour of the Dower House?'

'I'd love one!'

'Catch Ralph up. He'll show you round. Just offered to take me over the place.'

'Why didn't you accept?'

'I'm not dressed for that kind of thing. Besides, I'll never have a chance to live in a house like that. It would be silly to let myself get carried away with it.'

'Thought is free,' argued Polly.

'I get interested in things,' said the other. 'No, I'm much better off resisting the temptation . . . Cheerio.'

She set off at a canter, leaving Polly to ponder on what had happened, and to realise that it had actually made her forget the letter. Temporarily.

'But you can't, Polly!' protested Sid.

'I'm sorry.'

'It's all arranged.'

Sunday morning. It had taken Polly three days to get round to telling Sid. She had worked it out carefully. Sunday afternoon was the only possible time. The first cricket match of the season would keep Sid occupied for at least four hours. Just long enough.

'I said that you'd help with the teas,' he explained.

'Next week, Sid.'

'But I may not be picked next week. Let's face it, I'm only in the team to make up the number.'

Sid Perks was an enthusiastic rather than an accomplished cricketer. He had no illusions about himself. It was his willingness to run in the outfield which had earned him a place in the Ambridge XI. His highest score as a batsman was three runs.

'Not this week, love. Please. I really don't feel well.'

'Maybe you'll pick up by lunchtime.'

'I must take it easy this afternoon. I must.'

A look came into Sid's eye. Like his mother-in-law, he was nourishing some tentative hopes. Polly put paid to them. She was a little run down. Nothing more.

It was a dejected Sid who collected his cricket togs into his bag. Polly kissed him gently on the forehead and his spirits rose.

'Wait till I tell the lads!' he chortled.

'What about?'

'Dark deeds in the Dower House drive. As seen by Polly Perks.'

'Now don't you go spreading any scandal, Sid.'

'Me?' he grinned. 'Would I do a thing like that?'

Polly knew the way that Sid could turn the most innocent of facts into a vivid, technicolor story and she had no wish to be seen as the one who had started that story.

'Just keep it between the two of us,' she urged.

'I always knew Ralph Bellamy was a dark horse. These middle-aged bachelors are the worst.'

'He's not middle-aged,' she defended. 'Well, not really. In his own way, I think he's rather handsome.'

'With a very handsome cheque book. Amazing how dashing a bloke can look if his bank balance has got a big smile on it.'

'It's not only that, Sid!'

'Don't tell me that he turns you on! I've seen marble statues with more sex appeal.'

'You always think I mean *that*,' she complained.

'Hope springs eternal. . . .'

Remembering that she had pleaded tiredness, she gave up the argument and sat back heavily in the chair, letting Sid boast about what the Ambridge team would do to the Penny Hassett XI that afternoon. As he was about to leave, he made one more effort.

'If you do feel any better – '

'I'll join you there,' she promised.

'If you want me to slip back between innings . . .'

'No, no. I'll . . . probably be asleep.'

'In that case, I'll love you and leave you.'

He went out whistling and she waited till she heard the door bang downstairs before crossing to the window to watch him go. Then she rushed to the bedroom, brushed out her auburn hair, fastened it at the back with a slide, then went to take out her best suit from the wardrobe. Within minutes she was quite ready.

She paced the room impatiently, checking her watch and trying to work out how long it would take Sid to walk to the cricket ground. It would be perfectly safe and he would never find out – yet what if he did? The implications of what she was doing suddenly struck home and made her hesitate and reconsider. She weighed the conflicting loyalties and decided that she had to go through with it now, having committed herself in writing. Whatever the penalties, she had to see him this afternoon and get it over with for good.

Sid Perks was a popular character in the changing room at the cricket ground, where his fund of jokes always found a ready audience. As he speculated about Ralph Bellamy and the Dower House, he was in good form and had his teammates roaring with laughter. Forgetting all of Polly's warnings, he gave his imagination free rein and soon had the house equipped with a harem, a gambling casino and several bars.

'Crawling with bunny girls, of course,' he added, 'and I bet old Bellamy won't give *them* a touch of myxomatosis!'

There was a good response to all this, for Ralph was not popular, and then someone asked after Polly.

'She's not up to the mark this afternoon.'

'Sorry to hear that, Sid.'

'Yes, she's hoping to grab a spot of shuteye,' he said fondly, then started to explore a new vein of humour about Ralph.

A quarter of a mile away Polly found a seat on the bus and asked for a ticket which would take her some distance away from Ambridge and a long distance away from Sid.

Chapter Three

It was enough to make a horse laugh. Or so Red Knight seemed to think. He whinnied appreciatively and pranced about. Lilian Nicholson could contain her own mirth no longer. She burst into laughter. He looked up and saw them for the first time.

'What's so funny?' he demanded, reddening.

'You are,' grinned Lilian.

To be laughed at in this situation was bad enough. To be mocked by an older sister was unbearable. Tony Archer returned to his task with greater determination.

'It's a two-man job,' opined Lilian.

'I can manage,' he said, through gritted teeth.

'So I see.'

A fresh peal of laughter goaded him on to more strenuous efforts. He cornered the cow at the far end of the yard, cut off its retreat when it tried to double back up towards the milking parlour, then moved in towards it. The cow looked around, saw no way out and appeared to concede defeat. It drooped its head. Tony was relieved, but not out of the wood yet. He still had to coax the animal into the pen. He tried kindness.

'Come on, Katie, old girl. Come on, Katie,' he sang softly.

Katie was all obedience. She was quite docile now and allowed Tony to guide her with his stick towards the open door of the pen. He kept talking gently to the cow, delighted at the response he was getting. This would wipe the grin off his sister's face.

'That's it, old girl. In you go . . . in you go.'

Katie stopped at the door of the pen and inspected her new

quarters. They were not satisfactory. She served herself an eviction notice.

'Hey, come back!' yelled Tony, chasing after her.

But Katie had got her second wind now and was really enjoying the game. Whenever Tony came within a few yards of her, she accelerated with ease, dodging his stick and ignoring his imprecations. It was clear that Katie could keep this sort of thing up for a lot longer than he could. Tony leaned on the fence, breathing heavily. To be bested by a Friesian cow in the presence of his sister was a rather humiliating experience. Especially for a young man who had ideas of specialising in the dairy side of farming.

Lilian dismounted and removed her riding hat. She brushed back her fair hair and put her elbows on the fence.

'Katie's not playing ball, is she?' Lilian smiled.

'No, she'd rather play silly beggars,' snorted her brother.

Tony was taller and darker than his sister, but had the same slim build and open face. In his case that face was glistening with perspiration. He passed a forearm across his brow. Lilian took pity on him.

'Let me help you,' she offered, ascending the fence.

'Oh no!' he insisted.

'Why not?'

'Just leave it to me, Lilian, that's all I ask. It's my job not yours.'

She shrugged her shoulders and stayed on her side of the fence. Red Knight nuzzled up against her cheek. She patted his neck.

'What do you want Katie in the pen for, anyway?' she enquired.

'It doesn't matter,' he snapped dismissively.

'But I'd like to know.'

Her tone was pleasant and the mocking grin had disappeared. Tony was slightly mollified.

'She's been a naughty girl. Sucking. I want to put a plate on her.'

'And she's got other ideas.'

'Can't blame her. I suppose,' sighed Tony. 'She's been in all winter. I only turned 'em out a fortnight ago.'

'Does she know why she's here?'

'Yes. Cows are not that stupid. When you isolate them from the herd, they know something's up.'

She encouraged him to talk about his job because she knew it was the best way to make him cool down. Tony loved his cows as much as she loved horses, and he could discuss them for hours without a trace of boredom.

'No, if I let her get away with it, we'll have all sorts of trouble. She'll unsettle the herd, cause a lot of sore teats, impair the milk yield. . . . This is the only answer, I'm afraid.'

He held up a flat metal disc a few inches in diameter.

'How would you fancy one of these through your nose?'

'No, thank you!'

'It should cure Katie's bad habits. Won't stop her lifting the grass or chewing the cud, but it'll keep her away from the udders' udders!'

'You know a lot about dairy farming,' she grinned. 'Why don't you go in for it?'

'I might at that,' he laughed. 'When I've finished looking after all these cows!'

His anger had now vanished and he had forgotten all about it.

'What are you doing over this way?' he asked. 'You don't usually exercise Red Knight near Manor Court Farm.'

'Ralph won't mind, will he? After all, he did buy the horse for me.'

'That's nothing. He bought eighty cows for me!'

'Oh well, if you're going to pull rank . . . but what I came to see you about was your invitation.'

'Oh that . . .' he muttered.

'If the offer still holds, I'll accept. I'd love to go to the Y.F.C. dance on Saturday.'

'Oh, would you?' he said, dully.

Tony was on the committee of the local Young Farmers'

Club and was the driving force when it came to social events, loving nothing more than to organise dances. This time, however, Lilian could see that his enthusiasm had waned.

'I know that it was Dad's idea,' she explained. 'He twisted your arm to ask me because he thought the dance might "take me out of myself", whatever that means.'

'Well, no, I was going to ask you, anyway,' offered Tony, gallantly.

'Tell that to Katie,' she grinned. 'Anyway, I won't be there to cramp your style, so don't look quite so downhearted.'

'Eh?'

'I only expect to be taken *to* the dance. I daresay you'll find someone a bit more interesting than me to take home.'

'In that case,' he said, brightening, 'we'd better fix a time for me to pick you up. Eight?'

'On the dot. And thanks.'

'It uh . . . it gets a bit wild sometimes,' he warned her.

'I know what Young Farmers' Dances are like.'

'A lot different to some of those pukka efforts Ralph's taken you to.'

'I was only part of the scenery at those. On Saturday, I want a chance to let my hair down.'

She put her foot in the stirrup and mounted Red Knight again.

'Talking of Ralph, what's all this about you and him at the Dower House?'

'I don't know what you mean – '

'Sid Perks was going on about it. Yes, according to him, you and – '

'I shouldn't listen to Sid Perks if I were you,' interrupted Lilian sharply.

'But Polly saw you and Ralph – '

Tony got no further. Lilian waved her goodbye and rode off. Tony was annoyed with himself for having frightened his sister away like that. He was very keen to discuss the subject of Bellamy's interest in the Brigadier's estate. Lilian might have been able to clarify a few things for him. Tony Archer had worked for Ralph Bellamy at Manor Court Farm ever since he had left school. His employer had even sent him away for a year to the Walford Farm Institute, and took a keen interest in his progress. If Bellamy was going to enlarge his farming enterprise, it would have a direct bearing on Tony's job.

He remembered what he was doing in the yard and turned back to the unco-operative Katie. A surprise was in store for him. Thinking better of her earlier decision, Katie had investigated the pen and taken to it as a temporary home. She was standing inside, surveying Tony with large, soulful eyes. He ambled across, then closed and bolted the door. He smiled gratefully at Katie.

'I knew you'd get round to it in the end.'

Ralph Bellamy was not finding the purchase of the Dower House as straightforward a transaction as he had hoped. His agent had assessed the property carefully and Ralph had made what he considered to be a very fair offer. He had been confident that Lady Isobel Lander, embarrassed as she was by the need to pay sizeable death duties, would accept his offer. But this was not so. Lady Isobel had retired to her house in Sussex and the sale of the property was in the hands of a firm of estate agents from Borchester.

Ralph was having great difficulties with the firm of Wiley, Smith and French. He had grown impatient of working through his own agent and had decided to take the matter in hand himself. This brought him into direct contact with Stephen Wiley, an ambitious and self-opinionated young man, who was responsible for the sale. He and Ralph were like oil and water. Ralph found him bumptious and unhelpful, a hustler with a public school accent. For his part, Stephen was not going to be pressured by anyone into an early decision to sell. He was convinced that an auction would fetch the best price for the property. Interviews between the two men tended to be short and abrasive.

'What does Lady Isobel think of my offer?' demanded Ralph on one of his calls at the Borchester office.

'We have advised our client that it is unacceptable,' said Stephen smoothly.

'I want her views, not yours!' blustered Ralph.

'Our client is guided by us,' retorted the other.

Ralph took a deep breath, and tried to suppress his anger.

'Mr Wiley, all that I wish to know is this: will Lady Isobel agree to sell the Dower House separately?'

'That's out of the question, I'm afraid.'

'But why? Are you sure you've discussed it with Lady Isobel?'

'Naturally,' replied Stephen. 'I've discussed *all* the offers we have so far received for the property. You're not the only person in the hunt, you know.'

Ralph was getting very irritated. It was time to leave. He would have to think again.

'If Lady Isobel does change her mind –' he began.

'I shouldn't bank on that, Mr Bellamy,' warned the younger man.

Ralph thanked him curtly for sparing his time then left the office at speed. If he was to make any headway in the purchase of the Dower House, it would not be with the blessing of Stephen Wiley. There was only one course of action open to him.

Lilian Nicholson relaxed in her bath and wondered what to wear that evening. It was a long time since she had been to a local Young Farmers' Dance, but she remembered them as rather boisterous affairs. She must choose something light and thin. It would get very warm in the Village Hall. Mentally flicking through her wardrobe, she came to the most suitable garment. Then she recalled the occasion for which it was bought and put it back on its hanger. There were some memories with which she had still not come to terms.

Her hair imposed problems of choice as well. When she had got out of the bath, dried herself and dressed, she sat down in front of the mirror and experimented with various styles. First, she put her hair up. It made her look too old and she was already skirting the upper age limit of the Young Farmers. She tried plaits, but they only looked ridiculous. A single plait was more effective but seemed to need a more formal occasion than the one she was going to. She let her hair hang loose, but that was not the answer either. Finally, she opted for a pony-tail.

'Your hair looks nice,' complimented Tony.

'Thanks,' she said. 'You're early.'

'Force of habit,' he laughed.

Tony had arrived at her cottage at Hollowtree Flats a good twenty minutes before the time arranged with Lilian. He reeked of after-shave lotion and had been too liberal with the hair cream as well. His head positively shone. A light blue suit completed the transformation of the young farmer into the potential playboy.

'Thought we should call in on Mum and Dad first,' explained Tony, adjusting his tie in a mirror.

'Fine. Give me two minutes,' said Lilian, slipping back into the bedroom.

She collected some things into her handbag then inspected her hair once again. It was a rare achievement to wrest a compliment from her brother. As she was about to leave, she noticed the framed photograph on the dressing-table. Lilian paused for a moment, then crossed to turn the photograph face down. He would prefer it that way. He would not want to inhibit her at all.

'Do you have to go around and check all the locks?' asked Tony, as they left the cottage.

'Of course not, silly,' chided Lilian.

'But you're supposed to be the caretaker here, aren't you?'

'There are caretakers and caretakers,' she said. 'And I'm not one of the kind you're thinking about.'

'I stand corrected,' grinned Tony. 'Hop in.'

His sports car was soon making the short journey between Hollowtree Flats and the Bull.

As soon as they walked into the lounge bar, Lilian felt slightly guilty. She often helped behind the bar on a Saturday night. Yet this evening, when the place was exceptionally busy, Lilian was leaving her mother in the lurch. Peggy Archer had no objection to this. Though in the middle of serving a customer, she managed a smile and a quick word.

'Have a nice time, love,' she called.

'Thanks, Mum,' nodded Lilian.

'What are you having?' asked Tony.

'Let me get them,' decided Lilian, stepping behind the bar.

'Oh no, you don't,' interrupted Peggy. 'You belong on that side tonight.' She disposed of a few more customers and was soon ready to serve her own children.

'How's Dad today?' enquired Tony.

'Much as usual,' sighed Peggy, looking down the bar. 'He doesn't seem to change one way or the other.'

Jack Archer was helping Nora Salt, the Irish barmaid, at the far end of the bar. He was simply passing the odd glass or getting change from the till. Jack was unable to do anything more strenuous. Since he had been forced to give up his job at Brookfield Farm through ill health, he could do no more than go through the motions of working. Peggy would much rather that her husband stayed upstairs watching the television. But Jack was too naturally gregarious to put up with that.

'I'll tell him a few of my jokes,' offered Tony.

'Do that,' encouraged Peggy.

'Tony's full of himself tonight,' commented Lilian, as her brother strutted down the bar towards his father.

'What's he put on?' asked Peggy, sniffing and pulling a face.

'Too much.'

The women laughed, then Peggy was called by another customer. Lilian was not left alone for long.

'No prizes for guessing where you're going,' said Sid Perks.

He had come to the bar to buy another drink. From the suit he was wearing, Lilian deduced that he was off to the dance as well.

'Where's Polly?' she asked.

'Um, she's . . . gone on ahead,' he muttered. 'To the Hall.'

This struck Lilian as rather odd. When Sid and Polly went out for an evening they were usually inseparable.

'I just popped in to lay the dust,' confirmed Sid, indicating his empty glass.

While Peggy Archer pulled Sid another pint, he and Lilian chatted about the dance. For some reason he did not seem to be looking forward to it. Lilian was puzzled. But she had another score to settle with Sid. As he paid for his pint and tried to move away, Lilian stopped him.

'What are all these stories, then?' she enquired.

'Stories?' said Sid uneasily.

'The ones you've been spreading about Ralph Bellamy and me.'

'Ah yes, well . . .' mouthed Sid.

'I don't see that it's any of your business,' asserted Lilian, a light coming into her eye.

Lilian was known to have quite a temper when she was roused. Sid Perks had no wish to be on the receiving end of it.

'I'm sorry,' he apologised. 'Idle chatter, that's all. Idle chatter.'

'You're quite wrong, whatever you've been saying,' announced Lilian. 'So please. No more stories.'

'No, no, of course not,' promised Sid, backing away.

Lilian had got her point across.

The Young Farmers' Dance which was held at the Ambridge

Village Hall was no place for the weak or the faint-hearted. It made real demands on those who attended, as Lilian soon found out. Within minutes of stepping into the Hall, she and Tony found themselves in the thick of a game of Musical Chairs. At least, that was how it was described by the organisers. Lilian recalled Musical Chairs as a game which she had played and enjoyed at children's parties. The version played by the Young Farmers' Club had little in common with anything she had seen before. Competition took the form of naked, if good-natured, aggression. It was not enough to be in possession of a chair when the music stopped. One had to hang on like grim death as the chairless members tried to dislodge any sitting tenants.

Lilian was eliminated fairly early on but Tony was intent on battling through to the finish. His sister joined the others in shouting advice as the music played and the competitors circled the chairs at speed. Suddenly the music ended and over a dozen large, healthy young men fought for seats. Lilian admired Tony's agility and ferocity as he won a place in the last three. By now the dance was well and truly launched with everyone entering into the spirit of things and with partisanship developing among the audience. Lilian heard bets being exchanged with the odds against Tony. It made her cheer him on even more.

The two remaining chairs were placed either end of the hall and the three contenders moved around them like speedway bikes. Tony was giving away a few stone to each of his rivals, but Lilian reckoned that he had the edge on them for speed. The lad in charge of the music waited until all three of them were midway between the chairs, then lifted the arm of the gramophone. Amidst yells and shrieks, the trio converged on the same chair and hurled themselves at it simultaneously. The chair was unequal to its sudden popularity and collapsed with its back broken off. Tony and his two companions tumbled to the floor in a heap, then remembered the other chair. They scrambled to their feet, struggled with each other, then charged off down the hall, only to find that some wag had whipped it away. General acclamation declared the result a draw.

Lilian thoroughly enjoyed the evening and she threw herself into the wildest games with abandon. She could not recall a time when she had danced so often and so vigorously, and she complimented Tony on booking the Pop Group.

'They're great for this kind of gig,' he said, holding his latest girlfriend by the hand.

'Aren't you going to introduce me?' she asked.

'Don't even know her name myself.'

The girl giggled, then dragged Tony off in search of food. Lilian decided that she needed some refreshments and took her turn in the queue at the table. When she had filled her plate, she went over to sit in a corner with Polly.

'Mind if I join you?'

'Uh, no . . . do.'

'I haven't seen you on the floor at all, Polly.'

'Not yet,' she admitted, uneasily.

'It's a bit hectic out there. It's every girl for herself.'

'Then I think I'll sit it out.'

'Sid seems to be getting his share of dancing, though. Why shouldn't you?'

'I'm not really in the mood,' she said, defensively.

'Makes a change. Tony always says that you and Sid are the life and soul of these dances.'

Polly glanced nervously in the direction of the Refreshments Table and Lilian followed her gaze in time to see Sid munching at a sandwich and sharing a joke with a young girl.

'Isn't he getting any food for you, Polly?'

'I'm not hungry.'

'Sid certainly is. Look at him tucking in.'

Sid realised that he was being watched, said something to the girl and then lost himself in the crowd. Polly's face registered a kind of baffled anxiety.

'Have you ever noticed how few of the Young Farmers actually *are* young farmers?' asked Lilian, trying to cheer Polly up with a change of subject.

'No, I hadn't.'

'Look around. Farmers are very thin on the ground. We've got what you might call a good cross-section of society.'

'Yes.'

Polly was not ready to talk about anything and Lilian was rather glad when the music started again and she was asked to dance. The next time that she looked for Polly, the latter had disappeared.

Sid, by contrast, was very much in evidence, dancing for all he was worth with Michelle, the *au pair* girl from Brookfield. Lilian could not understand why he was throwing himself into it so vigorously. Most of the people there were enjoying themselves, but Sid had the look of a man desperately set on getting every ounce of pleasure out of the evening.

She was not allowed to reflect on Sid and Polly for long. Her dancing partner was suggesting that they took a walk and that was not the reason she had come along. She excused herself, waved a hand to Tony over the heads of the dancers, then slipped out.

The night was clear and the fresh air was a tonic after the stifling heat of the Village Hall. Lilian headed towards Hollowtree Flats, recalling some of the highlights of the evening. From her point of view it had been a complete success and she was glad she had gone. Her only regret was that he had not been there. He had loved dancing. She grew sad for a moment but the feeling passed. Lilian had learned to be realistic about it.

When she let herself into the caretaker's cottage at Hollowtree, she trod on an envelope. She switched the light on and found a note addressed to her. It was written in a firm, neat hand by Ralph Bellamy. Apparently, he had called at the Bull in the hope of speaking to her. The note conveyed a tone of mild disapproval, as if Ralph did not think a Young Farmers' Dance was quite the place for Lilian. At first, she bridled. What business was it of his where and how she spent her evenings? Then she smiled. There was something rather comforting in Ralph's old-fashioned attitudes. And she was fond of him.

The last paragraph of the note halted her. She read it with a mixture of surprise and excitement. It was the second unexpected invitation in a week. Dare she accept it?

Chapter Four

Polly Perks was mystified. She could not understand it. He had been like it for some time now. His performance at the Young Farmers' Dance was the culmination of days of strange behaviour towards her. As she lay in bed, waiting for him to return from the Village Hall, Polly tried to pin a definite date and time to it. Wednesday. That was it. Wednesday evening at the Bull. When she and Sid had set out for a drink, he was his usual happy-go-lucky self. By the time they had reached home again, he was withdrawn and sullen. What was really disturbing was that he would not talk about it. He fended off any discussion, insisting that nothing was wrong. Sid Perks, the apostle of frankness and cheerfulness, had clammed up on her.

A confrontation was overdue. She would sit up in bed and tackle him when he came home. This uncertainty and awkwardness between them must be resolved. At this time especially, when she needed her husband's support and love, Polly could not bear the thought that there was some rift between them. Yes, Wednesday evening had marked the decisive change. But how? And why had Sid alternately ignored her or watched her in a rather wounded manner ever since? And what was she to make of his behaviour at the dance? A pillow talk was the only answer. Like most married couples, Sid and Polly found the bedroom the most fruitful place for discussion.

At what precise time she dropped off to sleep Polly did not know. She only recalled looking towards Sid's side of the bed and wondering why he was so late. Then she drifted off into a deep, welcoming sleep. When she awoke sunlight was slanting in through the windows. Sunday morning was already well advanced. She reached out instinctively but he was still not there. He had slept in the bed, for part of the night at least. His suit lay in an untidy pile on the floor and his pyjamas were missing. Muffled scraping sounds from downstairs gave Polly a clue as to his whereabouts. She clambered out of bed and went to the shop in her bare feet.

'Sid, whatever are you doing?' she gasped.

'Making a few changes,' he said, casually.

'But you can't just heave shelves around on your own,' she argued.

'Why not?' he challenged.

The shop was already a vastly different place from the one which Polly had locked up the previous night. Shelves had been unloaded, counters reorganised, and the till moved nearer to the doorway. The floor was covered in cans and magazines and paperbacks. Sid was playing about in the middle of the chaos like a child playing with sand.

'Do you know what you're doing?' asked Polly, bewildered.

'Of course,' snapped Sid. 'It's on the plan.'

Polly picked up the piece of paper he pointed to. It was a ground-plan of the shop with counters and shelves set at entirely new angles to each other. A series of arrows indicated what she took to be the flow of customers.

'You go back to bed,' he suggested. 'I can manage.'

'You'll be here till Doomsday at this rate,' she pointed out.

'If it keeps me happy,' he mumbled, struggling with a display rack.

Polly herself was only half-awake but she could see that Sid was in a far more delicate state. A white face, hollow eyes, dishevelled hair and a grunt every time he stooped down confirmed that he was suffering from a bad hangover. And yet he was forcing himself to carry on. It was nothing less than self-inflicted punishment. Polly's concern had a practical application.

'Have you had any breakfast, Sid?'

'Not hungry,' he growled, as if he had signed a pledge never to touch a morsel of food again.

'What about coffee?'

He made no reply, but gazed distractedly into the refrigerator, puzzled vaguely by its contents. Polly repeated the question but still got no reply. She took the law into her own hands.

'Drink this,' she said, returning soon with two mugs.

'Ugh – I couldn't!' he protested, wincing at the sight of liquid.

'It'll do you good.'

Polly persuaded him to take a few sips. He even agreed to sit down and rest for a moment. As he drank the coffee, he pulled faces that were far more comical than anything he had achieved when really trying. Polly was tempted to laugh but rightly controlled herself. It was not the moment for laughter. She picked up Sid's plan of the shop.

'What's it all in aid of, though?' she wondered.

'Efficiency,' he countered. 'Better service.'

'But won't your plan make things difficult for me?'

'In what way?'

'The till, for instance. You've put it by the door. Yet if I have to cross to the Post Office section or serve behind the – '

Sid handed her the half-full mug of coffee and started work again. He was evidently in some pain. Polly pressed her point.

'Sid, I don't see how one person can run the shop if we follow your system,' she complained.

'One person can't,' he agreed.

'Well?'

He turned to face her and looked her in the eye for the first time. 'There'll be two of us from now on, Polly.'

Polly's immediate reaction was one of delight. She and Sid had often talked about his coming to work full-time in the shop. Jack Woolley, the owner of the Ambridge Village Stores, was very much in favour of the idea. He realised that the business could not expand so long as Polly ran it on her own, and it was certainly ripe for expansion. The last set of shop accounts showed that it could certainly support the work of two people. Polly was thrilled that Sid had finally come round to deciding to work alongside her. It was something she had wanted him to choose for himself without any direct pressure from her.

What soured her pleasure and caused her misgivings was the way in which Sid announced his decision. There was no warmth or optimism in his voice. He spoke as if delivering a kind of threat. Polly was hurt. Something which should have brought so much simple joy to both of them had taken on the character of an imposition.

'You do *want* to work here, don't you?' she enquired.

'I'd like to stay close to you,' he said, bluntly.

'It'll make all the difference, Sid,' she promised, bravely. 'Mr Woolley is always saying that this shop needs – '

'Church,' he interrupted. 'Your mother will be waiting.'

Polly went off to dress herself. When she left to pick up Mrs Mead, Sid was still busy moving things in the shop.

By lunchtime Sid looked marginally more alive, having dressed, combed his hair and consented to shave. But he was still not willing to be drawn into conversation. He sat hunched over the table, picking at a roast potato, as Polly tried a variety of topics. She told him who had been at church, and what her mother's golden hamster had been up to, and why she felt they could both make a living from the business if they put their minds to it. Eventually, she worked up the courage to broach the topic which had been tormenting her.

'Sid, why were you so late home last night?' she whispered gently.

'Because I didn't think you'd want me home early,' he replied, almost in a whisper.

Polly was bemused. Sid seemed, for a brief moment, so vulnerable, so absurdly unprotected. Before Polly could ask him to explain what he meant, he regained his distracted air, pushed his plate away and got up.

'I'm going to carry on in the shop,' he announced.

'It's Sunday. What about your cricket?'

'I'll give it a miss this week,' he said.

'But you love a game of cricket,' she urged.

'I used to,' he said rather wistfuly. Then added, firmly, 'Anyway, this is more important.'

Polly got no more out of him. He worked remorselessly all afternoon and well into the evening. Polly helped where she was permitted but said nothing for fear of upsetting him. Sid went to bed early, leaving Polly in the middle of some ironing. When she joined him in bed, he was fast asleep. Saturday night had finally caught up with him. Polly would have to wait until she finally caught up with the truth about Saturday night.

Dan Archer was the first customer to see the changes made to the shop. He stood in the doorway on Monday morning and blinked.

'Am I in the right place?' he chuckled.

'Come on in and find out, Mr Archer,' invited Sid, putting the finishing touches to a sign with a magic marker.

'It's our new system,' explained Polly. 'Sid's idea. We're hoping it'll speed things up a little.'

'Not sure I like the sound of that,' confessed Dan. 'At my age you want a system that slows things down.'

Dan Archer was a big, heavy man who favoured a crumpled old tweed suit and an open-necked shirt. His face was as seasoned and full of character as English oak. Dan had been calling in at the Village Stores in Ambridge for over half a century and had seen many so-called improvements. Like most farmers of his vintage, he was wary of change and sceptical about anything describing itself as progress. He read the sign which Sid had now fixed up above the Grocery section. He sounded unimpressed.

'Self-service, eh?'

'It's sort of experimental,' Polly said. 'Isn't it, Sid?'

'To save time queueing,' he announced.

'I don't see any queue,' grinned Dan.

Polly served Dan, who had come into buy some stamps and a postal order. As a rule she enjoyed chatting to him. Dan Archer was a mine of information about what was going on in Ambridge. He liked to keep in touch and Polly always found his gossip both interesting and amusing. This morning, however, she was conscious how she kept deferring to Sid, how she sought his approval for almost any remark she made. Polly could see that Dan sensed the tension between herself and Sid. She was glad when he took his leave.

'Well, I'd better get off, I suppose,' he said, opening the door and causing the shop bell to ring. 'I know I've retired but I like to keep an eye on the way Phil runs Brookfield.'

Polly was willing him to leave for she could see that he sensed the tension between Sid and herself. But Dan never rushed things and at the door he remembered something else he wanted to ask them.

'Enjoy the dance?'

'Uh . . . yes,' she lied, colouring.

'Lilian was saying what a rare old evening everyone had.'

Polly and Sid exchanged an embarrassed glance, neither feeling up to a reply.

'She had a nice surprise from Ralph Bellamy. Wants her to ride in a point-to-point. Someone's dropped out of the field, so Ralph's put Lilian in.'

'I'm sure she'll do well,' said Polly, glad that the subject of the dance had been left behind.

'Ralph has been looking for a chance to race Red Knight,' noted Dan.

'He might beat him if he ties the horse's back legs together,' quipped Sid, but there was nothing of the old punch in his voice.

Polly was relieved when Dan finally went out and she sat down on a stool for support. Sid went back to work, talking over his shoulder.

'Wonder how he does it?'

'Who?'

'Dan Archer. It's their Golden Wedding Anniversary this

year. Fifty blinking years of it and he can still manage a smile!'

Polly was hurt by the insinuation but she said nothing, fearing Sid when he was in this mood. It was late afternoon before she felt ready to tackle him, seeing that it was up to her to take the initiative. The passage of time was not improving Sid's attitude towards her. He was growing steadily more offhand with her. Polly had to act firmly. She chose her moment as they were shutting up the shop.

'We must talk, Sid,' she announced.

'What about?'

'You know quite well.'

'Forget it, will you?' he mumbled, turning to walk away.

Polly's cry stopped him. 'Sid, please!' There was pain and appeal in her voice. It made him face her again. Polly pleaded with him silently. They had always talked things out before. Why not now? If only she knew what she had done to provoke this black mood of his. He must tell her.

'All right,' he nodded. 'But not here.'

'We can go for a walk.'

'After tea,' he suggested, trying to buy time.

'Now,' she insisted. 'This is more important.'

The Ambridge Country Park was a valuable amenity for villagers and visitors alike. It was owned by Jack Woolley, the Birmingham businessman who had also bought the Village Stores when he moved to Ambridge. Woolley's ambitions for the Country Park did not always meet with the approval of local people, but there was no doubt that the Park provided acres of pleasant and interesting walking across open field and through woodland. At this time of year, with May approaching fast, the Park was a feast for the eye and a delight to the ear. Cowslips, wood anemones and wild daffodils carpeted whole areas of the Park, and bluebells filled many of the wooded glades.

April, as usual, had been a cruel month, capricious, headstrong and quite unpredictable. Into a single day it had sometimes compressed elements from all four seasons, spreading confusion gleefully among both flora and fauna. It had made a nonsense out of the proverbial wisdom about the joys of spring and dampened the most ardent spirits with its rain and wind. By the same token, it had been a kind month, a time of promise, of encouragement, of the first real signs of growth in the countryside. As the days lengthened beyond the scope of the nights, colour and blossom had appeared in earnest in the Ambridge Country Park. It was at its freshest and greenest with the beech in particular, the tall, elegant Lady of the Woods, looking at her best as her broad, oval leaves darkened and shone.

The beauties of nature did not impinge upon the consciousness of Sid and Polly Perks as they strolled along. They had no time to notice the hawthorn coming into blossom or listen to the varied programme of birdsong offered by the chaffinch, the thrush, the willow warbler, the robin, the skylark, and the early cuckoo. What gave the Country Park its special attraction was its demonstration that nature was no idyllic backdrop but a living, growing and totally inhabited place. For all the notice that Sid and Polly took of it, the Park might have been a desert.

'Looks as if we were wrong about them, Sid.'

Polly had walked in silence long enough. She must get him talking somehow and break down his morose, injured expression. 'About Ralph Bellamy and Lilian, I mean,' she amplified. 'I don't think there is anything between them. Not serious, like. No, if he's after a wife for the Dower House, he may even decide on Lady Isobel.'

This speculation washed over Sid and left him unmoved.

'Didn't he use to fancy Lady Isobel at one time?' she asked, vainly trying to engage Sid's interest. 'Save him a few bob if he marries her. He could have the Dower House for nothing. I wonder if that's Ralph Bellamy's game.'

But even this discussion of the more sordid, commercial aspects of marriage did not elicit any response. The couple, who had so often walked hand in hand through the Park, now moved along as strangers. They came to a rustic bench near an old elm. They sat down and Sid stared in front of him for a while. Then he chuckled out loud.

'She gave me a right old telling off,' he recalled.

'Who did?'

'Lilian Nicholson. Had a go at me about it in the Bull.'

'When was this?'

'On Saturday. Before the dance.'

Mention of the dance brought the gloom to his face again. Polly continued quickly, anxious to keep the conversation going. 'What did she say, Sid?'

'To stop spreading stories. To mind my own business.'

'There – I warned you not to go telling any tales at the Cricket Club.'

'I remember,' mused Sid. 'It was the afternoon we played Penny Hassett. The afternoon you were supposed to be too tired to help with the teas.'

'I was tired,' claimed Polly.

'Were you?'

He looked at her, accusing her, interrogating her with his eyes. Polly began to feel hot and uncomfortable.

'Were you, Polly?' he repeated.

'Of course,' she replied as firmly as she could manage.

Sid was unconvinced and Polly grew fearful. She watched him as he picked a blade of grass, chewed it for a moment, then tried to split it with his thumbnail.

'Where did you go that Sunday afternoon?' he persisted.

'I told you. I was resting.'

'Is that the truth?'

'Yes,' she said, unable to hide the tremble in her voice.

'I don't believe you,' he said, simply. 'I think you went somewhere when I was out of the way.'

Polly's mind was in a turmoil. Had he found her out? It was impossible. She had been back at the shop a good twenty minutes before Sid had got home from his cricket. He had shown nothing but concern for her. There had been no shade of suspicion. Polly must stick to her story.

'Chap I bumped into at the Bull on Wednesday. Reckons he saw you getting on a bus that afternoon.'

Polly's story disintegrated.

'He . . . must be mistaken,' she offered, weakly.

'I don't think so, Polly.' He looked her full in the face. 'Where did you go?'

'Not where you imagine I did,' she blurted out.

'Then you did go somewhere. You admit it.'

Polly's confusion was almost total. Her alibi had been exposed, her husband's trust in her shattered. Yet somehow she could not bring herself to tell him the truth. She hoped she could keep that blow from him. Sid had other ideas.

'I must know,' he insisted, gently.

'Look, there's nothing to worry about, Sid!'

'Then why get all dressed up in your best things!' he sneered, tiring of the gentle approach.

She went scarlet and realised that she could hold it back from him no longer. Though she could not take away his anger, she could at least rescue him from those particular thoughts. She dipped into her handbag and took out the crumpled letter which she had received over ten days before.

'This came for me . . .'

'Why didn't you say?' he demanded, snatching it and reading it.

'I *had* to see him, Sid.'

'That's not what we agreed, Polly.'

'I had to. Just one more time.'

'But you promised.'

His bitterness was as great as she had feared and there was no persuading him. In her desperation, she thought of the one piece of news which she had been keeping and which might win him round. 'Sid, I must tell you something good . . .'

'After *this*?' he snarled, throwing the letter down.

'I went to the doctor again on Monday and he says . . .'

But she was talking to thin air for Sid had walked away in a fury. Polly looked down at the letter, then picked it up and tore it into tiny pieces.

Chapter Five

Ralph Bellamy pressed his foot down angrily on the accelerator and raced his car through the country lanes which he knew so well. The week had frowned upon him in a most signal fashion. Nothing had worked out as he had hoped it would. On every front, Ralph had met with spirited resistance. In Sussex, at the offices of Wiley, Smith and French, in the jeweller's shop, and on his own estate, he had been confronted by the kinds of setbacks which incline a man to believe in the malignity of fate. It had been a cold, merciless, uncompromising week. At the end of it, Ralph was fatigued and very embittered.

Seeing the junction in the distance, he changed down to second gear and applied the brakes. The car slowed to rolling speed, its left indicator flashing. Ralph saw that the main road was clear, and stabbed his foot down again. Vehicle and driver turned on to the main road with a screech and sped off in the direction of Borchester. The clock in the dashboard told Ralph that it was only a quarter to nine. He would be there in five minutes, well ahead of the worst of the Saturday morning traffic. Saturday. The day of the point-to-point races. The thought of what lay in store that afternoon helped to dilute his general annoyance. He even tried to review his week with something akin to calm objectivity.

Inevitably, he began with Lilian. A dispassionate observer would see no reason why Lilian should not have gone to the Young Farmers' Dance. She was young, single, fairly gregarious and fond of dancing. Again, she had been invited by Tony. She had every right to go along. Ralph Bellamy, however, was no dispassionate observer. For all his bluff manner, he was a person whose emotions could be engaged. And in this case those emotions were more deeply engaged than even he had suspected. He had never known himself be so possessive about a woman. When Peggy Archer had told him that her daughter had gone to the Village Hall that night, Ralph felt that Lilian had committed an act of treachery.

All week he had nursed resentment against the Young Farmers' Dance and against Tony Archer, who had been responsible for taking Lilian to it. Ralph had gone out of his way to pick an argument with his young employee on some aspect of herd management. Tony had been understandably baffled by Ralph's sudden outburst. Thinking back on it, Ralph could see that his objections were not really against the dance itself, and certainly not against Tony. What needled him was the fact that the dance reminded him of the barriers between Lilian and himself. Ralph Bellamy could never have taken her to a function like that. There was the social barrier, which deterred a man with Ralph's pretensions from going to an occasion of that kind. And there was the age barrier.

Reaching Borchester, Ralph had his first piece of luck. He found a parking-space in the very street where the jeweller's shop was located. It was just opening when he arrived at the door. His last visit to the shop had been a frustrating one, involving apologies and delays. This time there were no problems. They had exactly what he wanted. He signed the cheque and left the shop with a smile of satisfaction. Perhaps his luck had changed, after all.

It was this slight indication that fortune was at last ready to concede him a smile which took Ralph past his parked Scimitar and on towards Main Street. Reflecting on the previous Tuesday, he decided that that was the worst day of his week. It had been one of the most comprehensively irritating and wasted days of his life. He had driven all the way down to Sussex to see Lady Isobel Lander at her home, confident that a direct approach to the owner was the only way to secure the purchase of the Dower House. Lady Isobel had been hospitality itself. Ralph had been welcomed, dined and urged to stay for a few days. But when he had broached the topic of the Brigadier's estate, she had been less than helpful.

'Of course, I'd like *you* to have it, Ralph,' she had announced, 'but I fear that it's not up to me.'

'I would have said it was entirely up to you.'

'No, I've no head for business. Not like some I could mention.'

Ralph rejected the compliment. His business acumen had hardly been in evidence of late.

'That's why I've put everything in the hands of that nice young man, Stephen Wiley,' Lady Isobel had continued. 'He's so clever and so full of useful ideas.'

To hear anyone speak well of Stephen Wiley was in the nature of a personal insult to Ralph, who had been the victim of some of those 'useful ideas'. As he thought of Wiley's air of well-bred truculence, Ralph had had difficulty in holding his peace. He had gone on to present his arguments to Lady Isobel, explaining that all he really wished to buy was the Dower House and a few acres surrounding it.

'That is out of the question,' Lady Isobel had said sweetly.

This quotation from the Book of Stephen Wiley confirmed that Ralph's journey was pointless.

The final indignity had occurred on the return journey to Ambridge. Tension and frustration are not ideal car passengers. Late at night, in blinding rain, Ralph had let his concentration wander. Misjudging a bend, he hit a slippery patch of road and skidded uncontrollably on to the grass verge. After thirty yards or so, a telegraph pole halted his progress. The damage to the Range Rover was enough to keep it off the road for a fortnight, hence his use of the Scimitar to drive to Borchester. The physical damage to Ralph was negligible and amounted to no more than a soreness around the ribs where the safety belt had jerked against him. But the damage to his pride was extensive. And not covered by insurance. Looking back on that Tuesday, Ralph hoped he would never have a day quite like that again.

His recriminations had taken him as far as Main Street and

he stood outside the premises of Wiley, Smith and French. In the window, pinned up in the middle of the properties on display, was a photograph of the Dower House. The two phrases which had connected with Ralph's imagination earlier still retained their potency. With one of those phrases – Ideal Family Residence – he had no quarrel. Of the other phrase – Unless Previously Sold – he was beginning to entertain serious doubts. He glanced up to the office which overlooked the street and which belonged to Stephen Wiley. The last time he had been in that office was on Wednesday, trying to extract a grain of use out of his visit to Sussex.

'Lady Isobel is very keen that I should buy the property,' he had told Stephen Wiley.

'She is entitled to her opinions.'

'Don't you take your clients' views into consideration at all?' Ralph had barked across the desk.

'Naturally. They are noted, Mr Bellamy. They are noted.'

Ralph had glowered at the estate agent, wondering which of his repellent aspects he disliked most. Was it the fashionably long hair which touched Stephen's shoulders as he leant forward with his elbows on the desk? Was it the trendy three-piece suit and the broad tie? Was it the unassailable self-confidence of the man, that cultured brashness, that impeccable rudeness? Or was it simply his appalling youthfulness?

'If that is all . . .' Stephen had said, rising from his chair by way of a hint that Ralph should leave.

'I intend to put in a bid for the property,' Ralph had declared. 'For the whole property, that is. Dower House and the thousand acres.'

'Then I look forward to seeing you at the auction.'

'I was talking about a bid prior to the auction.'

'Oh, I see.'

Ralph added a new aspect of Stephen to his list of dislikes. This studied indifference with which he spoke. This total lack of respect.

'What is the reserve price?' Ralph had asked.

'I'm expecting it to go well above the reserve price, Mr

Bellamy. We have some good buyers interested in the property. Some very good buyers.'

'What is the reserve price, please?' Ralph had demanded. 'If I am to put in a realistic figure, I need a realistic guideline.'

'The most realistic guideline of any property is what that property is worth to you as an individual.'

That smoothness, that educated superciliousness. Ralph would put that on his list, too.

'However, if you want it in nice round figures . . .'

And with a bland smile, Stephen Wiley had told Ralph what the reserve price was. It was high.

Reflecting on this interview with Stephen, he realised that there was no point at all in trying to see the man again until he was ready to make a firm offer for the property and he could not do that until he had organised the sale of some land in East Anglia. He was about to turn away from the offices but there was something about the photograph of the Dower House which held him and which eventually compelled him to go in through the door.

'Oh it's you again, Mr Bellamy,' smiled the receptionist. 'You're getting to know your way here.'

'Yes . . . is Mr Wiley here, by any chance?'

'Mr Raymond, Mr Charles or young Mr Stephen?'

'Stephen, please.'

'I'm afraid that he's not in today. I could make an appointment for Monday, if it's urgent. Or get him to ring you over the weekend perhaps?'

'Uh, no . . . it was just a thought.'

'Shall I tell him that – '

'No, not necessary. I was passing, that's all and . . .'

He backed out, wishing that he had not gone in at all, resenting the hold which the Dower House had over him. Without looking at the photograph again, he went swiftly back towards his car, pausing to buy a copy of the weekly *Borchester Echo* on the way.

As he had expected, the paper had devoted a special feature to the point-to-point races and it included tips about the form of horses and riders alike. There was only a brief mention of the Ladies' Open Steeple Chase, to be run over three and a half miles, but just to see it in print was enough for him. Ralph stopped looking back over the wreckage of the past, and looked forward to the future instead. The afternoon might yet redeem his week from total disaster.

The annual point-to-point always attracted fairly big crowds. Enthusiasts came from some distance, assured of a high standard of riding over a testing course. This year's point-to-point had a special significance, not to say poignancy. It would be the last fixture of its kind organised by the Ambridge Hunt which, for financial and other reasons, could not continue its separate existence. Next season the Ambridge Hunt would amalgamate with the South Borsetshire and lose its own identity. All those involved were thus particularly anxious to make this final fixture an occasion to remember and cherish.

Notwithstanding the heavy cloud and the swirling wind, an exceptionally large crowd gathered at the course. The car park was full, the betting lively, the speculation about the horses informed. Five steeplechases were to be run, the main event of the afternoon being the race for the Lawson-Hope Challenge Cup. Ralph Bellamy had himself competed in this race in previous years, though never successfully. His chief interest, however, was in the fourth race on the card – the Ladies' Open. He kept checking his racecard and halting at the fourth name on the list: 'Mr Ralph Bellamy's Red Knight, ridden by L. Nicholson (Ambridge)'. A bracketed number five indicated the age of the horse.

'We've arrived now. You can tell them to start.'

It was Dan Archer and his wife, Doris. Like many members of the Archer family, they had come to support Lilian. Ralph acknowledged them both with a smile.

'What are her chances, Mr Bellamy?' asked Doris.

'Lilian will walk it,' chuckled Dan. 'She'll leave the rest of 'em for dead.'

But the homely, silver-haired woman beside him wanted a more honest and objective assessment. Ralph shook his head slowly.

'Lilian has got a lot of competition, Mrs Archer. She'll do well to get placed.'

'Have more faith in your horse and rider,' chided Dan.

'The important thing is that she'll gain valuable experience by taking part,' consoled Ralph. 'She has an outside chance, naturally. But I wouldn't put it higher than that.'

Dan and Doris thanked Ralph and went off towards the paddock where Peggy and Jack Archer were studying the horses in the first race on the card. Ralph looked across at Peggy and Jack, who had left the Bull well before closing time in order to be at the course. With Peggy was Jennifer, her other daughter. Grandparents, parents, sister. Ralph was impressed by the way her family had rallied round Lilian for what was a difficult test for her.

The course was not an easy one. It was in a pleasant, park-like setting, enclosed on two sides by trees and on the other two sides by the River Am which bent around at right angles to itself. Riders had to contend with a right-handed, undulating course with a long pull uphill to the last two fences and some very tricky downhill jumps on the way. It was a course for stayers and tacticians. The viewing was excellent with a hill providing a natural grandstand near the finish and with the whole course visible throughout each race. In spite of the threatening cloud, the going was relatively firm.

Ralph did not show his usual interest in all the races on the card. He was too preoccupied with the Ladies' Open and spent most of the time repeating advice to Lilian or patting Red Knight encouragingly. He was even immune to the excitement of the race for the Lawson-Hope Challenge Cup, an event which was contested with daredevil courage over a distance of four miles. Ralph's thoughts were entirely with Lilian.

'How do you feel?' he enquired as she came out of the weighing-in tent.

'Nervous,' she confessed.

'It'll pass,' he reassured her.

Red Knight gained a lot of attention in the paddock, and responded to it rather skittishly. The various members of the Archer family cheered Lilian as she mounted, and she waved to them before checking the strap on her crash helmet. Ralph repeated his warnings about the awkward fences yet again and then it was time for the horses to go to post. The spectators left the paddock to resume their seats. Ralph found a vantage point on the hill and trained his binoculars on the start.

There were ten riders in the Ladies' Open but for most people the result was a foregone conclusion. The clear favourite was a horse called Black Jet, the mount of Anne Hawkes, who was without question the leading woman rider in the Midlands. The previous season she had collected ten wins. This season she had ridden seven winners already and was anxious to improve upon that figure. Ralph wondered how far behind Black Jet his own horse would come.

'Aunt Lilian is in with a chance, isn't she?' piped someone beside him.

Ralph recognised Shula Archer from Brookfield. Shula was Lilian's niece and as fiercely loyal as the rest of the family. She loved horses as much as Lilian. That her aunt was actually competing in a point-to-point made it a very special day for the twelve-year-old girl.

'Of course she has a chance,' reassured Ralph.

He offered her his binoculars but Shula had already gone. She was going to spend the whole race on the move.

When Ralph focused on the horses again, they were under starter's orders. The flag fell, the heels dug and the crowd came alive. Ralph's eyes never left Lilian. She got off to a slow start but soon made ground to take her place in the middle of the riders. Ralph thought that she was too circumspect at the first fence and it cost her a few lengths. She would have to attack the jumps more purposefully if she was to gain a placing. There were too many bends in the early stages of the race for any sustained galloping, but already there was a definite leader. Anne Hawkes, on Black Jet, was vindicating her reputation as a front-runner. The horses came uphill towards the finish for the first time and the crowd yelled and cheered. Above the noise the sound of the hooves could be heard pummelling and gouging the turf. At the fence directly in front of the main body of spectators, one of the horses fell and sent its rider somersaulting crazily. Lilian had to draw Red Knight sharply to the left to avoid hitting this early casualty.

The field swept past the finishing post in a bunch. Only Anne Hawkes was riding out on her own. It was almost as if two races were being run. Ralph concentrated on the second, hoping that Lilian might at least be up with the leaders when she next came to the finish. The horses now began a long downhill run, coping with an awkward ditch and two solid fences in quick succession. Red Knight took these obstacles boldly. Ralph was more pleased now. Lilian was clearly settling down and shaking off all traces of nervousness. She was standing up out of the saddle, putting all her weight on her knees and on the fragile irons. Red Knight's hooves were flashing forward.

By the time they had reached the halfway stage, the riders had stretched out over a distance of some thirty lengths or more. Two of the runners had lost contact with the others and could now be virtually discounted. Lilian was battling it out with the other five, and Anne Hawkes was pulling even further ahead. Ralph was proud of the way Lilian was riding. She was not over-taxing Red Knight, and was picking her line on the fences sensibly.

Six fences from home Black Jet and its rider made their first mistake. The horse came at the obstacle too fast, hit it hard and pecked. Anne Hawkes lost a stirrup and seemed in danger of being unsaddled for a brief moment. She showed great presence of mind, found the stirrup with her foot, and rose high to continue the race. But her ascendancy had been broken. The other horses had been given priceless seconds to make ground. Three had caught her up, Lilian among them. Ralph was on his feet, goading her on.

The next fence, which had been a problem all afternoon, put paid to the hopes of one of the challengers. Her horse jumped it at an awkward angle, landed badly, rocked, buckled and seemed about to go. It regained its balance but was by now right out of contention. Lilian had shown commonsense at this difficult fence, steering Red Knight towards a gap made earlier in the afternoon. She was conserving his energy admirably and Red Knight was running well within himself. Black Jet, by contrast, decided that it was not his afternoon. He struggled to stay marginally ahead of his two rivals at the ditch and at the following fence, but when they started the long uphill climb, he elected to drop behind. Anne Hawkes was unable to get him to lengthen his stride. It was now a two-horse race.

Red Knight against a grey. Lilian against a lady wearing pale pink and green colours. Stamina and skill against skill and stamina. Ralph's throat was dry with excitement. There were only two fences to jump. Lilian was virtually certain of a placing. From the way she took Red Knight fearlessly over the second from home, it was evident that she had set her heart on first place.

The grey and its rider put in a strong burst and drew a few lengths ahead. Lilian called for more from Red Knight and pulled up alongside her rival. They raced neck and neck with no more than a yard's width between them. It was all on the last fence and the gallop home. The horses jumped together and landed safely. Both were tiring as they struggled uphill but they were not done yet. When Lilian gave Red Knight his head, he managed a final spurt which put him a length and a half ahead. The grey looked the stronger horse but somehow was unable to improve its position. To cheers and applause, Lilian and Red Knight galloped past the winning post.

Ralph ran on to the course and was the first to reach Lilian as she slowed Red Knight to walking pace.

'Well done! Well done!' shouted Ralph. 'Good boy, Red Knight!'

'Never thought we'd make it,' said Lilian breathlessly.

She looked exhausted and was trembling a little. Red Knight was coping much better with the pleasures of victory and was tossing his head in triumph. Ralph led the horse proudly to the unsaddling enclosure. He did not mind the gentle ribbing from Dan Archer. He enjoyed talking about the more technical aspects of the race with Shula. And he watched happily as Lilian received the congratulations of family and friends alike. It had been a glorious afternoon. Memories of the dark week at the back of him had been utterly obliterated.

'Champagne?' she said in surprise.

'What else?' laughed Ralph. 'This is a celebration.'

'Marvellous!'

They were dining together later that evening. Lilian had now changed out of the thin, white cotton breeches and the blue silk colours. She was no longer panting and covered in perspiration. But the glow of victory was still in her face. As she sat there in new pale green evening dress, her hair caught up behind her in a chignon, she seemed more beautiful than ever to Ralph. He felt for the box in his pocket, then talked excitedly once more about the race. For him, as for her, the last Point-to-Point Races held under the auspices of the Ambridge Hunt would be an unforgettable occasion. Lilian had displayed courage, ability and character. Ralph could ask for no more.

The afternoon's success had sharpened their appetites and they both enjoyed a full meal. Ralph called for a second bottle of champagne as the first was drained. He was drinking rather more than Lilian but she did not seem to notice. She was relaxed and happy, glad that the trial of the race was behind her. As the meal progressed, Ralph grew more and more nervous. Doubts began to crowd in upon him but he kept them at bay. Over coffee he judged that the right moment had arrived at last.

'The Dower House,' he announced suddenly.

'What about it?' she asked.

'I'm thinking of buying it.'

'You're not the only one, I'm afraid, Ralph.'

'Oh?'

'We've had several people in the Bull this past week, asking the way to the Brigadier's estate. It's created a lot of interest.'

It was an unpromising start for Ralph. He certainly had no wish to talk about the past week. He sipped at his coffee then tried again.

'It's time for a change,' he explained.

'A change?'

'Of address, of direction, of . . . well, I suppose you'd call it life-style.'

'Ralph,' laughed Lilian, 'I can't honestly imagine you ever changing your life-style.'

She was not making it easy for him. Perhaps she saw what he was working around to and was attempting to deflect him. This thought made Ralph even less confident.

'Do *you* like the Dower House, Lilian?' he enquired.

'How could anyone not like it?'

'I meant . . . would you like to live there?'

A rather wistful look came into her eyes. She finished her coffee and pushed the cup away.

'I'd love to, Ralph. But there's little hope of that. Hollowtree Flats will have to do me for a while.'

Was Lilian so blatantly unaware of what he was talking about? Or was she gently stone-walling him? Ralph no longer put his trust in language. He let actions speak in place of words. He reached into his pocket.

'Ralph!'

Nestling in a black velvet dimple was a diamond engagement ring. Lilian made the connection in an instant. She stared at the ring, and then at Ralph, shaking her head slowly in disbelief. He tried to read the expression in her eyes. He could discern the surprise and the mild shock easily; but he also saw, or believed that he saw, a kind of hesitant pleasure. Words began to tumble out of him.

'I had to have it altered, you see, because it was too big. Ah yes, you may wonder how I knew that. Well, let me tell you. February. Last February when you were hostess at that party I gave. Do you remember? Do you remember that party, Lilian?'

She nodded. A half-smile formed on her lips and stayed there.

'I looked at your gloves. That's to say, I went out of my way to check your glove size in order to get some idea. Uh, in the event. I thought it a sensible precaution . . . well, that's it.'

His confession about his detective work helped to broaden the half-smile into a grin. Was she laughing at him or with him?

'Well?' he asked.

But Lilian could say nothing. She shrugged her shoulders, and looked uncertain. He leaned across the table.

'Try it on, Lilian.'

'I don't know . . .'

'Please. Try it on.'

She let him slip the ring on to the third finger of her left hand. Neither of them seemed to notice at first. Then both realised what had happened. Their embarrassment was mutual. The ring which Ralph had chosen and bought for Lilian shared her finger with another engagement ring and a wedding ring. Ralph blamed himself for his lack of tact. Lilian instinctively reached down to remove the new ring, but Ralph stopped her with his hand.

'Before you do that . . .'

Lilian paused, looked down at the three rings again, then came to a decision.

'Can I have time to think it over, please?' she whispered.

'Of course, of course.'

'Just a little time. A week or so.'

'As long as you like.'

She tried to remove the ring but it was rather tight. He helped her and it eventually returned to its home in his pocket. Time to think it over. Ralph Bellamy was well pleased. At least he had not been refused. At least she had taken his proposal seriously.

Chapter Six

'Ours is an age dedicated to noise', complained the Reverend David Latimer, hands resting on the edge of the pulpit. 'Do you know, I sometimes feel that progress is the enemy of silence. Look around you. And listen. Every single advance we make is marked by an increase in volume. More traffic, louder machines, bigger bombs.'

He paused for effect and surveyed the upturned faces of the small congregation in the Church of St Stephen.

'It is a great joy to remember that we still have one quiet place left to us. That there still exists even today a place which can offer peace and serenity and the many consolations of silence. I am talking, of course, about the English Parish Church. It can be a refuge against the clamour. And this delightful church of ours, here in Ambridge, is a good example of what I mean . . .'

According to David Latimer, a vicar is like an opening batsman. The rest of the day's innings can depend on the start which he gives with his sermon. He himself was certainly on form on the Sunday morning following the point-to-point. He dispatched metaphors to the boundary, swept anecdotes gracefully past square leg and took a series of quick singles with well-chosen quotations from the New Testament. It was a purposeful, attacking sermon, full of the kind of refined aggression that is the basis of cricket.

'You may have heard the story about the Loud Man and the Quiet Woman . . . oh yes, there are quiet women, I am told.'

He permitted himself some polite anti-feminist humour, then found himself facing his first awkward delivery. A page of his notes seemed to be missing. He was about to be caught in the slips. Then he located his missing page, picked up his thread and cheated the cupped hands of the fieldsman. Soon he was punishing the bowling once more, driving his story firmly and elegantly through the covers.

Lilian Nicholson was aware of neither the sermon nor its cricketing affiliations. Yet she was very much at one with the sentiments which the vicar was expressing. She, too, had come to church in search of peace and quiet. Sitting in a pew at the rear of the nave, she was grateful for the opportunity to be alone with her thoughts, to go over the events of the previous day, to question, to ponder, to revalue. If she could see David Latimer in the pulpit, she was listening to other voices altogether.

Ralph Bellamy had proposed to her. The element of surprise had not diminished in the least. Of course, she knew that he was extremely fond of her. They had been out together often, he had bought Red Knight for her, he had even arranged for an artist to paint her portrait mounted on the horse. But there had never been the merest hint that marriage was anywhere in Ralph's mind. Kind, attentive and considerate, yes. Wooing her with a view to a proposal most certainly not. Looking back now over the past few months – the party at which she had acted as hostess for Ralph, the Hunt Ball they had gone to together, the casual, friendly conversations while they were out riding – Lilian began to view them in a different perspective. What she had hitherto dismissed as no more than a pleasant and very proper relationship with Ralph now took on the quality of an elaborate, not to say devious, courtship ritual.

'Our final hymn this morning is number . . .'

The vicar's announcement postponed further thought until after Lilian had found the relevant page in her hymnbook and taken out some money ready for the collection. By way of introduction, Philip Archer played a few bars on the organ and the congregation rose. David Latimer stood ready to lead the singing. He believed that a family service should include at least one hymn especially suited to the younger parishioners and this morning was no exception.

> 'Fair waved the golden corn
> In Canaan's pleasant land,
> When full of joy, some shining morn,
> Went forth the reaper band.'

Singing the words softly, Lilian let her mind wander again. She had cause to feel indignant. The meal was, after all, ostensibly to celebrate her triumph in the race. Yet somehow she had been manoeuvred into a proposal scene. This sense of being almost set up, of being at the centre of a calculated situation, piqued her. Ralph had laid everything on with a sort of heavy-handed romanticism. Champagne, rich food, music, soft lights, every reason to relax and be right off her guard. And then, as if it were an item on the menu, the proposal. He had even bought the ring, denying her the possibility of choice. She began to feel quite exasperated.

> 'In wisdom let us grow,
> As years and strength are given,
> That we may serve Thy Church below,
> And join Thy Saints in Heav'n.'

As she knelt for the final prayer, Lilian considered the claims of another emotion. A sense of achievement welled up in her. A feeling of having won a first prize and defeated other contenders. She had call to feel flattered. On paper, Ralph Bellamy was devastatingly eligible. Single, wealthy, respected, ambitious, acute, generous – every adjective was a separate commendation. In cold commercial terms she could not do better; but in other, more important, ways she already had.

At the end of the service, the vicar stood at the church door seeing his parishioners off. He reserved an especially warm handshake for Lilian and even permitted himself a kiss on her cheek.

'Congratulations, my dear!'

'Thank you.'

'If I'd been there, I'd have bet my last penny on you.'

'I didn't know the church approved of gambling?' she laughed.

'But it wasn't gambling! You were a cast-iron certainty.'

She thanked him again and went out into the churchyard where further congratulations awaited her. Polly and Mrs Mead talked about her as if she had won the Grand National, Shula, a most reluctant churchgoer as a rule, had come along solely to relive her aunt's triumph, and Lilian's grandparents repeated their kind remarks of the previous day. Her uncle, Tom Forrest, gamekeeper at the Country Park, added his best wishes with a gap-toothed grin and a horny hand.

'Beat 'em hollow, you did.'

'It wasn't that easy, Uncle Tom.'

'One-horse race. You'll have to take it up professional.'

'We'll see.'

'Yes,' he persisted. 'Get Ralph Bellamy to put you under contract. You and him can clean up at all the point-to-points.'

Lilian enjoyed the delight of her family and was gratified when she was taken aside by her aunt, Jill, who wanted to thank her on Shula's behalf.

'You're such a good influence on her, Lilian.'

'I'm not sure I like the sound of that,' she smiled.

'Seriously, Shula looks up to you. You're her heroine. Phil and I are delighted she's modelling herself on someone worthwhile.'

'That's putting it rather strong, Aunt Jill.'

'Wait till you have kids,' warned the other. 'Honestly, you should see the cretins that some of Shula's schoolfriends idolise – film stars and pop singers and those dreadful long-haired footballers and heaven knows what else . . . in that company, you're a saint.'

'It puts a terrible responsibility on to me, though.'

'Not really. All you have to do is to go on enjoying yourself and keep winning races.'

Lilian was touched by what her aunt had said and thought

about it as she walked back to the Bull, where she wanted to help out for an hour.

'Here she is – the Queen of the Turf!' yelled Sid Perks, as she walked in.

'Not exactly, Sid.'

'Don't be modest,' he teased. 'Eh, what's next – the Derby, the St Leger or the London to Brighton Old Crocks Race?'

'The last one, I think.'

Sid laughed and told a joke about horse-racing, which she had heard him tell many times before. She obliged with a smile, glad to find him in something like his old mood again, though still wondering why he had been in such a peculiar state at the dance.

Her mother welcomed her and she went behind the bar to put on an apron over her suit. She served several customers and then found herself facing Sid again. He began to tell her the joke which he had told earlier.

'You've told me that once, Sid.'

'Ah no, this time it's different 'cos I've forgotten the punch-line,' he said, swaying slightly. 'But, talking horses, what happened to the famous Anne Hawkes yesterday?'

'It just wasn't her day.'

'Come on, tell us the truth,' urged Tony, leaning across the bar towards his sister and resting his elbow in the middle of some spilled beer. 'How did you fix the race?'

'Ground glass in the other horses' nosebags,' offered Sid, giggling.

'A fiver on the sly to Anne Hawkes,' asserted Tony.

'A bowl of spinach to Red Knight minutes before the start,' decided Sid, inflating his chest with dramatic suddenness and flexing his muscles. *'Popeye the Sailor Man!'*

Customers called for service and Lilian was rescued from their banter. Sid and Tony transferred their affections to the dartboard.

It would be another world altogether; Lilian understood that. Marriage to Ralph Bellamy would take her right out of this world that she knew and had grown up in. She glanced around the bar, assessing what she would be leaving behind. Firstly, the noise, a subject fit for any sermon. Laughter, argument, challenge, buying, selling. The thud of the darts into the board. The click of the dominoes being laid in position. The creak of old bones and the grating of old chairs. The sound of swallow and gulp and gurgle. Glasses on wood. Beer pumps sighing at their work. Feet shifting position. Coins jingling. The song of the till. Tops parted from bottles. Crisps. Peanuts. And all the other elements in a vast interlocking pattern of sound. Lilian could certainly bear to leave it. Peggy Archer might love the atmosphere of the Bull. Jack Archer, in healthier times, might have found it his spiritual home. But to Lilian there was something vaguely demeaning about having to serve behind the bar. It was a world she would not really miss with any sadness.

'Hurry up, Jack. You're keeping us waiting,' chided Peggy Archer, already seated at the table with Lilian.

'Sorry, my darlings,' muttered her husband, his movements slowed and his words slurred by the lunchtime's consumption. 'Coming.'

Jack Archer bestowed a kiss of apology on his wife's cheek then sat down at the table. It was three o'clock. They were at last ready to begin their Sunday lunch.

'Everybody was talking about you, Lilian,' beamed Peggy.

'Ar, yes,' agreed Jack. 'You did us proud.'

'You did Ralph proud as well,' pointed out his wife. 'Um . . . did you have a nice time last night?'

'Very nice, thanks.'

'Where did you go?'

'For a meal, Mum.'

'At Redgate Manor, was it? They do a wonderful meal, they say. We should go there some time, Jack.'

'Mm? Ah, yes. Whatever you say, Peg,' mumbled Jack, coping with a piece of Yorkshire pudding.

'Tell us what you had to eat,' invited Peggy.

'Another time, Mum.'

Lilian spent the next ten minutes wrestling with the

problem of how and whether to tell them. Her father seemed as subdued and listless as usual. Her mother was chattering away harmlessly, passing the morning's gossip on to them. Lilian did not want to speak, but they had the right to be told first. Their opinions – her mother's view, in particular – mattered to Lilian. She did not feel she could make up her mind all on her own. Eventually, she announced her news. There was a long pause.

'More meat, Jack?' asked Peggy, assaulting the joint with the carver.

'Oh, um, no thanks. Well, yes . . . all right,' he dithered.

Peggy put the slices of beef into his plate, then moved the gravy jug closer to him. Without looking up, she addressed herself to the joint, carving vigorously.

'Lilian?'

'Not for me, thanks.'

Lilian gave her parents time to assimilate the information. She could see that her mother was pleased, almost as if some long-cherished hopes had been fulfilled. But Peggy Archer was trying to hide her feelings beneath a flurry of nervous activity, serving herself and her husband more potatoes, moving things that did not need to be moved. Lilian turned to her father who seemed pleasantly bewildered by what he had just been told. She felt sad that he was not in the best of health. A few years ago his reaction would have been instantaneous. He would never have continued eating in the way he was doing. Lilian decided they had had time enough.

'Well?'

'We're both very pleased for you,' said her mother, cautiously. 'Aren't we, Jack?'

'Very pleased,' echoed her husband.

'It's . . . well, it's wonderful news, really.'

Lilian wondered why her mother's voice trailed away, why she did not sound as thrilled as she looked. She had told her parents in order that their response would clarify her own thoughts. But they were not helping her at all.

'Then you approve?' she asked, bluntly.

'Naturally. Don't we, Jack?'

'Naturally.'

'*If* it's what you want, Lilian,' added her mother.

'And if it's what *he* wants,' laughed her father, incongruously.

Peggy Archer cleared the plates away and brought the apple crumble from the oven. She was containing her own delight until Lilian had come to a decision. Sitting down again, she put a hand on her daughter's arm.

'Is it what you want, darling?'

'I don't know, Mum. I just don't know. One minute I think it is, and the next . . . I'm not so sure.'

'You never had this trouble last time,' blurted out her father.

'Jack!' scolded his wife.

But Lilian was glad of the reminder. Last time she had not needed to weigh and consider and test the reactions of others. She somehow *knew*. The very fact that she had asked for time to think it over was an argument against it.

'Whatever you decide, we'll be pleased,' said Jack Archer, trying to retrieve what he realised was a blunder.

'It's your decision, Lilian,' indicated her mother. 'But you'll have us right behind you . . . whichever way things work out.'

Lilian was right back where she had started. Completely at sea. The talk with her parents had not given her any of the bearings she had expected. It had left her adrift. Perhaps she should look elsewhere for advice?

It was some days before she found the courage to ride across his land. Though she and Ralph had agreed not to meet again until she had made up her mind, she feared a casual encounter if she went near his estate. At length she accepted that it was unlikely that they would bump into each other. Ralph had spoken about the large amount of work he had to do, about a few days in East Anglia, about other visits he would have to make away from Ambridge. She saddled Red Knight and cantered in the direction of Manor Court Farm.

All around her were visible proofs of Ralph's faith in mixed farming. The dairy herd had been turned out for some weeks now but the young stock had only just been given their first taste of freedom in the field. They were chasing about in groups, exploring every inch of their territory, pausing to graze for a few minutes, then racing off again. Sheep were grazing in an adjoining field, and in the distance beyond that Lilian could see a machine busy planting potatoes. She rode past land set aside for sugar beet and barley and wheat and grass. She skirted the woodland in which some of Ralph's workers were spraying with Paraquat. She recognised fields devoted to peas and beans and sprouts. Ralph Bellamy's farming enterprise was a tribute to planning and variety. The estate comprised nearly three thousand acres, some of it tenanted. Lilian could not suppress a thrill at the idea of being the mistress of that estate. All this and the Dower House to live in. They were powerful arguments.

She saw Tony long before he noticed her. He was walking down the field where the dairy herd was strip-grazing, moving the electric fence another six feet or so. He had switched off the fence and was lifting out the stakes before forcing them into the ground again. Lilian watched him and admired the sense of rhythm as he lifted, moved, re-positioned, then brought down his heel on the twisted metal at the base of the stake. As each new section of fresh grass was liberated for their attentions, the cows began grazing in earnest. A few walked behind Tony, one of them nuzzling him playfully. He turned to smack it away and saw Lilian. His wave and grin somehow deterred Lilian. This was not the place to tell Tony. She felt that she had to be on neutral territory. She waved her farewell.

'Come right on in, love!'

'Are you sure I'm not interrupting you, Grandad?'

'You're doing exactly that – thank goodness!'

Lilian had strolled over to the village and on down to Glebe Cottage, where she had found her grandfather working desultorily with a hoe. He had given her a royal welcome, seeing in her visit a means of escape from gardening.

'Doris, look who's come calling!' he yelled.

'What's that?'

Doris Archer came round the rhododendron bushes which screened one half of the garden from the other. She welcomed Lilian as warmly as Dan had done, sent him indoors to make a pot of tea, moaned about how she could not get him to do anything – but, *anything* – in the garden, then motioned Lilian to the deck chairs.

'It's looking beautiful,' complimented Lilian, sitting down.

'Needs a lot doing to it yet,' confessed her grandmother, pulling off her gardening gloves. 'But I haven't got the stickability I used to have.'

'Nonsense, Gran.'

'I could work in the garden at Brookfield for hours on end when we lived there. But here, I can only managed to potter.'

Lilian pointed out that the pottering had produced amazing results. The garden was a blaze of colour with the deep violet blue of the aubretia and the pale yellow of the alyssum especially arresting. White lilac had just started to put forth, and pink blossom was out on the flowering cherry. Lilian felt relaxed. It was a place where she could talk. Dan came out with a tray of tea.

'Put it down over here,' said Doris, taking charge.

'Can I do anything to help?' asked Lilian.

'You already have, love!'

'Dan!'

'Yes, I'll pour, love,' he volunteered happily, ignoring the reproving glance which Doris aimed at him.

Lilian did not have to wait long for an opportunity. Doris talked about the Brigadier and said how much he was missed at the point-to-point races. From the Brigadier, the conversation proceeded naturally to the question of who would buy his estate. Dan remarked that Ralph Bellamy would be a strong contender, and Lilian delayed no more.

'He's asked me to marry him.'

There was a moment's pause. Doris regained a voice first.

'Ralph Bellamy?'

'After the race on Saturday. We had a meal together.'

'Well, I'll be blowed!' mused Dan, in a way which gave no clue as to his true feelings about the situation.

'Uh, have you accepted, dear?' enquired Doris, tentatively.

'No. I asked for time to consider.'

Lilian noticed both her grandparents looking slightly relieved at this news. It was not a promising reaction.

'I'd like to know what you both think.'

'Oh, but it's your decision, Lilian,' said Doris.

'We wouldn't try to persuade you one way or the other,' agreed Dan.

'I'd just like to know your opinions, that's all.'

Dan and Doris exchanged a look. Doris acted as spokesman. 'What do your parents feel about it?'

'They're perfectly happy with the idea.'

'Are they?' Dan's tone had hardened.

'They both say they'll be behind me, whatever I decide.'

'So will we, dear,' promised Doris. 'So will we.'

Lilian was upset that her grandfather did not endorse this remark. He stirred his tea and stared into it.

'I think you should be very flattered,' went on Doris.

'I am. I don't get all that many offers,' smiled Lilian.

'I meant, well, bearing in mind what an important man Ralph Bellamy is. Yes, I know that that's not everything where a marriage is concerned, but I think it matters. It should be taken into account. Who he is. And what he is. Why, in five or ten years' time, you could be . . . Anyway, just think about it.'

Still no words from Dan. Lilian's embarrassment began to crimson her cheeks. This provoked Doris into a more effusive response. She crossed to Lilian and put her arms round her.

'Congratulations, Lilian. I'm thrilled!'

'Thank you.'

'I think you should . . . if it's what you want, of course . . . but I'd be very pleased if you accepted him.'

'Would you, Gran? Really and truly?'

The tears that formed in her grandmother's eyes confirmed the sincerity of her advice. Lilian helped her back to her seat.

She was pleased that someone at least had come out openly in support of the notion of her marrying Ralph. There were, however, reservations. Lilian was bound to wonder how far the older woman's opinions were dictated by her own experience in the village of Ambridge. For so very many years, Doris Archer had been in service with the Lawson-Hope family. She retained an exaggerated respect for the local squire and for the whole concept of a hierarchy. That someone in her own family circle should actually marry the local squire was bound to create a sense of awe in Doris. Those social divisions, which had been steadily removed or blurred throughout her lifetime, still had some meaning to her. Lilian appreciated all this. At the same time, she knew that her grandmother would never concentrate solely on the social implications. She would never urge anyone into a marriage which threatened the slightest unhappiness. No, Doris Archer had voted for the marriage. What did her husband think about the idea?

'Say something, Dan. Don't just sit there with a face like fourpence.'

Doris's scorn brought him back to life. He scratched his head, then turned to Lilian.

'I, um . . . I go along with what your Gran says.'

'No, you don't, Grandad.'

Lilian was too astute to be palmed off with a comment like that. Her grandfather nursed very definite objections. Lilian wanted to know exactly what they were. Chapter and verse.

'Speak your mind. Please,' she encouraged.

'Listen, love . . .'

'Do as you're told, Dan Archer. For heaven's sake, you're among family. Now give your honest opinion.'

'All right . . . look, I'm sorry about this, Lilian . . .'

'Please. Just say it. I prefer it that way.'

'Then I'm agin the idea altogether,' he declared.

'Whatever for?' said Doris, bridling.

'You've had your say, Doris. Now let me have mine. . . . The thing is . . . to put it baldly . . . I don't think Ralph Bellamy is approaching the marriage with the right motives.'

'And what are they when they're at home?'

Doris Archer was far from pleased with the way Dan was arguing.

'I must hear him out, Gran,' pleaded Lilian. 'It's important.'

Doris nodded. She glowered at her husband but she did not interrupt him again. When he spoke in his mellow, measured tones, he came straight to the point.

'Ralph Bellamy is a very ambitious man. Wants to be the big wheel around here. Ideally, he wants to put the clock back fifty years or more and be another Squire Lawson-Hope . . .'

This implied reproach of her former employer drew a snort from Doris, but it did not halt her husband.

'Why mince words? Ralph wants to own this village. He wants to get his hands on every bit of Ambridge that he can. He wants to buy the Dower House. He wants to take over the Brigadier's estate. He's even got his eye on Brookfield . . . yes, he has, Doris, so it's no use you frowning at me like that. He's after *our* farm.'

'I don't believe it,' intervened Lilian.

'It's true, love. That's why he's got our Tony working for him, chasing a promise of being his farm manager one day. And that's why . . .' His voice faded. Lilian could see that he was trying to shield her from some blow.

'Go on,' she pressed. 'I'd rather you said it.'

'That's why *you're* on the shopping-list as well.'

Further discussion was superfluous. Lilian was torn between anger and pain. She mumbled her thanks and went out through the gate. Before she was out of earshot, Doris Archer was ridding herself of a few acid remarks about her husband's tact and commonsense.

Dusk was falling as Lilian walked away. She felt weary, hurt, jaded, beleaguered. She was at once afraid of being alone with her thoughts and yet desperately wanting the complete isolation in which to sort out her own mind. Almost insensibly, her footsteps turned towards the church. She went up through the churchyard, following the path as it twisted between the gravestones. When she reached the church itself, she sat down on the stone bench in the porch. The cool breeze and the cold stone were refreshing.

Lilian Nicholson did not love Ralph Bellamy. She knew that all her reasoning must proceed from this fundamental fact. The question she kept coming up against was whether or not she could, in time, come to love him. Who was this man? Slowly but bravely, she began to collect together in her mind all the opinions she had heard about Ralph Bellamy. She built them up into an Identikit picture. Lilian let the most caustic comments of her grandfather determine the profile. She let other features be governed by the views of her brother, her grandmother, her parents, her friends. Ralph Bellamy was much talked about and she had no difficulty recalling phrases or individual words used about him in the village. When she had completed her mental picture, it was not an appealing one. Ralph Bellamy emerged as a cold, objective, fair-minded yet ruthless man. Lilian seemed to be no more than part of a plan.

'Is that you, Lilian?'

'Oh yes . . . hello, vicar.'

David Latimer had been crossing the churchyard on his way back to the Vicarage when he caught sight of the figure huddled in the porch. Concern registered on his wrinkled face.

'Are you all right?'

'Yes, I'm fine, fine.'

Lilian could see that he wanted more than a simple assurance. 'I was just resting. Thinking.'

'We're always open for that.'

She got up and they walked through the churchyard together. When they reached the gate, he turned to her as if he was giving her the chance to say what was on her mind, but she was unable to tell him.

'I've been to Glebe Cottage. I was . . . just walking past.'

'How were your grandparents?'

'Madly busy in the garden, Gran, anyway.'

'They're a remarkable pair when you think about it, you know. Your family must feel proud of them.'

'We do,' she said, hiding the resentment she still harboured against her grandfather.

'What a wonderful advertisement for marriage those two are,' observed the vicar, casually.

The remark stayed with her all the way home and it helped her to arrive at a decision. As she fell asleep that night, she knew exactly what her answer to Ralph must be.

CHAPTER SEVEN

HE LIKED the idea immensely. Polly could see that. She had long ago cracked the code. If he remained in his chair, rubbing the palm of his hand across his chin and humming through his nose, then he was signalling disapproval. If he stood up behind his desk and swayed gently to and fro, he was indicating interest. But when he paced around the office and talked to himself, he was very much in favour. This time he was on the move, holding an urgent conversation with himself, making sudden turns, gesticulating, slapping the desk. Polly knew that he was quite convinced. Still circling, he pronounced his verdict.

'Go ahead. Send me the bill.'

'Do you mean it, Mr Woolley?' asked Sid, excitedly.

'I believe in getting on with things. Delay is foreign to me.'

'That's great! That's marvellous!'

Polly was touched by the glow of pleasure on Sid's face. It was worth it just to see that.

'Start as soon as you like, Sid,' exhorted Jack Woolley. 'If you need any cash in advance, just give me a yell.'

'That's very kind of you,' observed Polly.

'See – what did I tell you, Poll Doll? I knew he'd go for it. I mean, well . . .'

Sid coloured slightly, fearing that he had phrased his remark rather badly. The older man chuckled and patted him on the back.

Polly liked Jack Woolley. It was true that he was volatile by nature and had a temper as warm as his enthusiasm. Many of the staff at Grey Gables Country Club found his moods unreliable and tended to fear him. Polly judged the man by her own dealings with him. Though some villagers might dismiss him as no more than a thrusting businessman trying to pass himself off as a country gentleman, she thought him fair, tolerant, hard-working and open. She knew where she stood with this dapper little man, who was running to fat and who was always buttoning his coat over the tell-tale pot-belly.

'Well, if that's all . . .'

'Uh, yes, Mr Woolley,' said Sid. 'I'll get on with it tomorrow.'

'Perhaps not tomorrow,' cautioned Polly.

Woolley's sharp eye caught the change of feeling in Sid, even though the latter tried to control it.

'Got something on tomorrow?' he quizzed.

'Nothing special,' shrugged Sid, the grin resuming its old tyranny over his features.

'Sid had forgotten, that's all,' clarified Polly. 'Well, it's very good of you to see us at such short notice, Mr Woolley. We won't take up any more of your time.'

'Pleasure, Polly. The night is young yet. Why don't you let me buy you both a drink in the cocktail bar?'

Sid was eager to accept but remembered something and declined the invitation on their behalf. Woolley saw them to the door, telling them how glad he was that they were now working in harness at the shop.

'Young married couple. Best team there is. Gives you a psychological advantage from the start.'

'I'm not with you,' puzzled Sid.

'Polly will explain,' assured the older man, buttoning his coat.

He waved them off. It was another thing which Polly admired about the man. This genuine fondness he had for them as a young couple. Given his own marital difficulties, Jack Woolley might be expected to talk about marriage with a well-informed cynicism. Instead, he spoke of it with longing. He had a rare ability to be happy in the happiness of others, and drew a kind of naive strength from the example of Sid and Polly.

'Right, leave this lot to me, love.'

'Sid, you can't!'

'Who's the gaffer round here, then?' challenged Sid, holding up his fists ready for a mock fight.

'You can't go on doing *everything.*'

'That – as the A said to the B – remains to be seen, my love.'

Polly protested as he eased her into a chair and switched the television on for her. But Sid was adamant. Before long he had washed up the dishes which they had had to leave after tea in order to be at Grey Gables for their appointment at seven. He had made her a coffee. He had fetched ner some slippers. He had settled down beside her. And, true to form, he forgot that she was supposed to be watching television and read snippets out to her from the evening paper.

'Hey, here's a good one. VICAR ATTACKS MOTHERS' UNION. There's a laugh for a start. . . .'

Polly got up and switched off the television.

'Hey, what are you doing!' he remonstrated.

'Switching that off doesn't take much effort, Sid.'

'You're supposed to rest.'

'Only according to you.'

'Don't be ridiculous, love. You've got to take it easy. And Sidney is here to make you do just that.'

'But the doctor said . . .'

Polly was talking to a wall of newspaper and not making an impact. She sat back and reflected on the meeting with Jack Woolley. A loud guffaw came from behind the newspaper.

'Oh yes, we must have that! We simply must!'

Sid carefully tore a section out of the newspaper and read it to himself with renewed amusement. Polly did not bother to ask him what it was. She would doubtless see it in time. Sid was always tearing things out of newspapers – jokes, cartoons, photographs, headlines which tickled his fancy. He usually pasted them on to a large board, which was hung in the shop between a poster about Supplementary Benefits and another concerning Savings Accounts. Polly saw no harm in what her husband called his 'chuckleboard'. It provided a lot of humour for the queueing customer and was an unfailing talking-point. She decided to bring Sid back to the problem arising out of their interview with Jack Woolley.

'Colours, Sid.'

'Eh?' he asked, folding the piece of paper up.

'Now that Mr Woolley says we can paint the outside of the shop, we'll have to choose some colours.'

The decorator in Sid took over and he let his imagination off its leash.

'Something bright, daring, eye-catching. What about a Gentian Violet or a Canary Yellow or even a Vermilion? There's endless possibilities, Poll,' he promised, flicking through a mental colour chart. 'Autumn Green, Pale Mimosa, Dawn Pink, Mediterranean Blue. . . .'

'Sid, we're painting a shop not designing a rainbow.'

'We want people to know we're here,' he countered. 'What do you say to Scorched Earth woodwork and Flame Orange brickwork?'

'Ugh!' replied Polly, pulling a face.

'Okay, if you prefer something with a touch of class, we'll settle for Royal Blue woodwork with gold lettering, and brick-work in a nice rich cream.'

'We have to consider the houses all round us,' Polly reminded him.

'Why? I'm not painting them as well.'

'But we have to match in with the rest of the village.'

'Do you know your trouble? You're too conventional, love. Your mind needs liberating from its own run-of-the-millery. You leave it to the professional. I'll come up with a colour combination that will take Ambridge by storm.'

'Black woodwork, white brickwork,' insisted Polly.

'Please, now! Don't insult an artist. Black and white? How corny can you get?'

Polly let him rhapsodise about a whole range of garish and wholly unsuitable colours. Then she played her ace.

'Black and white, Sid. It's what Mr Woolley would like.'

He tightened his jaw, pointed a finger, racked his brain for an answer, then sat back and grinned.

'Black and white, then,' he agreed, capitulating. 'Um, stripes?'

'No, you daft thing.'

Polly crossed to him and kissed him. She loved to see him back in moods like this.

On balance, Polly was glad that she had told him when she did. It had lifted the cloud that was hovering over them and brought them closer together. Sid's joy had been unfeigned. He had undergone a transformation. After their talk in the Country Park, when he had been shown the letter, Sid had been bitter and uncommunicative. Polly had put up with it for a few days and then, almost in desperation, she had sprung her news upon him. It had changed everything. Sid had been wonderful, taking control, planning, protecting her. He had decided to sort her major anxiety out once and for all. It was he who had suggested the visit and he who had insisted on coming along himself. Polly was no longer as fearful as she had been. With Sid beside her, she could face anything. Even him.

'Here we are – breakfast is served.'

'Oh Sid, you shouldn't have!'

'But I have, all the same. Now sit up and have the tray across your knees.'

It was Polly's one reservation. Sid was treating her like some sort of invalid. Not only had he taken on the lion's share of the work in the shop, he was cooking the meals and doing the washing up and generally relieving her of anything which required the most minimal physical effort. The sequence of breakfasts in bed had now lasted beyond a week. Polly was finding it rather oppressive. She raised an arm in token protest but Sid overruled her. He put the tray on her lap, plumped her pillows behind her back, then went off whistling to have his shave. Polly, who liked a soft-boiled egg in the morning, tackled Sid's defiantly hard-boiled egg out of loyalty. There was a limit. Polly sensed that she was approaching it.

Her natural apprehension grew throughout the morning. She was not at all certain that a visit was the best solution, if, indeed, it was any kind of solution at all. And why did they have to go that very afternoon? Polly could think of a dozen arguments against it, each more persuasive than the last. They ought to postpone their outing for a fortnight. Even a month. What kept her from suggesting this to Sid was the fact that he seemed quite unruffled by the prospect of the visit. He worked away in the shop with zeal and enjoyment, sustaining Polly with his own geniality. As a diversion, she glanced at his chuckleboard, which was covered in a strange array of cuttings. She smiled, less at the items themselves than at what they said about Sid's boyish sense of humour. One thing which Polly could not see was the piece of paper which Sid had torn out on the previous evening. It had been a sizeable section, far larger than anything on the chuckleboard. Polly concluded that he had rejected it after consideration.

Closing time was at hand and there were only two customers left in the shop. She wanted them to stay, to delay the moment when she would have to get ready to set out on the visit.

'I can't seem to see the bread, Sid.'

'Right behind you, my love. Top shelf.'

'I wanted a medium sliced.'

'Further along. Second shelf.'

Lilian Nicholson was not the only person who was having difficulty adjusting to the new self-service arrangements at the Village Stores. Polly herself had not completely mastered the system. She totted up the items in Lilian's basket and rang up the price on the till.

'It'll have to go, Sid Perks. It's like doing your shopping in that there 'Ampton Court Maze.'

'You'll get used to it, Walter.'

'I likes hindividual service. A ready smile and a saucy remark.'

'You got a barmaid fixation,' joked Sid. 'To you paradise is a saloon bar full of free beer, sly winks and pinchable bums.'

Walter Gabriel's laugh sounded like gravel being tipped in large quantities on to corrugated iron. Both Lilian and Polly smiled as the old man terminated his laugh with a cough and a wheeze. Walter pulled at the lobe of an ancient ear, out of which a small forest of hair was growing.

'Serious, though, what's the point of all this 'ere new-fangled, 'igh-falutin' rhubarb about Self Service? Am you a-trying to satisfy your customer, baffle 'im, or bamboozle 'im?'

'All three – in that order.'

'Don't tease, Sid,' scolded Polly. 'It's only an experiment, Mr Gabriel.'

'Can you make 'ead or tail of where things is, Lilian?' asked Walter, waving a despairing arm in the direction of the shelves.

'I'm having difficulty,' admitted Lilian.

All four debated the advantages and disadvantages of self-service. Polly was not surprised that Walter was totally against it. He was one of the oldest inhabitants in the village, and had been born and bred in Ambridge. His concept of what a Village Stores should be like had been formed decades before Polly was born. Like Dan Archer, Walter was a countryman with a healthy suspicion of basic changes in the routine of living.

'Coming to more himportant topics, who's a-going to get 'is 'ooks on the Brigadier's hestate?' asked Walter, settling into the chair by the counter, and removing his crumpled hat.

'Now you're asking,' said Sid.

Polly noticed that Lilian did not find the speculation as interesting as the others. Three of them exchanged opinions willingly, but Lilian seemed to be holding back. Polly felt obliged to offer her a way into the conversation.

'Several people have been in and asked the way to the Dower House. Daresay it's been the same at the Bull?'

'Yes,' nodded Lilian. 'We've had enquiries.'

'Big field. Make it more unpredictable,' noted Sid, rubbing his hands.

Walter hooked a thumb into his tattered and gravy-stained waistcoat and sounded authoritative.

'Bellamy'll get it, mark my words. 'E gets all that's going round 'ere. Ralph Bellamy. 'Im'll be the new Squire.'

Out of the corner of her eye, Polly saw Lilian redden slightly. The mention of Ralph Bellamy's name had discomfited her. Sid took his turn at crystal-gazing.

'Not a chance. Ralph Bellamy won't get a sniff of the property.'

'Then who will?' asked Lilian.

Polly thought she detected a slightly defensive tone.

'The big White Chief himself, of course. J. Woolley, Esquire. Our Father Which art in Grey Gables.'

'Jack Woolley,' snorted Walter, scratching his neck above the collarless shirt. 'What does 'e want with a thousand acres of farming land?'

'Room to expand,' explained Sid.

Polly recognised the look in Sid's eye. He was about to sound off in his most characteristic way. She tried to check him with a cough but it was unheeded. Sid spoke airily and confidently.

'Woolley's the typical self-made man. He's got to keep going. He can never stop. Okay – so he wants to make the Country Park bigger. What does he do? Swallows up the Brigadier's estate and uses the Dower House as a kind of Hunting Lodge.'

'We don't know that, Sid . . .' began Polly.

'As a matter of fact, I was chatting to him in his office at Grey Gables only last night,' continued Sid, assuming the status of personal friend to Woolley, if not that of business consultant. 'He as good as told me then that he'd be bidding at the auction. And when it comes to putting cash down on the table, there's nobody to touch him. No, if he's set his mind on having the Brigadier's place, then Ralph Bellamy and a dozen like him won't be able to shift him.'

By the time he had finished speaking, Sid had convinced Walter, Lilian and himself that Jack Woolley was a serious contender for the estate. Polly knew that it was no use pointing out that Woolley had not actually said half the things which her husband had imputed to him. Sid was impervious to hard fact at a time like this. Besides, Polly was not thinking about the auction any more. As soon as she saw the two customers out of the shop and locked up, her mind reverted to the afternoon's visit.

Mrs Mead had been the first problem. She had a long-standing claim on Thursday afternoons as far as Polly was concerned. The regular tea with her daughter was a real supportive factor in Mrs Mead's life. Though she saw Sid and Polly at other times in the week, a Thursday afternoon was a special occasion to her, and she did not want to be deprived of it. Polly had explained that that afternoon Sid was taking her to Borchester to visit the Ante-Natal Clinic. Mrs Mead had then insisted on replacing Sid, but Polly had been firm. Her mother could go with her to the Clinic another time. The father must take precedence.

Eventually, Mrs Mead had accepted this ruling. She had been so thrilled by the news of the baby that Polly had wished she could have told her mother earlier. Mrs Mead had burst into tears and been inconsolable for minutes. Then she had recovered, expressed her delight, and confided details of Polly's own birth to her. She had talked for a long time, happily confusing memory with nostalgia. That evening, she had determined, Sid and Polly had to call round to her to celebrate. When they had arrived, Polly had been moved by the trouble to which her mother had gone. She had bought a card, a cheap bottle of sherry, and a book of names; and she had made a whole range of savouries and cakes. Polly had found it a heart-warming evening. Looking back on it now, she regretted that her mother was going to miss her Thursday afternoon with her daughter. She also regretted having to lie to Mrs Mead. But she, above all people, could never be told where they were really going.

Polly ate no lunch. Apprehension had developed into a gnawing worry which subdued her appetite. She was glad that Sid did not have the same anxieties, or that he was managing to cope with them better than she was. Polly watched him as he ate heartily and boasted about how fresh the shop would look once he had painted it. He had other plans for the business and aired them importantly. Soon, however, it was time to go. They got ready, went downstairs and unlocked the shop door. Before they stepped out, Sid took Polly by the shoulders and kissed her lightly on the forehead.

'Let me do the talking, love,' he said, gently.

'All right.'

It was in a country area about twenty miles due south of Birmingham. To reach it one had to turn off the main road into a narrow lane, then follow that for a quarter of a mile. Overhanging trees obscured it from view until one got to within fifty yards of it. Then it disclosed itself, tucked away comfortably in an impressive woodland setting. At first glance, it looked very much like an ordinary hospital, but this impression was soon dispelled by the height of the perimeter wall and by the row of metal spikes running along the top of it. The massive gates, which were opened freely to visitors and to staff, were closed against the patients themselves. This hospital mixed medication with restraint. It had to contain as well as cure.

Polly tried to ignore the more obvious security arrangements as she and Sid went up the drive, obeying the sign marked 'Visitors'. Signs were very much in evidence throughout the grounds. They reduced both the rules of the establishment and its architectural shape to a series of terse phrases. The buildings themselves, which had seemed relatively modern from a distance, were slightly neglected when one got closer. Not for the first time, Polly noticed the perished brickwork in some of the walls and the lack of paint on much of the woodwork. Sid seemed to be less troubled by the environment than she had anticipated.

After taking the advice of several signs and a few arrows, they came to a large garden at the rear of the main block. Several people were sitting about on benches or standing in groups or walking dully along. Polly knew where he would be and took Sid straight there. They found him on the bench by the pond. He looked up without surprise and spoke as if he saw them every day.

'Have you any idea what's happened to them?' he asked.

'Uh . . . to what?' wondered Sid.

'The goldfish in the pond. There's no sign of them.'

'Sorry. Not a clue,' shrugged Sid.

The other came to a decision and spoke with bitterness.

'It's that man from West Block again. That so-called fisherman. I'll bring this up at the next Council Meeting. You'll support me there, won't you?'

'Uh, well . . . yes,' agreed Sid uncertainly.

'What about you?' he asked Polly.

She nodded, sat beside him on the bench, and indicated that Sid should sit on the other side of him. She noticed that his hand was clasped tightly around something, just as it had been on her other visit.

'How are you, Dad?' Polly enquired.

'Me? Oh, I'm fine,' he chuckled. 'Never felt better.'

'Good.'

'What about you two? Let me see, it's Sid, isn't it? How are you both keeping?'

'Not too bad,' answered Sid for both of them.

Polly caught a glance from him which invited her to keep quiet. Before they had left home, they had agreed that Mr Mead was not to be told about the baby. It was an emotive subject and was hardly a thing to be discussed under the circumstances.

'They're looking after you all right, then, Mr Mead?' Sid

regained the familiar jocular note in his voice. It brought a rich chuckle out of the older man.

'I don't let them get away with much, you know. I keep them up to scratch. I maintain standards.'

An old lady hobbled past, leaning on the arm of a nurse. Polly's father hailed them both cheerfully by their Christian names, then talked volubly about the old lady's case with a kind of brisk compassion.

'She's been here for over twelve years now and the treatment they've given her has varied tremendously. At first, of course, they started her off with . . .'

Listening to him, Polly thought he sounded less like a patient himself than a senior member of staff. He seemed so totally plausible. Polly had always known her father as a man who took trouble over his appearance and the habits of a lifetime had not deserted him in hospital. His short hair was neatly combed, his face clean-shaven, his nails were shining. He even contrived to look smart in his old brown pin-striped suit, which he wore over a dark green shirt and tie. To all appearances Frank Mead was a perfectly normal and healthy man in his early fifties, slim, alert, quite rational. As at their earlier meeting, Polly felt a great onrush of sympathy for him.

'I've been elected on to the Council, by the way,' her father said.

'Oh that's . . . that's an achievement,' offered Sid.

'Well they need someone to provide ideas and I seem to be the only one round here with any drive. Do you know what I think we need? A magazine. A magazine which we produce ourselves. I've worked it all out, even down to the title . . .'

Frank Mead talked intelligibly about his projected magazine for the patients and Sid nodded dutifully. Polly was given time to remember why her sympathy for her father should not be wholly uncritical. He had made her mother intensely unhappy. He had brought a lot of suffering and humiliation to his family for a number of years. It was right to be sorry for the mentally disturbed, and to accept that they were not responsible for their actions. But Polly felt that the true sympathy belonged to her mother who had carried her husband for so long, explaining away his peculiarities, stage-managing his appearances, disguising the full truth about her husband. It had taken years off Mrs Mead's life. By comparison with her, Frank Mead seemed quite sprightly. Polly believed that he had far more actual happiness inside his private world than ever her mother would now find. Sitting beside her father now, her compassion for him was much more guarded. Sid seemed to read her thoughts. He cut right across his father-in-law's monologue.

'This will be the last time we come,' he declared firmly.

Frank Mead seemed not to have heard him, but went off on another tack altogether. His tone was mildly accusatory.

'Polly, why didn't you tell me?'

'Tell you, Dad?'

'About the Brigadier's death. I read it in the *Borchester Echo*. We sometimes have old copies passed around. There's a man in East Block from Borchester. His son brings in . . . anyway, I read the obituary there. Why didn't you tell me he'd died?'

'That's all in the past,' muttered Sid.

'But I'd like to have been there,' insisted Mr Mead. He held up the small black book which was in his hand and tapped it with a finger. 'I should have liked to have read something at the funeral. A good man, the Brigadier. I respected him.'

Polly glanced at Sid again. It was time to make sure that her father understood their position as clearly as he was able.

'This will be the last time,' affirmed Sid. 'Don't expect us again.'

Frank Mead examined him calmly for a moment, then turned to Polly. A wistful expression came into his eyes. 'How is your mother?'

Polly was thrown slightly off balance by the question. She mumbled an answer. Frank Mead adopted a ponderous sincerity.

'I miss her. I miss her a lot. Tell her that, will you? She won't read my letters, you see. She tears them up. That's why I wrote to you instead, Polly.'

'I didn't know that you were allowed to write letters,' said Sid.

A look of cunning settled briefly on Frank Mead's face. 'We can get things out,' he explained.

Polly had stayed long enough. She was finding it very difficult to control her emotions in the situation. She stood up and offered her hand to Sid. He took it, and got up to stand beside her.

'Goodbye, Mr Mead,' he said, meaningfully.

'Goodbye, Dad.'

'Is she lonely – that's all I ask?' demanded the older man.

'Not any more,' answered Sid. 'We've bought her a hamster.'

'A golden hamster? What's its name?'

'Come on, Polly. We must go.'

'Tell me its name at least. I like animals.'

'Benjy,' conceded Polly. 'Mum calls it Benjy.'

'That's a name and a half for a golden hamster,' chuckled her father. 'Benjy, eh?'

Polly felt Sid tugging at her hand, but somehow she could not leave. It was her father, after all. She did not want the departure to be too brutal.

'And the shop?' continued Frank Mead, calmly. 'How is the shop?'

'Doing quite well,' snapped Sid.

Polly could see her husband's irritation rising, but she was still unable to make the final break. Her father realised and exploited the fact. He sat back on the bench, crossed one leg over the other, and patted the place beside him. Polly felt Sid's hand grip hers hard. She shook her head and backed away from the bench. Her father was not in the least upset by this.

'What are your plans for the shop?' he asked, casually.

'We must go, Dad,' whispered Polly.

'Has it changed since I was last in Ambridge? Must have. Do you have any ideas?'

'Plenty,' said Sid, gruffly. 'Polly, please.'

'Such as? I mean what sort of ideas?'

Polly suddenly began to talk at speed, answering his question as quickly and fully as she could. It seemed to her that once she had replied to him she would have the strength and the will to leave. 'We've changed the whole shop around, Dad. It was Sid's doing, really. We've gone Self-Service. Well, partly, anyway. And we're carrying more lines than we used to. Oh, and Mr Woolley says we can paint the outside so we've settled on black and white. We've even got him to agree to let us try and sell wines and spirits in an Off Licence section and Mr Woolley thinks that . . .'

Polly's voice died and she realised what she had said. At the mention of the Off Licence, Frank Mead had stiffened. He stared angrily at Polly and flipped through the book in his hand, as if feeling his way to a particular page. Polly needed no encouragement to leave now. She and Sid walked away quickly, Sid supporting her under the arm. After a hundred yards or so, she turned back. Frank Mead was still on the bench, reading aloud from his bible. Polly had no wish to see her father ever again.

Chapter Eight

HER TELEPHONE call came out of the blue. Ralph was so pleased to hear from her after all this time that his feelings broke through the constraints he normally placed upon them. He talked freely and affectionately. After all the unsatisfactory business discussions he had had over the telephone recently, this conversation brought with it a sense of release. It was only when a meeting was suggested that Ralph's manner changed.

'I thought I might come and see you, Ralph,' she said.

'Oh . . . fine. When?'

'This weekend. I feel the need for some country air. Quite naturally, I thought of Ambridge. And you.'

Mild panic seized Ralph. It was hardly convenient for her to make an appearance in Ambridge that weekend. Things had altered considerably since he had last seen her. The voice at the other end of the telephone was not aware of these alterations. It merely sensed Ralph's misgivings. 'Of course, if you don't *want* me to come . . .'

'It isn't that. I'd love you to come . . . the fact is that I'm away on business this weekend. In London.'

'Then *you* can visit *me*!' she ordained.

'Uh, well . . .'

'Even you can't talk business all weekend, Ralph. I shall expect you to pick me up on Saturday night at eight.'

'Yes . . . all right . . . what about – '

'Ask me on Saturday. 'Bye, darling.'

'Goodbye,' said Ralph, speaking to the dialling tone. He replaced the receiver and considered the arrangement he had just made. He was immediately alive to the dangers. Guilt brought its friends to visit him. One of them lit a slow fire inside Ralph's skull, while another busied himself around his neck with an invisible darning needle. No, Ralph must not meet her. She was a voice from the past which had no real place in his future. Nearer the time he would contact her and make some polite excuse, explaining that he was unable to see her on Saturday. Yet part of him wanted to see her, wanted to go through with the arranged meeting. She had always been such lively and intelligent company. She might provide a refreshing diversion. It was possible – Ralph was coming more and more to think it likely – that she might be in a position to offer him some consolation.

Ten days had passed since the proposal and there had been no word from Lilian. Though she had asked for a fortnight, Ralph felt sure that she would have accepted him by now if she had any intention of doing so. The more time Lilian was letting pass by, the more doubts she must have. Ralph was becoming increasingly fatalistic about her answer. He had almost persuaded himself that she was going to turn him down. If this were the case, why should he not enjoy himself in London? He was a free agent.

'How are things, Tony?'

'Oh, so-so . . .'

Ralph had walked across to the milking parlour where he had found Tony changing the filters in the milking machine. He had promised his employee that he would spare him some time that morning to talk about modernising the dairy arrangements on the farm. Tony, however, had other priorities. He finished what he was doing then squared up to Ralph.

'Do you mind if I speak frankly?' demanded Tony.

Ralph was amused. Tony was at an age when he could never be serious without sounding pompous.

'You usually do,' observed Ralph, drily.

'I want to know where I stand. I mean, I want to know exactly what my future is here.'

'I see.'

Ralph was too busy answering questions about his own future to want to be drawn into a debate about Tony's. He tried to deal with the request summarily, assuring Tony that his job at Manor Court Farm was safe and that he hoped to be able to offer Tony promotion in the foreseeable future.

'You said all that six months ago,' complained Tony.

'The situation hasn't changed since then.'

'I think it has – or is about to.'

The emphasis which he placed on the last phrase alarmed Ralph. It was evident that Tony knew. He had been taken into Lilian's confidence and told about the proposal. Judging by the slight surliness in his manner, Tony had not taken too kindly to the notion of having Ralph Bellamy as a brother-in-law. Inevitably, it had made him revalue his own situation.

'So – where do I stand?' repeated Tony.

'Andrew Sinclair has been talking about going back to Scotland. Give him a year. Eighteen months at most. Then his job is as good as yours, Tony.'

'I wonder,' mused the other.

'Show some gratitude at least,' snapped Ralph, getting impatient. 'You're only twenty now and, capable as you are, you've still got a lot to learn.'

'I know that,' accepted Tony.

'Then stop being so damn awkward! How many other people of your age are likely to become farm managers inside a year or two? And farm managers of an estate *this* size?'

'I'm not worried about other people.'

'That's rather obvious.'

'I've got a right to be told what's going on. What changes you plan.'

'Tony . . .' said Ralph, trying to calm down and find words to end the conversation.

'I can't go on working in the dark.'

'You're not in the dark!' barked Ralph, his temper rising again.

'What happens if you go ahead, then?'

'I don't know what you're talking about.'

'The Brigadier's estate. And all that.'

Ralph did not like the suspicion of a sneer in Tony's voice and told him so. The row escalated and both were soon exchanging what they considered to be home truths. At length, Ralph squelched Tony by reminding him that if he was not happy working at Manor Court Farm, he could always leave. Tony made no reply, but glowered in silence. Ralph was upset. He and Tony had always got on well in the past, and had always been able to discuss things in an open and friendly fashion. What upset him about the row was that it had forced him into sounding testy and intractable. It had lost him some of Tony's respect.

'Look, I've got things to do. We'll have to talk over the modernisation plans at some other time.'

'That suits me,' muttered Tony.

Ralph was about to leave, but Tony had reserved his Parthian shot.

'There may be some competition for you . . .'

'I beg your pardon?'

'At the auction. I gather that Mr Woolley is interested.'

Tony went off to feed the beef cattle, who were calling loudly for table service.

Ralph was astonished by the news. Whatever else he might be, Jack Woolley was no farmer. If he was after the Brigadier's estate, it would certainly not be with a view to farming it. Woolley would want to retain the sporting rights over the estate and would doubtless re-negotiate these with the new owner. But if he himself wanted to be that new owner, he must obviously have a purpose in mind for the land. Ralph's astonishment gave way to irritation. Why had Woolley made no mention of his interest? Ralph had spoken to him at the weekend when he had called at Grey Gables for a business luncheon. It said little for their friendship, that Jack Woolley had kept off a topic which he must know Ralph had a consuming interest in. Ralph believed what Tony had told him.

Tony would never speak out of spite. Jack Woolley posed a new and definite threat. Ralph acknowledged him as a stern competitor in any property deal.

That afternoon Ralph had an appointment to meet Stephen Wiley in Borchester. He was going to make a firm offer for the Dower House and for the thousand acres. He was going to hand it over in writing. Driving towards Borchester, he wondered if the property had not already slipped through his hands. The longer it was on the market the greater the number of potential buyers who could appraise it. Ralph decided that it was imperative to push things ahead. He would apply more pressure to Stephen Wiley.

'Do sit down,' invited Stephen, with grudging civility.

'Thank you,' grunted Ralph, settling into a leather armchair. 'Sorry I'm late.'

This time he had not been so fortunate with a parking space. He had had to walk some distance to the office and was five minutes late. Stephen wanted to make up for the lost time.

'You said it was urgent, Mr Bellamy.'

'Yes, I want to make a formal offer.'

'Well?'

Stephen leaned forward across his desk, hands clasped. He seemed to Ralph to be challenging, taunting almost. Ralph handed him an envelope.

'Here it is.'

'Under plain cover,' noted Stephen, darkly.

He opened the envelope and studied the information on the piece of paper inside. For a brief moment, the mask slipped. He looked at Ralph with something verging on contentment and nodded appreciatively. The professional manner resumed its duty. He thanked Ralph for the offer, assured him that he would communicate the relevant data to Lady Isobel Lander, and that he would report back to Ralph when the matter had been fully discussed.

'How soon will that be?' pressed Ralph.

'Quite soon. Quite soon, Mr Bellamy.'

Ralph was about to indulge in some more special pleading when the younger man got up and walked to the door. It was a signal for Ralph to leave, but he was going to ignore it.

'Do you take milk and sugar?' enquired Stephen.

'Mm?'

'I thought you might like a cup of coffee. We usually have one at about this time of the afternoon.'

'Oh I see. Uh . . . thank you. Milk, please, but no sugar.'

'Excuse me a moment.'

Ralph was left alone to cope with his surprise. Instead of the usual courteous eviction, he was being offered hospitality. Ralph wondered if he had misjudged this young man, if he had written him off too hastily as no more than a bland opportunist. The office in which Stephen worked was small but well-appointed. Everything had been chosen with care to celebrate a marriage of old-style comfort and modern efficiency. The leather armchairs were matched by the leather-backed upright chair behind the desk and the studded leather-topped desk itself. This desk was cleared for action. Files were stacked neatly on open shelves.

Ralph had often noticed the photograph on the desk but had only ever seen the back of it. He crossed and stood behind the desk to examine the contents of the leather-backed frame. It was a picture of Stephen's wife with their two children, twin boys. The very fact that he was married seemed to humanise Stephen in Ralph's eyes. He was touched that the estate agent should keep the photograph of his family on his desk. Other thoughts were triggered off by the sight of Mrs Wiley, an arm round each of her sons, smiling at the camera. Ralph would dearly love to have such a photograph of Lilian on his desk. One son would complete the picture for him.

Reality intruded. She had not even accepted his proposal of marriage. What was more galling was the fact that she had seen fit to take counsel concerning it. Tony had been told, hence his modified attitude towards his employer. Dan Archer had been apprised of the facts, too. Ralph was fairly certain of that. When he had met him at the garage some days earlier, he had perceived ragged edges to Dan's joviality. The older man had shown hints of real animosity towards him.

At first Ralph had put this down to the fact that Tony, who represented the third generation of the Archer family in Ambridge, worked for him. Dan had made no secret of his ambition to have his grandson working at Brookfield, the farm which he himself had run for so many years, first as a tenant, then as its owner. Ralph understood what a blow to Dan's hopes it had been when Tony had elected to strike out on his own and seek employment at Manor Court Farm. It was natural that Dan should resent Ralph as a man with inherited land and wealth. It was natural that he should be bitter about his grandson. But when he had talked with Ralph at the garage, there had been something deeper and more overt about his antagonism. It could only be explained as downright opposition to the idea of Ralph's marrying Lilian.

If Lilian had told her grandfather and her brother, then she must also have told her parents and her sister, Jennifer. She may even have sounded out Philip and Jill Archer at Brookfield Farm, and taken the opinion of her other grandmother, Mrs Perkins. Ralph found this notion of his marriage proposal – something private and intimate – as an item of public property very disquieting. It hurt him that Lilian seemed to be unable to make up her mind on her own. Was she holding a family referendum?

'I'm sorry to keep you waiting,' said Stephen, returning with a tray.

'Quite all right,' replied Ralph, sitting again.

'Yes, I've just telephoned Lady Isobel,' announced Stephen, handing a coffee to his guest.

'Oh yes?'

Ralph was impressed by Stephen's speed off the mark and eager to know what had transpired.

'I'm afraid she's indisposed for a few days. Gone away.'

'When will she be back?'

'Not till Friday afternoon, according to the housekeeper.'

Ralph's exasperation showed clearly, but it was checked by the one of appeasement which came into Stephen's voice.

'I'll speak to her the moment she returns, Mr Bellamy, I promise you. You've made a very realistic offer and I think she should be informed as soon as possible.'

'Unfortunately, I shall be away on business this weekend,' explained Ralph. 'I leave on Friday.'

'Can I get in touch with you somewhere? Not that I can guarantee a firm decision, mark you.'

Ralph shook his head. He could wait a few more days. Stephen thought his offer a good one and that in itself was encouraging.

'I'll leave it till Monday morning,' he said. 'Lady Isobel can have the weekend to sleep on it.'

'Right, Mr Bellamy. Leave it with me. I'll be in touch first thing on Monday morning.'

They drank their coffee and talked about the elder Mr Wiley, who had founded the business over fifty years ago and who still liked to put in his stint at the office. Ralph liked the pride with which Stephen talked about his grandfather. It was a new side to his character, and made him altogether less objectionable. Before he left, Ralph had grown to admire something else about Stephen Wiley.

'If you don't mind my asking, Mr Wiley, who is your tailor?'

'My tailor?' laughed the other.

'I rather like that suit.'

It was a dark-blue three-piece suit with fashionable flared trousers, and Ralph thought it was smart without being flashy. It certainly made his own charcoal-grey seem sober if not obsolete.

'To be honest, I got it off the peg.'

'Where?'

'Gillford's in Queen Street . . . um . . .'

'Yes?'

'No, it's nothing,' said the estate agent, clearly being discreet.

'I shan't be offended, Mr Wiley.'

'Gillford's is a shop for . . . the younger man.'

'All the more reason for me to go along,' said Ralph, and he took his leave.

He spent a long time looking in the shop window in Queen Street and ignoring the comments of some of its young patrons who walked past him. Ralph had no intention of buying a suit like Stephen's, realising that on him it would look ridiculous, but he was in search of ideas to brighten up his image. When he made his way back to the car, he had already made a few tentative decisions about ways in which he might acquire a bit more dash and style.

For a man with a rooted objection to cities as such, Ralph always found London a tremendous ordeal. To avoid driving in the traffic, he travelled by train then took a taxi to a hotel in the suburbs. Even here, miles from the city centre, he was oppressed by the noise and the greyness and longed for the sight of plough and field. He had little sleep that night, still racked by the problem of what Lilian's answer would be.

Saturday morning began with a working breakfast and brought him some welcome news from his agent. Ralph learned that some of his land in East Anglia had been sold to a property developer at a price well above that originally expected. He suddenly had an additional £30,000 with which to play and it strengthened his bargaining position in the battle for the Brigadier's estate, which now seemed to be within his reach. He did not dare to allow himself to think the same about Lilian, and he reflected how ironic it would be if he secured the Ideal Family Residence and then had no wife with whom to share it.

His business commitments kept him occupied until late afternoon and then he decided to brave the traffic and travel to Regent Street, where he did some shopping. Glad that he had not cancelled the evening with Sarah, he was ringing the bell of her Knightsbridge flat well before the arranged time.

'Ralph, how marvellous to see you!'

'Hello, Sarah!' he said, kissing her.

'And there was I, thinking you wouldn't turn up . . .'

'Of course I turned up!'

'You didn't sound too keen on the telephone. I began to wonder if you were forgetting me. . . .'

She gave him a longer kiss, on the lips this time, then looked annoyed when he broke away. He took something out of his pocket and offered it to her, changing her pique into soft purr.

'Oh Ralph, it's beautiful!' she said, admiring the brooch.

'Just a little present . . . for old times' sake.'

'That sounds rather final. You're not going anywhere, are you?'

'Here, let me pin it on for you, Sarah,' he said, then stepped back to appraise it from a distance.

'I love that dress,' he murmured into her ear. 'Pink suits you.'

'I think it makes me look like a pale and interesting version of a Scarlet Woman,' she said, turning to him.

'And why not?'

They laughed, then Sarah moved to the cocktail cabinet. Ralph did not regret coming. Already he was feeling more relaxed and welcome than he had done for weeks. Sarah even remembered his preference for whisky and soda, with a cube of ice. There was a rustle from the silk dress as she crossed to hand him the glass. She sipped her own dry martini and took a proper look at him.

'You look *rather* dashing,' she decided.

'Do you think so?'

'I do indeed!'

Ralph was reassured by her approval. The new suit which he had bought earlier had been the result of an impulse. He had only decided to wear it that evening after some hesitation. Sarah's admiring gaze convinced him that the new blue mohair suit had been a wise purchase. Ralph had bought a light blue shirt to wear with it, and a matching tie and handkerchief. Sarah tugged this handkerchief a little further out of his top pocket, and then stood back and nodded. Ralph's confidence was given a great boost. He noticed that he had finished his drink.

'Help yourself, darling,' she invited.

'Thanks,' he said, crossing to the drinks.

Sarah arranged herself on the sofa so that the long dress was not creased. She looked far younger than her true age. Ralph put her near forty years of age, but had the sense of spending an evening with a woman who was barely thirty. He glanced around the luxury flat.

'You've made some changes since I was last here.'

'Do you approve?'

'Very much. I've always admired your taste.'

'So you should – being an example of it.'

He grinned and moved to sit opposite her.

What Ralph liked about the flat was the way it combined the ultra-modern with the traditional. The set of original sporting prints did not look out of place beside the lime green television set which was suspended from the ceiling by a steel spring. The Jacobean court cupboard which occupied one wall achieved peaceful coexistence with the modern three-piece suite in a shade of ginger. Sarah had struck the right balance. But then she had the time and the money to spend on striking that balance.

'What's all this work that brought you up to town?' she asked.

'Buying and selling.'

'What have you bought?'

'Nothing as yet.'

'Then what have you sold?'

'Some land. Not in Ambridge.'

'Mm.' She purred quietly, running a finger round the rim of her glass. It gave Ralph the opportunity to acknowledge why he felt so easy in her company.

Sarah Latham was a very handsome, witty and self-possessed woman. A private income had relieved her of the problem of having to work or, in her own phrase, of having 'to buy a meal-ticket' and marry. Ralph was not blind to the more mercenary side of her character, but he thought it unimportant beside the warmth, intelligence and natural charm. People meeting Sarah Latham for the first time – and Ralph recalled making this mistake himself – were apt to view her as a social butterfly, flitting through a life that was rather like a glorified cocktail party. Ralph had come to know her better. Looking at her now, and admiring once again the sharply attractive features, framed by the short black hair, Ralph thought about some of the things he had found out about her.

'Have you collected any new charities lately?' he asked.

'Several. I'm on two more committees and a working party.'

'Anything special?'

'Aid to Redundant Landowners – a worthy cause,' she smiled.

'You can divert some of the aid my way then!' he chuckled. 'But, seriously, which charities are they?'

'It doesn't matter,' she said deprecatingly. 'It's only compensation anyway. The shrinks explain it all in their textbooks.'

Ralph did not agree. He believed that her concern for others was authentic. It was something he was impressed with all the more for being unable to emulate her example. He drained his second glass and was ready to leave. Sarah had certainly made the decision as to where they would be going. This had always happened in the past. Sarah was an instinctive organiser.

'Right – were are we going?' he enquired, getting up.

'Relax, Ralph. You've been playing the dynamic businessman all day. Leave decisions alone.'

'But I thought that you – '

'Various things crossed my mind,' she explained, 'including a party in Hampstead.'

Ralph's face showed disgust and apprehension. Sarah had gained the response she had been after and laughed.

'However,' she continued, archly, 'since you don't exactly care for some of my friends . . .'

'It isn't that, Sarah. I just feel like a fish out of water. Look what happened last time.'

'But that was over a year ago.'

'I still have nightmares about it,' he confessed. 'I spent the whole evening drinking an inferior white wine and listening to people telling me about their divorces.'

'It's that kind face of yours, Ralph. You're marked down as a good listener.'

She got up and put an arm around his neck. 'I thought we'd miss out on the party,' she whispered.

'That's a relief.'

'For a change, I thought I'd demonstrate some of my more domestic accomplishments.'

'I'm not with you.'

Sarah crossed to the curtain which divided the dining area from the main room. She drew it back along the copper curtain rail. Ralph saw the dining table, set out for two. Sarah had omitted nothing. The candles were already alight.

'Well?' she asked.

'Yes . . . fine by me,' he muttered.

But Ralph had suddenly begun to have qualms. Sarah asked him to give her a few moments to get things ready. Ralph stopped her.

'I wonder . . . could I possibly make a telephone call?'

'*Now?*' Her voice had acquired a metallic edge.

'It is rather urgent.'

Sarah shrugged, indicated the telephone, then went into the kitchen which led off the dining area. Ralph looked around for a directory. From the kitchen, Sarah anticipated his needs.

'You can't dial Ambridge direct,' she called. 'Go through the operator.'

'Right . . . uh, thanks.'

First he tried the Cottage but she was not at home. Next he asked to be put through to the Bull. Peggy Archer answered and became slightly breathless when she learned it was Ralph. She explained that Lilian was not there yet but was expected at the Bull later in the evening. Could she take a message? Ralph declined her offer and rang off. As a last hope, he thought of the Stables. It was a light night, still early enough for her to be there. He waited for a long time as the number rang out. He did not notice Sarah coming out of the kitchen and back towards him. After a painful silence, the telephone was picked up. Ralph heard the voice at the other end of the line.

'It's me. Ralph!' he said.

'Oh.'

She sounded nonplussed, but it was too late to stop now. Ralph had to know. He had, after all, waited a full fortnight.

'I just wondered . . . what you had decided,' he stuttered.

'Yes,' she replied.

'Do you mean that!'

His joy made him forget where he was. He made Lilian repeat her answer then promised that he would see her on the following morning.

'I'll have to go now,' she explained. 'Mum's expecting me.'

'Yes, of course . . . till tomorrow then.'

Ralph put the telephone down and stood there in a daze for some minutes. A great rock had suddenly been rolled away to admit light and warmth. He could not believe his luck. Lilian had accepted him. This mattered far more to him than the acquisition of any property. She had agreed to be his wife.

Pleasure gave way to misgivings. He became aware of where he was and why he was there. He turned to see Sarah standing there, and felt uncomfortable. To tell her everything would hardly make it the kind of evening Sarah had planned. Yet to say nothing would be to betray Lilian at the very moment when she had agreed to share her life with him. Ralph was on the horns of a dilemma. He stood where he was looking hopelessly lost.

Sarah Latham rescued him with her usual calm authority.

She made the decision which he was unable to reach himself. Coming down to him, she kissed him full on the lips then led him into the dining area. She sat him down, then went round and sat opposite him.

'Tell me all about her, Ralph. Come on.'

Chapter Nine

The heavy rain, which had fallen earlier in the day, had left its traces everywhere. Hedgerows glistened, ditches gurgled with employment, and grass verges were pitted with patches of mud where hooves had autographed their progress. Road surfaces were darkened by wetness and a passing car could still produce the hiss and the spray with its tyres. But it was the trees who were the most reliable witnesses. Not only were they visible reminders of the rain with their sodden leaves and moist branches and rivered trunks; they could miraculously reproduce the rain itself as evidence. With a little prompting from the wind, they would sway and groan and swish before sending down a complete impromptu shower.

Walking slowly from the stables, Lilian Nicholson had cause to regret that the trees had such talents as mimics. She was twice soaked as she strolled beneath a covering ash and elm. Her annoyance was only momentary. A whole forest of dripping leaves could not distract her for long. Lilian had just come from her telephone conversation with Ralph Bellamy. She kept interrogating herself with the same question: when she had made up her mind firmly to reject Ralph Bellamy's proposal of marriage, why had she done the opposite?

Lilian was disturbed. In some mysterious way, she had lost control. She had found herself saying what she did not intend to say. And yet the words must have been inside her in order for her to come out with them to Ralph. Had she been acting on instinct? While her reason told her not to accept Ralph, some deeper force had done the talking at the crucial moment. It was disquieting, and yet at the same time it was invigorating. She did not regret having agreed to be Ralph's wife. Indeed, she suddenly thought of many things in favour of the idea which had never occurred to her before. She was not responding with the same kind of bursting joy which she had felt the last time. But then that kind of experience only came once in a lifetime. From Ralph she must look for something else. At the moment it appeared to be a mixture of simple pride, pleasing warmth and a kind of distant happiness. Good marriages had been built on far less promising foundations.

As she entered the village and made her way to the Bull, she decided that she would tell nobody yet. She would wait until Ralph's return on the following morning. It would be wrong to make anything public when the two people involved had not committed themselves to each other face to face. Lilian was glad that she was going to be working in the bar. It would occupy her, separate her from her thoughts. She smiled as she thought of Ralph. He had sounded elated over the telephone but would probably have to spend the evening alone in some hotel room, with nothing to keep him company but business documents and a Gideon Bible. At least she had the anaesthetic of other people at her disposal.

'Hello, Lilian,' said Polly chirpily, as she walked in.

'Congratulations!' smiled Lilian. 'I haven't had chance to speak to you since I heard.'

'To be honest, I'd much rather you *hadn't* heard,' admitted Polly.

'Why is that?'

'Because I didn't want to spend the next six months answering questions about how I was.'

Lilian nodded understandingly. Polly was sitting at a table just inside the door of the bar, which was fairly full. Sid had evidently gone off to buy some drinks.

'It was Sid's fault,' confided Polly. 'He let the cat out of the bag.'

'I hope you gave him a roasting for it,' said Lilian, siding immediately with the wife.

'What's the point? It's too late. Sid let it slip out to Greg Salt and, of course, Greg told his wife – '

'And, as we all know, telling Nora is as good as telling the whole village.'

Polly grinned and they both looked in the direction of the bar, where Nora Salt was pulling pints and talking nineteen to the dozen. Lilian was delighted for Polly, whom she had always liked very much. She knew that they had been trying to have a baby for some years and had had to weather many false alarms and serious disappointments.

'Mind you, I had one nasty shock,' giggled Polly.

'What was that?'

'When I went to the Clinic.'

'Is this the Ante-Natal place in Borchester?'

Lilian found herself taking a serious interest in the subject. In agreeing to be a wife she had subconsciously elected to be a mother as well. Any detail would be valuable.

'It's a smashing place and they're ever so kind to you. A bit brisk, mind, but considerate. They treat you as a human being.'

'That makes a change,' noted Lilian. 'But what was this shock?'

'Oh yes – I could have died, honest. You see, the nurse had this card with everything about me on it. Well, as she popped it on the desk, I happened to catch a glimpse of what it said at the top of the card.'

Polly giggled again as she recalled the incident. Lilian waited until she was ready to pick up the story.

'Do you know what it said – Polly Perks. Elderly, prim.'

'What?'

'Just that. Polly Perks. Elderly, prim. So I gets my dander out right away and no mistake. I mean, I don't think it's their business to go around writing down judgements about you.'

'Quite. Anyway, you're not elderly. And you're certainly not prim!'

Lilian caught her mother's eye. Peggy was asking for help behind a bar which was now besieged by customers. Lilian waved to indicate that she would be there directly, then turned back to Polly.

'What did the nurse say?'

'That any woman over a certain age – something ridiculous like twenty-five – is classed as elderly. It just means you're old in terms of having kids.'

'I suppose that makes sense. What about prim?'

'That's Latin. Stands for . . . now, let me see . . . Prima gravida. Yes, Prima gravida – or first pregnancy.'

Lilian was as interested as she was amused by the tale. She took her leave of Polly, who asked her to tell Sid she was still waiting for her drink. Lilian pushed her way behind the bar, acknowledged the many greetings, and helped to clear the backlog of customers. Eventually, Sid placed his order for a pint and a bitter lemon. While Lilian was getting the drinks, Sid was joking and laughing with Tony Archer. Lilian only caught snatches of what they were saying as they pored over some kind of form. Tony was reading out questions, Sid was suggesting answers, and both were taking it in turns to add a cross to sections of the form. The men parted when Lilian approached with the drinks.

'What's all that about?' she asked.

'Nothing,' said Sid, slipping the form back into his pocket.

'Polly is about to sue you for desertion, Sid Perks,' Lilian warned.

'Then I'd better hop it,' he said.

He paid for the drinks and went hastily back towards Polly. Tony was in a conversational mood, and Lilian guessed that one of his girlfriends would soon be joining him. She was not wrong. Before long, Michelle, the French *au pair* girl who worked at Brookfield, popped her head in through the door. Tony had downed the remains of his pint and was haring towards her in no time.

Lilian Bellamy. She tried the name a few times, while there was a brief lull in trade. It had a ring to it. Lilian Bellamy. It was not going to be that difficult to grow to like. It was a name that would stand for a great deal in the village. There would be some hostility from a number of quarters, notably from within her own family. Both her grandfather and her brother had resisted the music of the name. To them, Lilian Bellamy would always signify a kind of betrayal. But why should she be governed by their prejudices? It was her opinion which counted in the long run. And to her, the name Lilian Bellamy had increasing appeal. It stood for security; it conferred status; it would excite envy. Lilian was coming to believe that her answer to Ralph earlier on was the right one.

'Hello, love.'

'Hello, Grandad.'

'Uh, two pints, one half and a bottle of Walter's special.'

Dan Archer was playing dominoes with Walter Gabriel, Tom Forrest and Lilian's father. It was Dan's round. Lilian exercised the beer pump with a practised hand.

'How's Dad this evening?' she asked.

'Oh fine. There's not the old spark, but he seems a lot better.'

Lilian glanced across at her father who was sharing an anecdote with Walter and Tom. He certainly lacked the 'old spark'. Jack Archer had been an ebullient and tireless man before his illness. Lilian remembered his streak of inspired wickedness. It now seemed a thing entirely of the past. Echoes of it were occasionally seen in Tony but never in Jack. Lilian uncapped a bottle of beer suitable for diabetics and poured it into a glass. Walter Gabriel, a sufferer from diabetes, would drink nothing else.

'Heard about Sid and Polly?' asked Dan, handing over a pound note.

'Wonderful news,' said Lilian, searching for change in the till.

'Something to cheer Mrs Mead up,' commented Dan. 'Nothing like being made a grandparent for giving you a new lease of life.'

His colleagues at the domino table were keen to start a new game and called him impatiently. Dan hooked the glasses in his fingers and carried them off.

Lilian watched him go. She and Dan had long since overcome the slight awkwardness between them. On the day after his rather harsh comments in the garden of Glebe Cottage, Dan had called round to apologise. He had not changed his mind about Ralph Bellamy as a man, but he realised that he had spoken rashly. Lilian had forgiven him instantly. She loved her grandfather too much to be estranged from him for long by any outspoken remarks. Some of the things he had said about Ralph had an element of truth. All of them had been informed by Dan's compulsive honesty.

Fresh customers called for service and Lilian had no more time to ponder. It was only when 'Time' had been called by her mother, and the regulars began to drift out, that she was able to relax.

'You'd think some of 'em didn't have homes to go to!' observed Nora Salt tartly, collecting empty glasses.

'Saturday night is Saturday night,' sighed Peggy, philosophically.

'Then thank goodness it only comes round once a week,' said Nora, 'or I'd be after it with a broken bottle.'

'You and whose army?' asked Greg Salt, lazily. Her husband had drunk enough beer to take him to the drowsy stage. He was sprawled in a chair, waiting for his wife to finish work before walking back to their cottage with her.

'And you can get up off your whatsit and help, Greg!' scolded his wife. 'Look at him, Mrs Archer, since he's had that new job as a milkman in Borchester, he's nodding off every blessed minute!'

'The early hours,' yawned the disenchanted husband.

'We'll manage here,' smiled Lilian. 'You take Greg home.'

'Yes, we can cope,' said Peggy, as the last of the glasses were put on the bar. 'We'll wash these in the morning.'

'Come on, then, Light of my Life,' said Nora, jabbing her spouse in the ribs. 'Take me back to Paradise.'

They went out, Nora supporting Greg with accustomed ease. Peggy and Lilian were alone. Jack Archer had already retired to bed.

Her mother was hovering and Lilian was acutely conscious of the fact. She knew what her mother wanted, but she did not feel ready to talk about it yet. Ralph must return first and, in a sense, ratify their engagement in person. To tell anyone in advance – even her mother – would be unfair to Ralph. She made to leave but Peggy called after her.

'Ralph rang earlier.'

'When was this?'

'About eight o'clock.'

Lilian surmised that he had tried to reach her at the Bull, before getting through to her at the Stables. It made matters awkward for her. Her mother must have guessed why Ralph was telephoning.

'He sounded very anxious to speak to you.'

'I can . . . understand that.'

'What are you going to tell him?'

Lilian tried to dismiss the question with a shrug but her expression played the traitor. Her mouth tightened and her cheeks turned pink. Peggy needed no more. She crossed to Lilian and hugged her for a long time. In her mother's face Lilian could see real pride and happiness. It brought tears to her own eyes.

'Don't tell anyone till I say, will you, Mum?'

'Of course not.'

Peggy showed her daughter to the door. Lilian's decision had certainly brought joy to one member of her family.

She had expected him to call early on the following morning, but she had not been prepared for this. Ralph was ringing the bell of her cottage well before eight o'clock. Lilian clambered out of bed and groped around for her housecoat. In her half-awake state, she imagined that it could only be the milkman, ringing that early. She forgot that she had paid him the day before, went downstairs and found her purse. The bell rang more insistently. Lilian tried to tidy her hair slightly with a weary arm, then opened the door.

'Good morning.'

'Ralph!'

She was awake in a split second. The last thing she had

wanted was for him to see her like this. Confusion and embarrassment made her stutter and back away. Ralph stepped into the cottage, closed the door behind him and leaned heavily against it. He was very nervous and not quite sure what to do or say. Lilian observed that he looked drawn and hollow-eyed. His nervousness and her embarrassment kept the pair of them transfixed for a long time. They stood there rather foolishly, trying to shrug and gesture at each other. Ralph recovered first. He suddenly jerked himself forward, grabbed her by the shoulders and planted a hasty kiss on her lips. Lilian was galvanised into action.

'I must apologise. I didn't realise it was – '

'Not at all, not at all,' he interrupted.

'But I must look a state,' she said, her hands covering half her face.

'Not at all,' he repeated.

'I'll throw something on . . . come on in.'

'But I don't mind, really. You look fine to me.'

'I don't feel very fine,' she admitted, moving to the stairs. 'Why not make us both a coffee?'

'Oh . . . right,' he nodded, sounding less than confident in his assignment, but heading for the kitchen nevertheless.

Lilian darted upstairs to the bathroom, where she ran cold water into the basin. She applied it liberally to her face until she felt wholly and responsibly awake. Then she dried her face, before cleaning her teeth. Banging noises from down below suggested that Ralph was having difficulty finding the coffee mugs, but she had no time to give him directions now. She left the bathroom and nipped across the hall to the bedroom, shutting the door behind her.

As she looked around for some tights, she took off her housecoat and let it fall to the floor. Her nightdress followed. It was only when she walked past the cheval-mirror that she realised she was quite naked. She stopped to appraise herself, feeling oddly detached, as if she were looking at someone else. She did not feel the slightest shame or concern over the presence of Ralph in the kitchen.

'Uh, Lilian . . .'

A knock on the door confirmed that the presence of Ralph was closer than she had imagined. Lilian crossed to the door quite calmly.

'Yes?'

'The coffee mugs. I can't seem to find them.'

'In the cupboard to the right of the sink. Top shelf.'

'Thanks.'

She could hear him, standing outside the door. She was just about to open the door to repeat the instructions, when she heard footsteps departing. More banging soon charted his movements around the kitchen. Lilian stood there, thinking. She had learned a great deal about herself and her relationship with Ralph in the last twenty-four hours. When he had knocked, she had not grabbed the first available garment to cover herself. Somehow, his presence no longer perturbed her in the least. She had not felt threatened or compromised. She had answered him as easily and naturally as if they were married. She would not have minded in the slightest if he had walked into the bedroom. Part of her felt rather disappointed that he had not.

Over a coffee, which convinced her that she must be in charge of making it on all future occasions, Lilian learned that Ralph had driven back through the night in his eagerness to get to her. His appearance certainly confirmed his lack of sleep, but he was rallying with every minute. He kept asking her if she wanted to change her mind but each time she assured him that she would stand by her decision. At length he seemed to accept this and relax a little.

'What did you do in London?'

'Oh, it was very boring. One meeting after another.'

'Didn't you have any time to yourself?'

'Uh, no . . . none at all.'

Lilian noticed the defensive note in his voice.

'What about the evenings?'

'I spent them thinking about you,' he said, with a kind of amateur gallantry.

She let him take her hand and squeeze it. He asked if she had told anyone yet, and she shook her head. He seemed pleased. She disengaged her hand and made another coffee. It conformed rather more to some of the claims made on the coffee jar, and it revived both of them. Ralph began to talk about his offer for the Dower House, and he explained that Stephen Wiley was to ring him the following morning. He did not tell Lilian the amount of money which represented his offer for the property, but Lilian had some idea of what that amount might be. Her grandfather knew enough about land values to put a tentative figure of half a million pounds on the Dower House and the thousand acres. That Ralph could refer in such a matter-of-fact way to such enormous sums of money impressed Lilian. From what he was saying, the Dower House appeared to be as good as his. She checked herself. The Dower House was as good as theirs.

'Would you like to go and see it?' he suddenly asked, getting up.

'The Dower House?'

'Yes – why not?'

'But it's Sunday morning, Ralph. I mean . . . well, the place will be all locked up.'

'It does run to a few windows, you know. We could peep in.'

'That seems such an awful thing to do,' she complained, tempted by the idea all the same.

'I vote that we go this very minute. All in favour say "Aye".'

Lilian obliged and they were soon speeding towards the House. The last time she and Ralph had been at the property, he had invited her to take a look around with him and she had refused. She had no notion then of the feelings behind his invitation. This time it was vastly different. She was being driven, to what might well be her future house, by her future husband. It was a dislocating experience. She felt it was not really happening to her, that she was in the rear seat of the car watching two other people go to view their possible home.

If she had never had ambitions to live in the Dower House before, the visit implanted those ambitions now. It was a beautiful house in every way and Lilian fell for it as completely as Ralph had done. Peering in through the windows, she saw spacious, high-ceilinged rooms with friezes and mouldings and marble overmantels. She began to imagine what it would be like to hold a party there, or to dine alone with Ralph in the long dining room, or to spend a quiet evening with him in the drawing room.

It was a house that caught and kindled her imagination, and which made her see that it would be a wonderful home for children. Ralph led the way into the gardens, which were shielded by hawthorn hedges and laid out with expert care. As they walked across the rolling lawns and watched the goldfish in the pond and found endless things to admire, they started to plan and discuss for the first time. The Dower House was something on which they both agreed and it became a basis from which they could really work.

In the distance, the church bells began to ring and the same thought crossed both of their minds simultaneously. To be seen at church together would be a first step towards announcing the engagement, though Ralph accepted that she could not wear his ring until her family had been told formally.

'Are you sure?' he asked.

'Yes. I'd like it very much, Ralph.'

She could see at once that their appearance at church contradicted and confirmed weeks of gossip. Her grandmother was patently delighted and had to reach for her handkerchief during the first hymn, and even her grandfather, though less pleased, gave her an encouraging wink. Polly was rather overawed by it all, and Lilian recalled a remark she had once made to her about never getting the chance to live at the Dower House. Mrs Mead was curiosity itself, turning round at regular intervals to look at them. Her Uncle Tom seemed to have reservations but his wife, Prue, had none at all and simpered at Lilian whenever she caught her eye. David Latimer discerned the situation at once, and gave both of them quiet words of congratulation as they left the church. Lilian had thought that it might be difficult to endure, this hostility that some were bound to feel. But after that first experience of going with Ralph to church for all to see, she knew that she could sail over any criticism.

When the Bull closed for lunch, Ralph came round to meet Lilian's parents and the formal announcement was made. Peggy Archer kissed her future son-in-law in her excitement and Jack offered him his hand. It was a warm welcome and Ralph appreciated it, making a short and rather comical speech about how well he would look after Lilian. She herself was highly diverted by the speech, but dare not laugh because her parents were listening to it so solemnly.

The rest of the day they spent together, talking, planning, simply getting used to being together. On the following day, they would have a decision about the Brigadier's estate. Lady Isobel would have considered Ralph's offer, and reported back to Stephen Wiley. The chances were that she would accept the offer and close with it there and then. Ralph had persuaded Lilian and himself that this was likely to happen. He was so confident that he announced he would drive into Borchester first thing and be at the office when Stephen arrived. On impulse, Lilian asked if she could go with him, but he told her that he would prefer to go alone. The business side of things was his to worry about. However, he did let Lilian wrest from him the promise that he would telephone her from the office in Borchester as soon as he had some news.

Monday morning offered nothing to distract Lilian while she was waiting for word from Ralph. She tried reading the newspaper, but it failed to hold her interest. She switched on the radio, but the news bulletin about reactions to Britain's application to join the Common Market did not hold her attentions. She tidied the flat and did the washing up, but the suspense still tormented her. Lilian had never known herself feel so proprietary about anything before. She longed to live in the Dower House. It was exerting an almost physical pull upon her. Pacing the room and hoping that the telephone would ring, she began to understand how Ralph must have felt over the last fortnight. The tension seemed unbearable, the wait endless.

At length, release. The telephone rang. Lilian grabbed it.

'Ralph?'

'Yes, it's me. I'm at Wiley's office now.'

'Well – what's happened?'

She could tell from the pause that the Dower House was not theirs. Ralph sounded apologetic when he eventually spoke.

'They've received another offer. A good one. I'm afraid the ball is back in my court once again.'

Lilian put the telephone down without waiting to hear any more.

Chapter Ten

He had made a good job of it and Polly was the first to tell him so. They crossed over to the other side of the road to get the best view.

'It's like a new shop, Sid!'

'We aim to please,' he said modestly.

'It looks smashing. Real professional.'

'You know me, Poll Doll,' he sighed. 'Perfectionism in everything.'

'I'm so glad we settled for black and white,' she decided. Then, seeing the disapproval on his face, she added, quickly, 'Mr Woolley will be as thrilled as I am.'

'Good. We artists need encouragement, the same as everyone else.'

'Well I don't think the shop could possibly have been painted any better. How's that for encouragement?'

'It'll do for starters,' he grinned, slipping an arm around her.

'Come on. I'll make you a coffee. It's starting to get dark.'

'One final touch,' he insisted, walking back across the road.

'It looks finished to me,' she puzzled.

Sid took a piece of chalk out of his pocket and bent down to freshen up the signs along the pavement. Polly smiled as she watched him. Sid had written 'Wet Paint' in letters a foot high. He certainly believed in getting his message across.

'Where's my brush?' he asked, looking up.

'I thought you'd finished painting.'

'I just want to paint "Fresh Chalk" by here, so that people won't walk on it.'

'Time for coffee,' she laughed and led the way back into the shop.

'Wait for me!'

They were still at the stage of arguing about names. From the way that Sid kept dismissing her suggestions, Polly was starting to wonder if they would ever agree. As they sat watching the news on television, she brought the subject up again. Sid giggled, jumped up and went over to the sideboard. Polly winced as he grabbed a book and waved it at her like a flag. She had grown to resent the way that he used his copy of *Have You Named Baby?* as a kind of weapon against her.

'Fire away!' he invited, flopping back into his chair.

'It's not a competition,' she pointed out.

'No, of course not. Now – what's first on your list?'

'Adrian,' she said, bristling as he began to laugh.

'Here we are!' he announced, turning to the first page in the book. 'It says here that Adrian means "of the Adriatic. Black." That's out right away.'

'Why?'

'Adrian Perks. You can't call a child Black Perks. It sounds like a disease not a name.' Sid used one of his funny voices. 'The doctor diagnosed that he was suffering from Yellow Jaundice, Scarlet Fever and Black Perks.'

'I'll cross Adrian out,' conceded Polly. 'It was Mum's idea.'

'I bet it was!'

'Now don't you go on about Mum,' warned Polly. 'She's entitled to make suggestions.'

'No comment!'

'Oh, we're just wasting our time, Sid.'

'No, we're not, love. What's next?'

'Whatever it is, you'll just shoot it down in flames. You haven't liked any of the names I've come up with.'

'I liked David. I liked John. I liked Elizabeth. All you need to do is to have triplets!'

'See – you're at it again!' she exploded. 'Making a big joke out of it. Can't you be serious just for once? It's *important*.'

'Then let's forget your mother's ideas for a kick-off. Any-one who can saddle a poor, defenceless animal with a name like – '

'Sid!'

'No, not Sid. Benjy.'

Polly sat back heavily in her chair and folded her arms. When Sid was in this kind of mood she always felt so frus-trated. She pretended to watch television, but was only glow-ering into space. He got up and switched the television off, silencing her protest with a gesture. She turned away as he sat on the arm of her chair, but she let him kiss her on the cheek.

'I'm sorry, love. You go on.'

'It's hopeless.'

'Please. No more gags, I promise.'

She looked into his face which was boyishly apologetic and allowed herself to be won round. She referred to her mental list and went through the names. Sid either nodded in agreement or shrugged. It was an improvement on a battle against the contents of *Have You Named Baby?*, and Polly was grateful. At least he had not laughed at her suggested names.

Feeling pleasantly tired, she glanced at her watch and was surprised to find how late it was. She collected the cups from the coffee table, but Sid relieved her of them at once. She grabbed them back, only to have them taken from her again. She took them from him once more and walked away, but he intercepted her and claimed the cups. Polly was beginning to feel as if she were part of some comedy routine, and the sense of playing a game certainly appealed to Sid. He handed her the cups and then pulled them away again.

Weeks of being pampered by Sid had built up a feeling of anger and resentment inside Polly. These emotions now began to come to the surface in a great rush.

'Give them to me, Sid.'

'You go on to bed, love. I'll do the washing-up.'

'No, *I* will,' she insisted.

'Don't be silly,' he soothed, 'that's my job.'

'Not any more!'

Polly lunged at the cups but only managed to knock one of them to the floor where it shattered into pieces. Sid was maddeningly equal to the occasion.

'I'll fetch the dustpan and brush,' he smiled.

'Stay here!'

The force of her plea halted him in his tracks. Polly let the words tumble out of her, speaking quickly and intensely. Sid held his ground and listened as she told him that she could stand no more of his 'help'. She was not ill, she was still able to cook meals, she was still capable of cleaning the place.

'Can't you understand, Sid? It's driving me up the wall. It makes me feel so useless and humiliated. That's why it's got to stop. From now on – from this moment on – I am going to live as normal a life as I did before we knew about the baby.'

Sid stood there, unsure of what to make of Polly's outburst. She repeated herself, more calmly.

'As normal a life as before.'

She went into the kitchen to fetch the dustpan and brush and came back to clear away the bits of broken china. Sid remained in the middle of the room, looking hurt and rather lost, as if he had suddenly been robbed of his function. Polly took the second cup from his hand and went into the kitchen.

She washed the cup along with the other things waiting on the draining board, then spent some time putting various items back in their proper place. Only when she had removed all traces of Sid's reign over the kitchen did she feel ready to leave it.

By the time she reached the bedroom, he was already in bed, lying back with his hands behind his head. Polly could see that his pride was wounded, but his pride was far less important than her survival. She tried to get him talking again, complimenting him once more on his painting of the shop front. But Sid's mind was miles away, and he stared at the ceiling without hearing her.

At length she put out the light and climbed into bed beside him. She snuggled up to him so that her mouth was by his ear.

'Hello,' she whispered.

'Hello.'

'Remember me?'

'Yeah – you're the one who just tore me to shreds in there. Believe it or not, I thought I was on your side.'

'You are now, love,' she said.

Polly moved even closer to him and felt about for his hand. He turned to look at her and brought his face within inches of hers.

'Sid, when I said I want to live as normal a life as possible . . .'

'Well?'

'I mean just that.'

At first he did not understand, then he looked faintly shocked, then he began to consider, then he was simply curious.

'I spoke to the doctor about it. He said there was no reason at all to act as if I was ill. I'm just to carry on . . . as before.'

She felt his hand tighten on hers. Her toes curled around his and she moved her lips forward until they touched his.

'December's a long way off, Sid.'

'Don't I know it!' he confessed.

'Are we friends?'

Afterwards, they went through all the names they could recall and actually agreed upon some of them before they fell asleep.

Mrs Mead somehow managed to hold two conversations simultaneously. While talking to her hamster she was at the same time quizzing her daughter about her condition. Polly described some of the breathing exercises she had been taught to do and her mother became sceptical.

'What are they supposed to do for you?' she wondered.

'Make the labour easier.'

'I don't believe all that nonsense about so-called natural childbirth. There was an article about it in my magazine last week.'

'I read that, Mum. It made a lot of sense.'

Polly saw at once that her mother did not agree. Benjy lost his conversational partner as Mrs Mead gave her views on a topic which had lost none of its immediacy for her.

'Painless deliveries indeed! No such thing.'

'Not in your day, maybe.'

'I'll say, Polly! Do you know how *you* were born?'

And though she had heard the story several times in the past few weeks, Polly listened attentively. She had been born during the war, at a time before the existence of the National Health Service. Hospital deliveries were relatively unknown among ordinary people. In most cases a midwife took charge.

'I was fortunate to have Doctor Patterson,' remembered her mother. 'He was a lovely man. Very kind.'

Polly sat and shuddered quietly at the thought of having to undergo the kind of experience which her mother had suffered in order to bring her into the world.

Doctor Patterson had had to be called out at night, which had meant a larger fee. In the tiny bedroom with its low beams, he had needed to stoop as he worked by the light of the oil lamps. It had not been the best place to discover that he was dealing with a breech presentation, but he had not let Mrs Mead down. Throughout a long, difficult and arduous labour, he had talked to her and encouraged her.

Reliving the experience, Mrs Mead screwed up her face as she talked about the pain and the fear which went with it. Polly knew that her mother had desperately wanted some chloroform but could not afford it.

'It was three guineas, you see. Your father hardly earned that in a week. I just had to put up with the pain, Polly.'

Polly was expecting her mother to go on and describe the delivery, the cutting of the cord, the damage she had suffered.

Instead, a new detail found its way into the story, one which caused Polly some surprise.

'And so, because I couldn't ask for chloroform, I called out for your father and he came in.'

'You never told me that, Mum.'

'He didn't want to – I knew that. It was no place for a husband. But I'd called and he came. What we couldn't afford to buy he gave me just by holding my hand. I can feel him squeezing it now. Without his help, I don't know how I would have got through it.'

Polly had never heard her mother talk about her father in that way before. It explained something of the bond which her parents had had between them and which had only been cracked by his illness. The recollection had upset Mrs Mead, who held a handkerchief to her eyes.

'Can I get you something?' offered Polly, crossing to put an arm round her mother's shoulder.

'I'm all right,' sniffed Mrs Mead. 'Your father was a good man, Polly.'

'Let me get you another cup of tea,' said Polly, anxious not to talk about her father.

'No, you come with me. I want to show you something.'

Benjy was racing about his cage, trying to attract attention, but he had lost his hold over Mrs Mead. The older woman walked out into the narrow passage and across to the bedroom. Polly followed her with some trepidation, and watched as her mother knelt down by an old chest of drawers.

She was not sure what her mother was looking for as the latter burrowed about in a drawer, and even when a large biscuit tin was lifted out she still had no inkling.

'Do you know what's in here?'

'No, Mum.'

'Letters. The letters he wrote me then, when I was only your age. And the others.'

Polly was not certain what the others were but she had her suspicions as soon as her mother opened the tin. The brown envelopes and the spidery handwriting told all. From the postmark on the top letter, Polly could see that it had been received in the last week.

'I read all his letters,' confirmed her mother.

'Mum, I'm not sure that that's altogether wise.'

'He's still my husband,' reminded the other, defiantly.

'Yes, but you've got to remember what they said at the hospital. He's not going to get better. You're not helping him by letting him think . . . well, by letting yourself think . . .'

Polly could not go on. Tears were welling up in her mother's eyes, as she stood there looking through the collection of letters. It would be cruel to state things too bluntly. Polly took the tin gently out of her mother's hands, put the lid back on and slipped the tin back into the drawer.

'I only keep this place clean because of him, Polly.'

'Look, Mum – '

'He'll come back one day. And this bungalow has got to be ready for him. Your father will have a proper home to come back to. I'll see to that.'

Polly took her back into the living room and sat down on the settee with her. The very mention of her father had brought back a flood of memories about him and about the visit which she and Sid had made to the hospital. It had been wrong to imagine that that visit had ended the relationship with her father. Though out of sight, he would never be totally out of mind. He would always exert a real emotional claim upon her and upon her mother.

'Do you write to him, Mum?'

'No. Not any more.'

'Does he . . . say anything about me in his letters? The latest ones, I mean.'

Polly was fearful that her father had mentioned her visit, and that her mother would reproach her for not being told about it by Polly herself. The older woman shook her head.

'They're just . . . letters to me.'

Mrs Mead got up and went to let Benjy out of his cage. The hamster ran under the furniture, exploring every inch of the carpet. Mrs Mead began to clean out his cage, lifting out the old newspaper which she had put inside. She spoke to Polly over her shoulder.

'I think I want to visit him again.'

'Mum, you mustn't! For your own sake, you simply mustn't!'

Polly was on her feet, arguing strongly against the idea. But her mother had clearly made up her mind and could not be dissuaded.

'Have you forgotten how ill the last few visits made you? You had to stop going because it was upsetting you so much.'

'It'll be different now.'

'But it won't. You'd only be punishing yourself.'

'I want to see my husband,' said Mrs Mead, firmly. 'He needs me.'

Polly could find no more words. She sat down again and merely nodded as her mother talked about the baby again. While Mrs Mead tidied the room, she kept thinking about her father and the way in which he was refusing to be forgotten. It was several months since her mother had last been to the hospital, and she had been so distressed on that occasion that Polly had made her promise that she would never go again. Mrs Mead had seemed to welcome the advice and to adjust to the idea of putting her husband in the past. Now the problems were about to arise all over again, and Polly was numbed by this realisation.

When it was time to leave, she mumbled a few words of thanks for the tea and moved to the door. Her mother held her hand for a moment.

'Before you decide on the baby's name . . . you will think about your father, won't you? He'd love it to be called after him.'

It was a special mid-week match, beginning at six-thirty in the evening, and the weather was obliging. In the evening sun, the cricket pitch looked green and inviting; a good crowd turned up to watch the local team playing a limited over match against the Churcham XI. Sid was chosen to play for the Ambridge team, which won the toss and decided to bat first.

'Will you be okay, Poll Doll?' asked Sid.

'I'll find myself a seat,' she said, looking around for a vacant bench. She had come to watch the match in the hope that it would take her mind off her visit to her mother that afternoon.

'As long as you put your hands over your eyes when I take my turn at the crease.'

'But I want to see you bat, Sid.'

'You'll be lucky. Churcham have got a demon bowler. He's twice as fast as Tony Archer. Yes, they reckon he broke a batsman's arm last season. All in the spirit of the game, of course.'

'Sid, you will take care, won't you?' she urged.

'Discretion is the better part of cricket,' he chuckled. 'If that fast bowler is still hurling 'em down when I get out there, I won't pick a fight with him . . . anyway, I'll see you. Bye . . .'

Sid went off to join the rest of the team on the verandah of the pavilion. The Churcham XI had taken the field and were practising throws to the wicket-keeper. Polly looked around the team, wondering which of them was the feared bowler. When she glanced back towards the pavilion, Sid was chatting happily to Tony Archer. Polly could not help smiling at Sid's flannels, which she had ironed only the day before but which now looked creased and baggy. Something about her husband's legs defied smart trousers.

Polly took a seat on a bench beside Doris Archer, who made her very welcome. As usual on all village sporting occasions, the Archer family were out in numbers. Philip Archer and Tony were members of the team, while Dan Archer was acting as scorer. Polly noticed that Jill Archer had come along to support her husband, and brought her four children with her. Jack Archer was on the pavilion steps chatting to the vicar.

The umpires walked out to take up their positions on the

pitch and the game was soon in motion. Polly could see why Sid had such qualms about Churcham's fast bowler. He was a big, stocky, redhaired man with his shirt sleeves rolled up. After taking an enormous run-up, he was hurtling the ball towards the batsman with real venom. Polly was amazed when anyone dared to score runs off such a fiery bowler, and she hoped that Sid would not have to face him.

'Hello, Gran. Polly.'

Another member of the Archer family had joined them.

'Sit here, Lilian,' invited her grandmother.

'I'm not stopping,' warned Lilian, sitting for a moment. 'How are you, Polly?'

'Surviving,' smiled Polly, noticing the engagement ring on Lilian's finger. It was a beautful diamond ring and it had displaced the other engagement ring which Lilian had been accustomed to wear.

'Any news about the house?' asked Doris.

'Not yet,' replied Lilian, sadly.

Polly surmised that they were talking about the Dower House. She remembered something.

'I haven't really had chance to congratulate you on your engagement, Lilian. We were both very pleased.'

'So were we,' added Doris.

Lilian nodded her thanks but did not seem to be keen to talk about her forthcoming marriage. Polly could not help comparing Lilian's attitude to her own, when she had become engaged to Sid. In those days, she could not talk enough about the wedding.

'Well, I must be on my way,' said Lilian, getting up.

'Aren't you going to watch the game?' asked Polly.

'I'm not in the mood,' explained Lilian. She made her farewells and walked away. Polly watched her speak to her father, before leaving the ground altogether.

'I was delighted,' affirmed Doris.

'What's that, Mrs Archer?'

'About Lilian and Ralph Bellamy. Yes, I know that a lot of folk object to the idea of him being so much older than her, but my feeling is this, you see. Lilian deserves some happiness. After that terrible business of losing her first husband like that . . .'

Polly let her companion talk away at length. Doris Archer was entirely in favour of the marriage and made no bones about it, but what Polly kept wondering was whether or not Lilian herself shared her grandmother's views.

The fast bowler soon began to make his presence felt in the most literal way. Unable to beat the bat, he began to send down a series of vicious bumpers to intimidate the batsmen. One of these eventually struck a batsman on the side of the head and he was forced to retire hurt. The rest of the Ambridge team were unsettled by this and played well below their best form. Even when the fast bowler was taken off, the Ambridge batsmen made no rapid advance in scoring. Sid, who was at the tail-end, scored one run before being clean bowled.

'That's it then, me ole dears, me ole beauties,' wheezed Walter Gabriel, coming to sit beside Polly.

'I don't think they should have allowed that man to throw the ball like that,' offered Doris.

'He was terrifying,' admitted Polly.

'No, he were nothin' to a real good batsman, like I used to be. Doris will bear me out, won't you? I was the next best thing to W. G. Grace when I was a lad in my teens.'

Polly laughed as Walter invented anecdotes about his past. A wink from Doris confirmed that most of the feats which the old man claimed to have brought off were figments of his imagination. As she was listening to Walter's dubious memoirs, she happened to look up at the pitch. The Ambridge team were taking the field, but two of its members did not have their minds on cricket at that moment. Sid and Tony Archer were standing together and shaking with laughter as they pointed in Polly's direction. When they saw that she was watching them, they moved swiftly on to the pitch.

It was not the first time that Sid and Tony had been together in a situation like this. Polly recalled the time at the

Bull when she had seen them poring over a piece of paper and laughing mischievously. And there had been two occasions since then when Tony had come into the Village Stores to have a brief conversation with Sid. Polly knew that they were up to something, and from the way that they had pointed towards her bench she assumed it must have something to do with her.

'Yes, sometime in the near future, he says.'

'That'll be a nice surprise for you, Walter.'

Polly turned her attention back to Walter Gabriel in time to hear him announce that his son was going to pay a visit to the village.

'Doh! I don't fool myself that Nelson comes to see his ole Dad. It's them flats of his he comes to check up on.'

'Business before pleasure,' noted Polly.

'Oh no,' corrected Walter, with a wicked grin, 'now that's one way he does take after me. He allus puts pleasure fust.'

'Walter Gabriel, you're an old reprobate!' chided Doris, but this only produced more of the wheezy chuckle.

'Nelson doesn't know about Lilian and Ralph Bellamy, then, does he?' said Polly. 'I wonder how he'll take to the news that he'll be losing his caretaker from Hollowtree Flats.'

'Not very well, knowing him!' asserted Walter.

'Ralph isn't happy for Lilian to stay at Hollowtree any longer than she has to,' commented Doris.

'I don't blame him,' chortled Walter, nudging Polly. 'Pretty, young widow in a sicklooded cottage all on her own. If I were our Nelson's age, I'd be – '

'Behave yourself!' scolded Doris.

'They're about to start,' said Polly, diverting their attention to the pitch, where Tony was just beginning his run-up for the first over.

The Ambridge attack had nothing like the pace and aggression of the Churcham bowlers. The visiting team were never in difficulties and, at the cost of only three wickets, they passed the Ambridge total of 61, with overs to spare. Polly was glad of the early finish. There were several things she wanted to talk over with Sid.

Over a drink at the Bull, Polly told her husband about the afternoon's session with her mother. Sid was in too light-hearted a mood to ponder over it for long. He decided that his mother-in-law would not really go through with the notion of visiting the hospital. It was best for Polly to dismiss it from her mind altogether. When Sid and Tony began to exchange a series of signals across the bar, Polly ventured on to another topic which was puzzling her.

'What are you and Tony cooking up?' she demanded.

'Nothing,' he shrugged.

'Come off it, Sid,' pressed Polly and paraded all her evidence. She ended by pointing out that she knew him well enough to sense when he was up to something.

'Well . . .' said Sid, considering. He came to a decision. 'If I tell you, promise to keep it to yourself.'

'What is it?'

'Promise, first,' he insisted.

Polly nodded and Sid began to giggle loudly. He glanced around to make sure that nobody was watching, then took something out of his wallet. It was a crumpled piece of newspaper, and Sid spread it out on the table, holding it flat with the help of his pint tankard. Polly read the advertisement with care, but could still not appreciate the joke. The advertisement had been placed by a Computer Dating Agency, which promised to find 'the perfect date' for anyone who completed one of their forms. Sid was waiting for some grin of approval from his wife, but she looked baffled. He slipped the piece of paper back into his pocket, then leaned over to her.

'Tony and me sent away for one of the forms.'

'Whatever for?' asked Polly, colouring at the thought of Sid's seeking a Date by Computer.

'We thought we'd find him the perfect date. Like it says.'

'Who? Tony?'

'No, he doesn't need a bird. Got loads queueing up as it is. Our idea was to play cupid for someone else.'

'But *who?*' she hissed, eager to know.

'Wait – as the old lady said when she kissed the cow – and see.'

Polly was given no further enlightenment.

Chapter Eleven

While the Ambridge cricketers and their supporters were seeking some consolation in the Bull, Lilian Nicholson was wandering aimlessly around the little garden at the back of her cottage.

She had tried various ways to console herself, but each one had failed signally. Now, with the evening starting to darken and a wind springing up, she was still as distressed as she had been since the day had begun.

Lilian had been caught off guard. It would have been their second wedding anniversary, and she knew that she was bound to feel sad and cheated. Lester and she might so easily have been celebrating this anniversary with a child, because they had both been so keen to have children early in their marriage. Lilian had realised that she would reflect on these things and had made an effort to steel herself against it all.

What she had not expected, and not taken precautions against, was the violent upsurge of guilt which she felt, a sense of letting down one husband simply by considering another. Lester had been everything that Ralph was not, and could never be. He made any successor appear unworthy and inferior. He made Lilian regret that she had ever accepted Ralph's proposal.

She had spent much of the morning with her wedding photographs and with the many snapshots of Lester. They had been very happy in their brief marriage, and she would never forget the element of sheer infatuation which he had inspired in her. Looking at the bright, carefree smile on his face had brought it all back to her. But memories of the good times with Lester inevitably led to thoughts about the final few months.

Lilian remembered the plane crash in which he had been involved, the fears that he had been killed, the dramatic finding of Lester, still alive, the apparent improvement in his condition, the new plans they had made, and then the painful, gradual decline which had left him confined to a wheelchair and which had ended in his death.

In an attempt to shake off these morbid thoughts, Lilian had gone out riding immediately after lunch. But no matter how hard she galloped Red Knight, she could not get Lester or the significance of the day out of her mind.

She had called at Brookfield Farm, where Jill had been understanding and sympathetic, and where Shula diverted her by talking excitedly about riding. When she had left, however, Lilian was still dejected. Acting on Jill's advice, she had walked to the Bull to be with her parents. She had arrived in time to join them for tea.

Her mother had realised that she had come to talk about Lester and did not try to stop her. It had been her father, somnolent for most of the meal, who had objected strongly.

'Stop it!' he snapped, getting up from the table.

'Lilian is entitled to remember,' argued his wife.

'It's not healthy. The past is past,' insisted Jack Archer, slumping into an easy chair.

'That's a matter of opinion, Jack.'

'Best to forget, Peggy. Best to put it out of your mind. What's buried should stay buried.'

It was a rather brutal way to express it, but Lilian did not feel offended. In a way, she agreed with what her father had said. To pass the rest of her life mourning for Lester was as pointless as it was unrealistic. The problem was that at the very moment when he was trying to obliterate Lester's memory from her mind, her father was actually rekindling it.

As she studied her father in his chair, gazing vacantly in front of him, Lilian was irresistibly reminded of Lester, of the strange and terrifying wasting away of a human being. Without stopping to finish her meal, she had got up from the table and walked out.

Lilian had strolled across the fields, dropped in on the cricket match and walked back through the village. Now, after meandering around her garden, she succumbed once more to the pull of her memories and went back into the cottage.

How long she sat in the bedroom over letters and photographs, she did not know. Nor did she recall taking Ralph's ring off her finger. But when she heard the car draw up outside, she realised that it was quite late and that she was once more wearing Lester's engagement ring.

The doorbell rang and she prayed that it might not be Ralph, who was the last person she could face. She glanced through the window and saw the Jaguar parked outside. Lilian knew only one person with a car like that and he was hardly welcome at a time like this.

'Were you in bed?' enquired Nelson Gabriel, with a twinkle in his eye.

'No, I was reading. . . .'

'What a dreadful way to have to spend an evening,' he laughed and Lilian suspected that he had been drinking. 'May I come in?'

'It's very late . . .' she began.

'Nonsense. The night is young,' he said, and stepped into the house.

'Oh well, you'd better sit down for a moment, I suppose,' she agreed, wearily. 'Would you like a coffee?'

'Later, Lilian. A scotch would be more appropriate just now.'

He sat in a chair and stretched his legs out, not the least troubled by her obvious reluctance to let him in. Lilian found a half-bottle of whisky and poured him a small glass. When she handed it to him, he took hold of her arm and pulled her closer to him.

'You're looking very fetching, I must say.'

'Do you want anything in it?' she asked, detaching his hand.

'No, I take it as it comes – nice and neat. Oh, aren't you having anything yourself?'

Lilian shook her head, but Nelson ignored this. He crossed to the bottle of whisky and poured another glass, before finding and opening a bottle of dry ginger. He added some of the latter carefully.

'Now, that's about what you like, isn't it? There – get that down you. That'll make me seem far less of a nuisance descending on you like this.'

To her surprise, Lilian accepted the glass and even sipped from it. The drink helped to make her fully awake and to wonder exactly why Nelson had called at this late hour. He had resumed his seat and was toasting her in silence.

Appraising Nelson Gabriel, she could not help thinking yet again how totally unlike his father he was. Where Walter was essentially a dry old countryman, Nelson belonged to the town and to the world of business. There was no trace of his father's idiosyncratic diction or rough edges in Nelson. He was impeccably dressed in a dark lounge suit, and looked both successful and self-satisfied.

'How's everything going?' he asked, running a finger around the rim of the glass and keeping his eyes on hers.

'Fine, fine. No problems to speak of.'

'I wasn't talking about Hollowtree Flats. I was talking about Lilian Archer.'

'Lilian Nicholson,' she corrected, sharply, and he acknowledged his mistake with a mock bow of his head.

'Aren't you going to sit down?'

Lilian sat in the chair furthest away from Nelson. She asked him if he had been to see his father yet.

'First things first. I happened to be passing – to coin a phrase – and so I thought I'd call in. It's one of my flying visits, I'm afraid. I have to try and squeeze a lot of people in.'

He drained his drink and got up.

'Let me get you another,' he invited and Lilian was

astonished to see that she had emptied the glass. 'You don't seem to have all that much scotch left. Not to worry. I've got another bottle in the car.'

Lilian did not really want to sit there drinking whisky with Nelson, but she somehow did not feel sufficiently in command to make this point. She took the second drink from him and sipped at it. Nelson walked around the room, picking up an ornament here and a book here in order to inspect them.

'Tell me all about the Brigadier's estate,' he said.

'There's not much to tell,' Lilian shrugged, glad that the conversation had at least turned to business. 'It's up for auction soon.'

'Every auction has its own dark secrets,' assured Nelson, who was a professional property speculator. 'What's the local interest?'

'Ralph Bellamy is after it,' she blurted out.

'That figures,' he retorted, with a trace of a sneer. 'Ralph has always fancied stepping into the Brigadier's boots, though he might find them a few sizes too large. Is he after the Dower House as well?'

'Especially that.'

'Whatever for? It's far too big for a single person, unless he's thinking of bringing a harem to live there with him. Maintaining some of the best traditions of the old randy county set.'

'He's asked me to marry him,' she volunteered, simply.

Lilian could see that Nelson was genuinely surprised, but she could not decide whether it was amusement or cynicism which made him smile to himself.

'Are you going to accept?'

'I don't know,' she answered, honestly. The events of the day had certainly made her want to think again about the marriage. 'I really don't know, Nelson.'

He seemed to be relieved by her answer and gave her the benefit of his opinion on the subject, which was that Ralph was nowhere near good enough for her. Lilian suspected that he was speaking with real feeling, which was unusual for

Nelson. She thanked him for being so sincere and outspoken. Another glass was emptied and filled.

'No more for me,' she protested, but took the glass all the same.

'I can't drink alone,' he complained. 'Too sordid. Solitary boozing. Cheers! To you!'

'Cheers!' responded Lilian, who found the drink having a definite calming effect on her. It made her think once more about Lester, but not in any mournful or despondent way.

'A penny for your thoughts,' offered Nelson, ever the financial investor. 'Not that we have pennies any more.'

'It's something . . . rather private,' she confessed.

'Sounds interesting. I love things that are strictly private.'

Lilian did not see him move to a nearer seat. She had lapsed back into a reverie about Lester and felt Nelson as a kind of distant presence in the room, something which was oddly comforting.

'It's our wedding anniversary today,' she announced.

'Oh, I'm sorry . . .'

'Don't be. I'm not upset about it. Not any more. It's a positive thing. It's a thing you can draw strength from.'

'Do you miss him a lot?' he asked, gently.

'More than I could ever say. Lester was so . . . how can I explain?'

But Lilian did explain. For over ten minutes, she explained exactly how and why she missed Lester Nicholson. She talked more freely and easily than she had done all day and felt no need to restrain her feelings as she spoke. She did not observe Nelson's reactions at all, but was only aware that he was listening and helping her by doing so.

'It's the little things I miss most,' she concluded, 'the corny things like a friendly face, a cuddle, company.'

Recapturing some of the times she had spent with Lester made her want to get out his photographs and show them. She went upstairs and had to support herself slightly on the wall as she did so. In her bedroom she went straight to the wedding album and flicked through until she found the photograph of him which she loved most. It seemed to have caught the essential Lester for her.

The sound of the door closing behind her brought her out of her dream. Lilian was no longer a woman talking about her past to a sympathetic friend. She was a desirable woman, who had come into her bedroom of her own accord, and who had clearly given the man who had followed her there the wrong idea.

'I understand how it is,' whispered Nelson, moving towards her.

'No, I don't think so,' she said, backing away.

'There's no reason why you should miss out on everything . . .'

'Nelson – '

'Now come on, don't pretend it's not what you want,' he smiled, as she got herself trapped in a corner. 'That's it . . . that's it . . .' he murmured, as he put his hands on her shoulders.

Lilian froze but did not resist. She was too struck by the realisation that, from his point of view, she had deliberately led him on.

'I won't hurt you,' he purred, undoing the top button of her blouse and running his hand up and down her neck.

'Please. I don't want – '

'Let me decide what you want. Just this once. You won't regret it. Just leave it to me . . .'

He undid another button on her blouse and pushed her hand away when she tried to resist him. For the first time, Lilian appreciated what a strong man Nelson was. Her struggles were easily checked by him and only seemed to heighten his anticipation. Lilian's blouse was now open right down the front, and Nelson was trying to kiss her breast.

'Don't!' she yelled, only to find a hand pressed over her mouth.

'I've always wanted you, Lilian,' he admitted, taking his hand away so that he could kiss her full and hard on the mouth.

Lilian pushed him as firmly as she could but it was no use. He moved her sharply to the left and twisted so that they fell on to the bed. Panic now seized her. She may have misled him and landed herself in this dangerous situation, but she simply had to get out of it somehow. She tried biting him but he only laughed. As they fought on the bed, he somehow took off his coat and threw it to the floor, then began to feel for the catch at the back of her skirt.

'No!' shouted Lilian and swung her free hand into his face, causing him enough pain to stop him for a moment.

Nelson looked at her angrily and she became really afraid of him, wondering what he was going to do next. Headlights raked across the bedroom, and she heard the car door slam outside. When the bell rang it sounded very sweet to her. Whoever it was, he had rescued her.

She got up and reached for her blouse. Nelson was still very annoyed and was glaring at her, but he did not prevent her from leaving the room. Lilian went down the stairs, hurriedly buttoning up her blouse before tucking it into her skirt. When she reached the front door, she took a deep breath before opening it.

'Ralph!' she called out, with relief.

'Are you all right, darling?' he asked, seeing her distress.

'I'm fine now,' she laughed, almost light-heartedly. 'I'm so glad to see you. I mean that.'

'As I drove past, I noticed the car outside. Doesn't it belong to Nelson Gabriel?'

'Inspector Bellamy does it again,' mocked Nelson, joining them at the door. He had recovered all his smoothness and aplomb.

'What are you doing here?' challenged Ralph.

'Nothing,' interposed Lilian, anxious to avoid an argument between the two men, and wishing only that Nelson would leave.

'As you so rightly say, Lilian . . . nothing,' said Nelson, turning to her with an apologetic smile and shrug. 'Well, I suppose that I ought to . . . leave you to it.'

And with a nod to Ralph, he went out through the front door and closed it behind him. Only when she heard his car start up and drive away, did Lilian relax properly. She saw that Ralph was carrying a small parcel and was about to ask him what it was.

He got his question in first.

'What did he want?'

'It's all over now, Ralph.'

'What did he want?' he repeated, with emphasis.

'I'll tell you later, I promise . . . come on in.'

She made some coffee while he explained how he came to be at her cottage. He had been away on business in Norwich all day, and had returned home to find a parcel awaiting him, addressed to Lilian and himself. Ralph wanted her to open it, but Lilian now found herself making various excuses not to do so. The parcel embarrassed her since it was a reminder of something which she had more or less decided to call off.

Paradoxically, she was still eager to know about the fate of the Dower House. Though she had resigned herself to not marrying Ralph, she still had the same proprietary feeling about the house.

'What's the latest?'

'Not good,' he replied. 'Wiley has scrapped the auction.'

'Since when?'

'Since today. I rang him from Norwich. I've kept in close touch with him all along. Not through choice, mark you. I loathe the man.'

'You mean that Lady Isobel is not going to sell at all?' asked Lilian, affronted.

'She's selling all right and she'll get a tidy price. Wiley has opted for sale by letter of tender. In one way, it saves a lot of shouting in the auction room, but in other ways, it's not so satisfactory.'

'I don't follow. Will you have to . . . submit a tender?'

'Yes, in writing. By ten on Monday morning. There are four of us in the race, apparently. We're all what Wiley calls 'good buyers'. We send him our bid, he compares them and that's that.'

'Isn't that rather similar to an auction?'

'Let's not bother about that now,' he muttered, dismissing the subject with a wave of the hand. 'Why don't you open this?'

Lilian took the parcel and inspected the typed address. She could not make out the postmark, and wondered who could have sent it. Even as she began to tear at the brown wrapping paper, she knew that it was unfair on Ralph to pretend. She put the parcel down and finished her coffee before crossing to sit at his feet. She took his hand.

'What's the trouble, Lilian?'

For a long time she could say nothing, not wanting to hurt him by telling him her decision and yet not wishing to let him assume things that were not true.

'I've been thinking . . .'

His eye fell on Lester's engagement ring, and Lilian did not need to spell it out for him. Ralph seemed deeply hurt, then became angry.

'Is this anything to do with Nelson?'

'No, nothing at all.'

'I know that there was a time . . . in the past . . .'

'Please, don't think that. It's nothing to do with him. It's . . . something else altogether.'

Ralph's anger disappeared at once and he became gently curious about her reasons.

'I knew that . . . well, it might be difficult for you today,' he said. 'To be honest, I was trying to keep out of your way. I didn't want to . . . seem to be intruding.'

Lilian was moved at this proof of how considerate he could be. She had not even realised he knew that it was her wedding anniversary, and was grateful for his understanding. But she still felt that it would be a mistake to go ahead with their plans. Ralph listened to her as she described what had been going through her mind that day, then he tried to soften her decision.

'Why not think it over?'

'Ralph, there's no point – '

'There's every point. This is a special day. You're bound to . . . Just give yourself more time. Please. I won't press you.'

Lilian could see it from his standpoint and felt sorry for him, agreeing that she would reconsider yet again, though now convinced that she would never marry him. Behind his next words, she sensed an almost pathetic concern to save his face.

'You won't . . . tell anyone about this, will you?'

'No, of course not.'

'If you do . . . well, come back round to the idea . . . then nobody need ever know about this. I mean, we don't have to announce that everything is off. Just yet. Do we?'

Lilian shook her head and squeezed his hand. There was another awkward matter to be mentioned and Ralph reddened as he searched for words. Lilian anticipated what he was trying to say.

'Don't pull out now, Ralph. Put our . . . send in your tender for the Dower House. You must.'

He smiled and she feared that she had raised his hopes unfairly. In her heart she somehow felt that if he secured the Brigadier's estate, it might be a compensation for losing her. She dared not tell him this and he did not pause to ask. He got up and walked to the door.

'Goodnight, Lilian.'

'I don't want you to go,' she said, standing and going after him.

'But I thought – '

'Stay, please. For a little while, at least.'

'My car is outside. People will recognise . . .'

Lilian put a hand to his lips to stop him talking, then asked him if he could drink another coffee. He nodded and went back to his seat. He left at six the following morning.

The day was dry but cold and Lilian was glad of the stiff breeze as she strolled towards the village. She felt quite recovered from the shock of her encounter with Nelson, and had come to see that she was as much to blame as he was. While she would never forgive him for what he had done, she could at least understand it and view it in a calmer perspective. As Ralph had been quick to point out, there had been occasions when she had found Nelson attractive company, and had even encouraged his attentions in a mild way.

Though still wounded by the experience in her bedroom, she no longer felt that she must immediately resign from being caretaker and get out of the cottage. Nelson would not bother her again, she felt, and she would never again permit herself to mislead him.

When she passed Honeysuckle Cottage, she was surprised that Nelson's car was not parked outside. Walter Gabriel was in his garden, running a noisy lawnmower over the grass. They exchanged greetings but the old man made no mention of Nelson and Lilian decided that he had probably driven away from Ambridge after leaving her cottage.

She went on down to the Village Stores and admired the new exterior yet again. Inside the shop she interrupted an argument between Polly and Sid, who seemed embarrassed by her arrival. Sid began to stack some items on the shelves, while Polly served her, making an aside about her husband's sense of humour.

'It's only in fun,' complained Sid.

'That's what you call it,' muttered Polly. 'Sorry, Lilian . . . how many stamps was it?'

'Am I in the way?' Lilian enquired.

'Luckily for Sid,' asserted Polly. 'Otherwise, I'd be throwing something at him.'

'See what marriage does to you?' warned Sid. 'Think twice before you go to the altar again, Lilian.'

'Sid!' cautioned his wife.

Lilian paid for the stamps and commented on the shop front. Sid basked in her praise, but as soon as she left she heard him turn back to Polly to resume the argument.

Standing in the post office section of the Village Stores, she had remembered something and it made her walk briskly back towards Hollowtree. When she let herself into the cottage, it was still there on the floor. Ralph had obviously forgotten all about it when he left.

With the engagement now off, it seemed wrong to open the parcel. In any case, Lilian considered, she ought only to open it in Ralph's presence. Since that would only set up further misunderstandings, she resolved to put the parcel away and forget about it.

But her curiosity got the better of her. The parcel looked so neat and inviting that she could resist it no longer. Slitting the wrapping paper with a knife, she took out three boxes tied together with twine. She recognised the name of the exclusive London store stamped on the top box, and was given a clue about the price of this present.

She cut through the twine and opened the first box to find, nestling in tissue paper, an exquisite miniature, painted on ivory. Companion pieces in the other boxes made up the set, and Lilian began to imagine them on the wall of the drawing room at the Dower House.

Lilian still had no idea, however, who had sent this highly expensive gift and when she saw a card inside the last box she grabbed it hastily. The name on the card left her rather puzzled, and the message was enough to bring a sudden warmth to her cheeks and forehead.

'To Ralph and Lilian, with Love and Best Wishes . . . Sarah. (I shall be staying at Grey Gables this weekend in the hopes of seeing you both.)'

Chapter Twelve

The problem with trying to take on the mantle of Brigadier Winstanley was that it made him the centre of attention in Ambridge.

At first Ralph Bellamy had welcomed this and enjoyed being pointed at and looked up to and talked about. After Lilian had accepted his proposal, he had taken pains to be seen in the village more often, and had relished the feel of his new role as the potential squire.

The latest turn of events had made him regret all this and wish that he could escape altogether from public gaze. At the very moment when he felt that he could be sure about Lilian, she had rocked him with her decision to call the marriage off. His only instinct had been to keep her change of heart from everyone else, hoping vaguely that the passage of time would somehow bring her back to him again.

On top of this had come the news of Sarah's visit to Ambridge, and Ralph had felt quite shaken. Lilian had left it till Friday before telling him about opening the present and finding the card. He had told her that Sarah was a friend from his past, and implied that she was much older than was in fact the case. Then he had tried to ring her to put her off coming to Ambridge, but Sarah had not been at her flat.

It was going to be a long weekend for Ralph and he was not looking forward to it. The woman he really wanted was once more pulling away from him, and the one he least wanted to see at this point in time was actually making a special journey to see him.

He spent Friday afternoon walking across his estate, talking to his farmworkers, trying to lose himself in work. With June less than a week away, it was time to think about haymaking and sheep-shearing and spraying his sugar beet once the mechanical hoeing was completed.

Though he employed a farm manager, Ralph liked to keep directly in touch with every aspect of his enterprise and often made these tours of inspection. He had always considered himself to be a real farmer, ready to get mud on his boots, rather than merely an administrator of an estate.

His walk brought him round to the dairy unit, where the afternoon milking had just finished. He could hear Tony hosing down the parlour and whistling to himself, and was glad that he would not have to chat to Lilian's brother. Tony had other ideas and came out of the parlour in time to see and hail Ralph. The latter crossed over to him.

'How are things, Tony?'

'I was about to ask you the same question,' said the other, leaning on the fence that separated them.

'What do you mean?' said Ralph, on the defensive.

'The Brigadier's estate, of course.'

'Oh that . . . well, yes . . .' Ralph did not want to take Tony too much into his confidence, but he had to say something. 'It's in hand.'

'You're likely to get it, then?' pressed Tony.

'I hope to. I should know fairly soon.'

Tony nodded and did not seem happy, but Ralph could get no explanation out of him.

'We've got a spot of mastitis,' noted Tony, indicating the dairy herd in the standing pen.

'Serious?'

'No. Just the one cow. No problem.'

The men stood there rather awkwardly for a moment, not having anything to say to each other, yet not wanting to be the first to break away. At length Ralph took the initiative.

'They sound as if they want to get back out to pasture.'

'Mm? Oh yes . . .' agreed Tony, and he called the cow dog to help him.

From this rather muted conversation with his employee,

Ralph was able to draw an important comfort. Tony's manner showed that he still assumed the wedding to be on, having been told nothing to the contrary by his sister. Lilian had kept her word on that score.

Ralph returned to his house and passed an uncomfortable evening as he contemplated the difficulties that lay ahead over the next few days.

Saturday morning brought a light drizzle and a sharp breeze but this did not deter Ralph from driving once again towards Borchester. In his pocket was his written tender for the Brigadier's estate, ready to be delivered by hand because Ralph dare not trust to the postal service on so crucial a matter. Clinging to Lilian's remark that he should still go after the property, he was making the highest possible bid which he could.

He had persuaded himself that there was a definite link between ownership of the Dower House and his ability to attract Lilian. If he secured the former, he would win back the latter. He saw the whole operation in terms of a transaction.

The receptionist who greeted him at the offices of Wiley, Smith and French surprised him with the news that 'Mr Stephen' was on the premises. Ralph was shown into his office and was able to hand over his letter of tender personally. Without opening it, Stephen Wiley put it into a drawer and invited his visitor to sit down.

'One of the horses has scratched,' he observed.

'Oh?' Ralph was pleased and interested.

'He didn't approve of this method of sale. Thought I was going to run a Dutch auction.'

'And the other two parties?'

'They're still very much in it.'

Ralph tried to get some clue out of Stephen as to the strength of the competition but the young estate agent would disclose nothing. Instead, he opened a folder on his desk and took out some photographs.

'Lady Isobel found these among her uncle's effects. She thought that the future owner might like to have them.'

'May I?' asked Ralph, taking them.

'Certainly. I think some of them are extremely good.'

The photographs were aerial views of the Brigadier's estate and served to intensify Ralph's desire to buy the property. From the air the Dower House looked especially fine and he wished that Lilian could have been there to see the photographs.

'What did you have in mind for Monday?' asked Stephen.

Ralph looked up quizzically.

'I've arranged to telephone the other two people who have submitted a tender – or, at least, who are going to.'

'I think I'd rather be here, if you don't mind.'

'Even though it may be a wasted journey?' warned the other.

'Even then.'

Ralph handed back the photographs and took his leave, conscious of the other problems he now had to deal with. Stephen Wiley saw him to the door and wished him the best of luck.

The drizzle was heavier when Ralph reached Grey Gables and he had to scurry from the car park into the shelter of the building. He had established on the previous day that Sarah was booked in for Saturday and Sunday night. Since guests were not asked to vacate their rooms until noon, it was unlikely that she would arrive before lunch. But Ralph wanted to be there early, just in case.

He went straight to the coffee lounge, ordered a coffee and found a morning paper behind which he could be anonymous. The bar, though just opened, did not tempt him because he was more likely to meet someone he knew in there. His disguise behind the *Daily Telegraph* was soon penetrated.

'Ralph, darling!' she called, sailing towards him.

'Ah, you've arrived,' he observed, ridiculously.

'Don't get up,' said Sarah, sitting beside him. 'Is that coffee? I'd love one. I've done the journey in one. Well, you know what the coffee is like in those motorway places!'

As always, Sarah was beautifully dressed for the occasion, favouring a light green tweed suit with matching shoes and gloves. She did not wait long before asking the question which Ralph had feared.

'Well, where is she?'

'Who?' he burbled, momentarily losing the script for the answer which he had rehearsed.

'Who – he says! Lilian, of course. She's the person I've come all this way to meet.'

'Uh, that won't be possible, I'm afraid. She . . . isn't in Ambridge this weekend. I did try to contact you to let you know but I wasn't able to get through.'

'You're hiding her,' smiled Sarah, studying him shrewdly. 'You're keeping her locked up somewhere.'

'That's not true, Sarah. You just happen to have picked the wrong weekend, that's all.'

The arrival of the coffee interrupted the interrogation and Ralph felt that he had got over the first obstacle. It would be far too embarrassing for the two women to meet and Lilian had gone along with his suggestion that he should see Sarah alone.

'Did you like my present?'

'Oh yes, thank you. It was very kind of you. And very typical.'

'Did Lilian approve?'

'Naturally. You and she have similar ideas.'

'I know that,' she rejoined, archly. 'Anyway, I had to mark your engagement in some way. It's an historic occasion, after all. Someone's brought you to it at last.'

'Don't tease!'

'I think I'd like to see my room now, darling,' she announced, getting up. 'This place seems almost civilised.'

'It has its points.'

She looked at him levelly for a moment, then handed him the key to her car. While he collected her suitcase from the car park, Sarah signed in at the reception desk, Ralph then escorted her to her room, which she criticised but decided she could endure for two nights. He outlined his plans for the rest of the day, which entailed a drive around local beauty spots, notwithstanding the weather.

Sarah was ready to fall in with any suggestions and made no further mention of Lilian. She decided that she would change for lunch and Ralph went down to the dining room to find a table.

So far, he congratulated himself, everything had gone relatively smoothly. Sarah may not have believed his explanation for Lilian's absence, but she was not going to pursue him on the topic. She had come to the country to enjoy herself for a weekend and there was no reason why he should not take advantage of her company.

Over lunch he found himself flirting gently with her and she responded. He began to think that something which he had feared might instead turn out to be a refreshing experience. Chatting with Sarah over a bottle of Chablis, he forgot all about his tender for the Brigadier's estate and his problems with Lilian and the immense pressure under which he had been for the past few weeks.

It was only when they were about to leave that he was jerked out of his pleasantly relaxed mood. He saw Jack Woolley bearing down upon them and felt his embarrassment flood back. Characteristically, Woolley insisted on being introduced and Ralph mumbled that Sarah was staying as a guest at Grey Gables.

This widened the beaming smile on Woolley's face and he asked if the accommodation was to her satisfaction. Sarah took control, made a few admiring comments then promptly excused them before easing Ralph down the steps and into the car park. When Ralph looked back, Woolley was still standing there, happily dumbfounded. It was not the first time that he had been thankful for Sarah's ability to cope with all manner of social situations.

'Where are we going?' she asked, as the Scimitar started up.

'Everywhere,' he boasted.

'As long as we fit in these places,' she insisted, taking a booklet from her bag.

'I'm supposed to be the guide,' he protested.

'Fine guide you are, Ralph. You can't even guide me to your fiancée.'

'Let's forget about her,' retorted Ralph, with unintentional firmness.

'I'm game.'

'So am I.'

'Then don't spare the horsepower,' she urged, strapping herself into her safety belt.

'Sorry about the weather.'

'That phrase ought to be part of our National Anthem, you know. Or maybe you can have it translated into Latin and used on your family crest at the Dower House.'

'What's the first place on that list of yours?'

'Did you hear what I said?'

His answer was to accelerate and overtake a lorry, which replied by sounding its horn. Sarah laughed.

It was the kind of afternoon which Ralph had not spent for many years. Without feeling any tiredness, he drove well over a hundred and fifty miles to visit a succession of castles, stately homes, abbeys and churches. Sarah acted as navigator on the journey and commentator during the actual visit. Collecting such places was a hobby of hers and she knew all the jargon.

They arrived at Redgate Manor, where Ralph had reserved a table for dinner, early enough to spend an hour in the cocktail bar. He did not notice the quantity of drink which he was getting through, and was only gratified by its mellowing effect. The meal was praised by Sarah, which pleased him. An excellent cook herself, she was highly critical, and her approval seemed to set the seal on the plans which he had made for the day.

'You're driving, remember,' she warned, as he ordered another bottle of wine.

'I drink myself sober. Family habit,' he assured her.

'Seriously, Ralph . . .'

'I *am* being serious. Never was I more serious. Never was I less unserious.'

'Just . . . take it easy, that's all I'll say.'

'And I will be the first to drink to it,' he laughed. 'Now, tell me all about London. What have you been doing with yourself lately?'

'Getting more and more bored with the place.'

'That doesn't sound like the Sarah Latham I know.'

'Perhaps it's old age creeping up on me, but I'm beginning to feel I ought to settle down.'

'You have settled down. Delightful flat. Ideal place to settle down, I can testify to that.'

She raised her glass to acknowledge the compliment, then looked rather wistful for a moment.

'Will you show me round the house tomorrow, Ralph?'

'My place? You've already seen all there is to see,' he laughed, and then realised what she meant. It sobered him slightly.

'Well, do I get to see your future home?' she pressed.

'I wouldn't bank on it being that,' he remarked, bitterly.

'You'll buy that estate and you know it,' she reassured. 'In that respect, we're two of a kind. We *always* get what we really set our sights on. Don't we?'

He met her gaze for some minutes and an idea passed through his mind. Though eager to keep Sarah well away from Ambridge, he now began to wonder if it might not be in his interests to let her see the Dower House. They would only be able to walk around the building but this had been enough to excite Lilian. He promised that he would call for her on the following morning.

As they drove back towards Ambridge, he began to feel the effects of too much drink and did not need her prompting to stay well within the speed limit. They reached Grey Gables and she thanked him for his kindness in taking her out for the day, even though it was not quite what she had expected when deciding to visit Ambridge.

'It's such a pity that Lilian was . . . not available.'

'Uh, yes,' he agreed.

'But then, I can't complain. When one thing falls through, it's often the case that the next alternative, so to speak, is equally enjoyable. No reflection on Lilian, of course, but . . . well, I was glad to have you all to myself.'

'Same here,' he admitted, seizing on her words to clarify the idea which was now taking definite shape.

She leaned over to him and shook her fist at him in mock anger, screwing up her eyes.

'Why didn't you ever ask *me*?'

'I don't know,' he confessed, as if accepting that he had made a serious mistake.

She laughed and kissed him lightly on the lips. He put his arms round her, pulled her close and kissed her fiercely until she restrained him with a smile. Then she reminded him of his promise for the next day, got out of the car and went up the steps of Grey Gables.

The rain which had fallen throughout the previous day and night had died away by Sunday morning, leaving only a few token clouds behind to police an otherwise clear sky. Ralph had dressed and breakfasted by seven before working for a few hours in his study. He was pleased with the purposeful start which he had made to the day, and glad that it had left him no time to reflect on the previous evening.

His feelings towards Sarah were so ambiguous at the moment that he was almost afraid to examine them in depth. The anxiety to keep her away from the village itself had returned and he hoped that nobody would see them as they drove out towards the Brigadier's estate.

When he arrived at Grey Gables, he was greeted with his first shock of the day. Sarah was not there. She had left a message with Jack Woolley to say that she had taken a walk towards Ambridge. What embarrassed Ralph was the way in which Woolley delivered the message, assuring the former that he could rely on his discretion.

Woolley gave him his second shock by telling him that Sarah had been most interested to learn where Lilian lived. Ralph excused himself and ran back to his car, certain that he knew where he would find Sarah. He should have known that she would not be so easily deflected from her purpose.

As soon as Lilian let him into the cottage, he felt the tension. Sarah had been there less than a few minutes, but she and Lilian had already taken a marked dislike to each other. Ralph found himself taking on the position of a referee.

'You're not a bit like Ralph described you,' observed Sarah, with a kind of icy politeness.

'That works both ways,' replied Lilian, shooting him a glance.

'I didn't realise that you were coming back today, Lilian,' said Ralph, trying rather half-heartedly to maintain the fiction that Lilian had been away for the weekend.

From the expression on the faces of both women, he wished that he had not drawn attention to what all three knew was a patent lie. He determined to remain silent until the chance arose to get Sarah out of the cottage.

'You never told me that Lilian helped out behind the bar at her parents' pub,' smiled Sarah.

Ralph coughed and looked away.

'I'm sure they'll miss your assistance when you get married.'

'Not necessarily,' retorted Lilian.

'Mr Woolley is a far more reliable source of information about you than ever Ralph was, you know.'

'I'm sure you enjoyed checking up on me.'

'Naturally, I was interested to know what Ralph was letting himself in for, if you'll pardon the expression.'

Sarah seemed set on scoring points off Lilian, but the latter was holding her own spiritedly. The longer he stayed the more awkward Ralph felt and, though it gained him a cold stare from Lilian, he was relieved when Sarah mentioned that she was going to view the Dower House.

'Perhaps we ought to be on our way,' he ventured.

'Lilian and I have hardly had chance to get to know each other,' protested Sarah.

'Can I offer you a coffee?'

'Not for me, thank you. Ralph?'

He shook his head, resenting the pleasure that Sarah was taking in the situation. His sympathies were now entirely with Lilian.

'I do like your engagement ring,' said Sarah, holding Lilian's hand for a second. 'I see that you've been married before.'

Neither Lilian nor Ralph were ready to explain that the engagement ring was not in fact the one that he had bought. They merely exchanged another uncomfortable glance.

'May I see the other presents?' asked Sarah, getting up.

'They're not all here,' claimed Ralph, hoping to spare Lilian and himself another ordeal.

'Sarah is welcome to see what we do have,' replied Lilian, civilly. 'They're in here.'

She led the older woman into the small dining room, leaving Ralph alone for a few minutes. He could hear Sarah making comments about the various presents, which had been set on the table and sideboard. He was furious with Sarah for putting them all in this situation, and yet he accepted that it was partly his fault. The one consolation was that Lilian was pretending that the engagement was still standing, despite the embarrassment it was causing her.

As he thought about ways he could make it up to Lilian, and as Sarah's voice droned away next door, his eye fell on the red roses in the vase on the side-table. He guessed that there must be all of two dozen there and was curious to know what it said on the card that lay beside them.

'And this, of course, is your own present,' he heard Lilian say.

'Ralph has admired the miniatures in my flat so often that I knew he'd like them. I hoped you would as well.'

He stopped listening to the conversation and walked across to pick up the card. The message on it was blunt but explicit

– 'Many apologies.' Nelson had scrawled his name across the bottom of the card.

When the women rejoined him, he was still standing by the roses on the side table and moved away guiltily. He was surprised when Lilian came over to him and took his arm.

'Sarah was just asking why we haven't had a proper engagement party, darling.'

'I should have thought you'd have made a real splash,' laughed Sarah. 'In your position, I know that I would.'

'We wanted it to be a quiet affair, didn't we, Ralph?'

'Oh . . . yes.'

'That wouldn't do for me,' insisted the other woman. 'I'd want to be engaged and be seen to *be* engaged.'

'It's so much a question of personal choice,' replied Lilian, and he could see that she had caught Sarah slightly on the raw.

'Perhaps it's time that – ' he began, but neither of them heard him.

Lilian had let go of his arm and was rearranging the roses in their vase, while Sarah was settling down in her chair again.

'How long are you staying in Ambridge?' asked Lilian.

'I shall have to go back to London this evening.'

'But I thought you'd booked in for two nights.'

'Darling, please, I couldn't stick that dreary country club for another night. I'll drive back today . . . but before I do that, why don't we all have lunch together somewhere?'

The idea was so disturbing to think about that he could not even find words to oppose it. Lilian came to his rescue.

'I shall be helping behind the bar today,' she said, with some defiance.

'In that case, we must come to this pub of yours,' countered the other woman. 'It's years since I had a meal in a country pub. Might be rather fun. Ralph?'

He did not agree and announced firmly that he had already made other arrangements for their lunch. He then shepherded Sarah to the door, insisting that it was time for them to leave.

Sarah began dropping out invitations for Lilian to visit her in London, but he could see that this was unlikely to happen.

When Sarah walked out to get into his car, he stood at the door trying to convey to Lilian with his eyes that he was deeply sorry she had been caused so much embarrassment. For the benefit of the watching Sarah, he then stepped forward to kiss the impassive Lilian on the cheek before leaving.

Ralph showed Sarah around the outside of the Dower House without speaking, too annoyed with himself and with her to trust to words. Sarah was unworried by his anger and chatted away volubly, suggesting improvements in all the rooms into which they looked. Strolling round the garden with him, she made efforts to identify all the trees and shrubs, as if trying to convince him of her knowledge of such things.

It was only when they had come back to the drive and looked up at the Dower House for the last time that she made any mention of Lilian.

'Is she really up to a place like this?' she asked, bluntly.

Ralph led the way to the car.

Chapter Thirteen

Within days the news had gone right round the village and given fresh stimulus to the gossip. Polly had never doubted for a moment that Ralph Bellamy would add the Brigadier's estate to his own, and, from where she stood, the sale had seemed a remarkably straightforward and uncomplicated business. Now that it was finalised, she began to envy Lilian the advantages with which she was about to begin her marriage. Sid did not endorse her view.

'No, it wouldn't suit me,' he told the customers in the Village Stores one morning. 'Basically, the Dower House hasn't got what it takes. No swimming pool. No tennis court. No billiard room.'

'But you never go swimming,' argued Polly. 'You can't play tennis. I've never known you go near a billiard table.'

'I was speaking hypothetical, Poll Doll.'

'Good luck to 'em both, I say,' commented Tom Forrest, paying for the tobacco he wanted. 'Lilian will make a real go of that place.'

'What will happen to Ambridge Court when Mr Bellamy moves out?' wondered Mrs Perkins, sucking a peppermint audibly.

'You should know, Mrs P,' chuckled Tom. 'Hasn't Lilian let her grandmother into all her secrets?'

'She hasn't, Mr Forrest. To tell truth, she's not been ready to talk overmuch about her plans, at all. Not to me, at any rate.'

'It's the uncertainty,' said Sid, grandly. 'Not wanting to take the Dower House etcetera for granted until it was well and truly in her hot and sticky hand.'

Polly could see that Mrs Perkins wanted to ask her something and moved closer to her. The old lady spoke in an undertone, intending that the men in the shop should not hear her.

'Have you got any boil-proof elastic?'

Polly reached down a card from the wall and served Mrs Perkins. Out of the corner of her eye, she could see Sid smirking and drawing Tom's attention to the old woman's purchase.

'Someone was saying that Mr Bellamy was going to convert Ambridge Court into flats for his workers,' remembered Polly.

'Feather-bedding 'em,' sneered Sid.

'Ralph Bellamy won't feather-bed anyone,' said Tom.

Polly's glance was in time to stop Sid making a vulgar aside. She waited till the customers had left the shop and then turned to reprove him for the way he had mocked Mrs Perkins.

'I didn't mock her. I merely put it down as evidence of life's rich and ever-changing pattern.'

He was in a joking vein again and she had already had proof of the damage that could do. She was still angry with him over his sending off the form to the Computer Dating Agency, and had tried in vain to get from him the name of the intended victim.

'You mustn't make fun of everyone, Sid,' she scolded.

'A giggle never hurt anyone, love. Ambridge's own chuckle-board, that's me. Hey, we've learned one thing about Mrs P. . . .'

'If it's another joke, I don't want to – '

'Such insights we get into human frailty, serving in a Village Stores. It's obvious why she wants boil-proof elastic – she keeps her bloomers on when she takes a bath.'

The sound of a horn outside stopped her from telling him off. She did not want to miss the Mobile Library, which only called once a fortnight. She left him to keep an eye on the shop, urging him to stop laughing at the expense of some of the customers.

The large van was parked in its usual place by the village

green. The sliding door had been left open and the windows in the roof of the van were ajar, but it was still oppressively warm inside. Books were stacked neatly on the shelves along the sides of the van and three or four people were already browsing when Polly stepped inside.

The new young assistant behind the counter smiled a nervous welcome when Polly asked if the book which she had reserved had arrived. Mr Venables, the old man who drove the van, was telling the girl the names to look for and the girl went to a tray marked 'Reserved'. She found the book, a volume on childbirth which Polly's doctor had recommended.

'Reading up on the theory, are you?' asked Peggy Archer, coming up to the counter with half a dozen books.

'Sort of, Mrs Archer.'

'There are some things the books never tell you,' warned the other.

'So I gather.'

She let Peggy sign for her books, then explained that the book was not only for her own benefit.

'Ah, you're trying to educate Sid.'

'No, I want to put him off. I'm hoping that if he reads this, he'll forget all about it!'

'About what?' Peggy was interested.

More customers had come into the van, which was now crowded and even muggier. Polly signed for her book, and then stepped down on to the pavement with Peggy.

'He wants to be present. At the birth.'

'Does he . . . know what to expect?'

'He thinks he does. But, quite frankly, I fancy he'd be more of a hindrance than a help in the delivery ward.' Polly giggled as she imagined Sid's reactions. 'Yes, it would wipe the grin off his face, I'm sure.'

'Then you don't want him there?'

'Yes and no. In principle, it sounds like a good idea. And some husbands would be all right. Not Sid. He's got a squeamish streak.'

'Most men have,' confided Peggy.

'Anyway, if this book doesn't put the finish on him, then the film will.'

'Film?'

'It's one that the hospital have arranged to show us. Tomorrow night, in Borchester. Shows you everything – labour, delivery, the lot. I'm not sure that I'm exactly going to enjoy it, but Sid . . .'

'He might surprise you, Polly.'

'After all these years?'

The women laughed, then went their separate ways. Back at the Village Stores, Polly found a small queue of people at the post office section. She was kept busy until lunch time and was only then able to show Sid the book.

'I've read it,' he said, airily. 'The butler did it.'

'Sid!'

'He did, I tell you. Both twins had his nose. It was cast-iron proof. By the time they'd discharged her from hospital, hubby had filed a divorce suit.'

'*I'll* be filing a divorce suit, if you don't listen.'

And while he attacked his egg and chips, she told him why she wanted him to read the book. He agreed amiably to all that she said.

By the time they finally closed the shop for the day, Polly had learned to regret that she had given him the book. Every moment when not attending to customers he spent skimming through the pages and studying the graphic illustrations. Instead of frightening him off, it only strengthened his determination to be present at the actual birth.

Worst of all, he had picked up the technical phrases and used them again and again. Over tea, it was the dilation of the cervix and the breaking of the membranes. During a walk which they took out towards Heydon Berrow, it was second stage contractions and the techniques of induction. When they went into the Bull, it was episiotomy and involution.

She had complained about his over-active sense of humour for days, but she now saw that she preferred that to this profound seriousness. She had unwittingly converted a fairly normal husband into a self-appointed expert on childbirth, and she was grateful when the attraction of the dartboard came between him and new-found wisdom about obstetrics.

The Bull was comparatively quiet that evening, which made it odd that Lilian was helping behind the bar. Polly thought that anyone lucky enough to become the mistress of the Dower House would be spending practically all her time there, making plans, discussing ideas, simply enjoying being there. But Lilian did not look as if she was enjoying being anywhere, and Polly recalled that both Doris Archer and Mrs Perkins had found their grand-daughter's attitude towards the marriage a little restrained.

Having escape Sid in his medical mood, she began to think about his more usual condition and came up against the question of the practical joke which he and Tony were playing on someone. She had not been able to identify that someone by keeping on to Sid, but she wondered if she might have more success with Tony. He was sitting at a table with his grandfather, who was looking rather perplexed at something he had just been told. Polly decided to bide her time until she had a chance to corner Tony on his own. An ally suddenly presented herself.

'I'm just not needed this evening,' said Lilian, joining her on a stool at the bar.

'Have they made you redundant?'

'Something like that. I seem to be treading on Nora's toes tonight.'

'Too many cooks and all that . . . actually, I'm glad of a chance to speak to you, Lilian. It's about Tony.'

'What's he been up to now?'

'I'm hoping that you might be able to tell me.'

Polly retailed the story, as far as she knew it, about the Computer Dating Agency. At first Lilian was amused but she came round to Polly's argument that it might involve a lot of unnecessary embarrassment for innocent people. She could think of no obvious target for Sid and Tony but offered to help Polly tackle her brother. It was the kind of irresponsible thing which he tended to do.

'Not that I want to play the elder sister at him, mind.'

'He'll have to listen to you now, though.'

'Why, Polly?'

'You'll become his boss's wife. He'll have to kow-tow to you.'

Once again Polly discerned a reserve in Lilian's reaction to a mention of the wedding. Then she saw Tony getting up and heading for the bar.

'We'd like a word with you, Tony,' said his sister.

'You'll have to be quick,' he retorted, putting his empty tankard down. 'I've got a date.'

'So has somebody else,' piped up Polly. 'A date by computer.'

Tony looked hurt, then turned to glance across at Sid.

'He's told Polly everything,' confirmed Lilian.

Tony hunched his shoulders in annoyance, then burst out laughing, still finding the whole idea very funny. Polly wanted to ask outright who the victim was but Lilian knew how to handle her brother.

'Why pick on *him*?' she demanded. '*Him*, of all people?'

'You know what he's like. Always on about his fatal charms. Sid and me just took him at his own word.'

'I still don't think he deserves this,' pressed Lilian.

'Uncle Walter will lap it up, don't worry. We're doing him a favour in one sense.'

Tony took his leave and went out through the door after waving a farewell to his parents. At least they now knew who the mystery victim was, and Polly had to concede that Walter Gabriel was an inveterate boaster about his effect on women.

'What's the next step, Polly?'

'Get them to call it off.'

'I thought you said it was due to happen this Saturday?'

'That's what Sid thought, but he couldn't be sure. The letter from the agency will be sent to Honeysuckle Cottage.'

Lilian giggled, then remembered the serious aspects. Some

woman might come to Ambridge on what would be a totally humiliating trip. It was the woman, rather than Walter Gabriel, for whom she felt sorry.

'I sympathise with Mr Gabriel as well. This is the last thing he needs just now after the let-down he's had.'

Polly went on to explain that Walter had received a post card from his son to say that he would be visiting Ambridge towards the end of the previous week. Not only had he failed to turn up, but he had sent no word of apology since. Lilian listened to all of the criticisms of Nelson and nodded. Polly put down the pinkness in her cheeks to the warmth of the bar.

She let Sid resume his lectures on childbirth on their way back to the Village Stores, but she challenged him about the practical joke once they were back in their living room. Sid was not in the least repentant; he still saw only the comic possibilities of some eager, marriage-minded woman making tracks towards Honeysuckle Cottage at the appointed hour.

'It's disgusting, Sid!'

'How do we know what they'll get up to?' he quipped.

'Just imagine. Some poor, misguided old lady – '

'Oh she won't be all that old. Tony and I adapted some of the facts a bit. We've put Walter down as a sprightly fifty-five.'

'That's even worse!'

'Calm down, Poll. I don't see why you've got to get your knickers in a twist about it. We gave him a terrific boost when we sent that form in. Made him sound like the best thing since Errol Flynn.'

'Can't you see how unkind it is on the woman?'

'She'll get over it. If she was a blushing violet, she wouldn't be writing to a Computer Dating Agency, would she? Probably some hard-bitten old harridan who'll eat Walter for breakfast.'

'It's *wrong*, Sid!'

She went through the same arguments she had been hurling at him for days, but he withstood them. Only when she threatened to tell Walter all about the deception did she make him take notice of her.

'You can't blow the gaff on us now!' he exclaimed, as if some terrible outrage had been suggested.

'If you don't tell him, *I* will,' she repeated.

'Of course we'll tell him, love. We intended to all along. We'll tell him immediately afterwards.'

Polly could not believe her ears when Sid outlined their full plan. He and Tony had had to specify a date, time and meeting-place on the form, and they had opted for the approaching Saturday evening, electing Honeysuckle Cottage as the venue. Their idea was to be on hand when the woman arrived in order to enjoy the mutual embarrassment when Walter answered his door.

'Let's face it, Poll Doll. As soon as she's wise to the fact that it's a hoax, she'll beetle off back to where she came from.'

'Having spent all that time and money getting there?'

'It may be someone local, for all we know.'

'Sid, I'm dead serious about this. First thing in the morning, you ring up that Agency and call this whole thing off. It's no good looking at me like that. I *mean* it!'

A night's sleep seemed to have reconciled Sid to the idea that the joke had no more mileage in it. Breakfast found him thumbing through the book again, inspecting a diagram relating to breathing exercises. He got down in the position required and experimented, bringing the first smile of the day to her face.

His apparent change of mind made Polly feel more well-disposed towards him and she began to think that perhaps he might be an asset in a delivery room, after all. She remembered her mother's story about her own birth and the part which her father had played in that. When Sid had gone through his pompous phase of airing his knowledge, he might be a real help to her at the critical time.

As she opened up the shop, she reminded him of the undertaking he had made and his good humour evaporated.

Evasive and irritable, he said that he would have to discuss it with Tony first. But she stuck to her guns and sent him off to make the telephone call.

'Well?' she said, as he returned, grinning.

'No luck, Poll. They said their service was highly confidential. Wouldn't discuss anything over the blower. Said I'd have to write or call in.'

'It's too late for that.'

'My view, entirely. I reckon we just ought to let the scheme roll on its own sweet way.'

'We'll do nothing of the kind!'

Customers interrupted their argument and it was an hour before she was able to reiterate her case. He would have to go to Honeysuckle Cottage and own up, a course of action which had as much appeal as sticking pins into himself.

It was the shop's half-day so she was able to walk with him the short distance to Walter Gabriel's cottage. He was not at home and Sid was overjoyed at what he saw as a kind of stay of execution. Polly went off to visit her mother, warning Sid that they would keep calling at Honeysuckle Cottage until they found Walter there.

Fortune seemed to favour Sid because a second visit to the cottage after tea produced no occupant. It was time to go into Borchester to see the film, so the confession would have to be postponed until later. Sid's good humour was restored by the temporary reprieve and he was at his most garrulous as they left the village, quoting new extracts from the book about childbirth.

The Ante-Natal Clinic was a small, purpose-built extension at the rear of the Borchester County Hospital. Plastic chairs had been set out in a row in the waiting room, facing a screen. At the far end of the room a technician was winding the film on to a large spool. Sid and Polly were among the last to arrive and found themselves in the company of about a dozen expectant mothers, in varying stages of pregnancy. Sid was the only husband there and Polly could see that he was proud of the fact.

'Two in the stalls, please,' he informed the nurse who greeted them.

The woman, a West Indian, chuckled loudly and showed a row of sparkling teeth.

'By the way, what's the supporting picture?' he asked in an aside, and she chuckled again.

'Come on, Sid,' said Polly, tugging him towards the chairs at the back and feeling that everyone was looking at them.

'Talk about shutting the stable door,' whispered Sid, nodding towards a poster on the wall.

Polly read the advertisement for Family Planning and told Sid to be quiet. Coming to the Ante-Natal Clinic always made her excessively self-conscious and she did not want any attention drawn to her. She was glad when the blinds were drawn, the midwife's introductory remarks were over and the lights put out.

There was a slight technical hitch and the lights had to be put on again for a moment, just long enough for Sid to observe that it was a rather short film. Polly's elbow told him to keep his voice down, and then the lights died again and the film flickered upon the screen.

It was a colour film with a soundtrack and it claimed to be a record of a fairly normal delivery. The opening shot was of a young woman, introduced by the narrator as Margaret, being wheeled in her bed into a labour ward. Instinctively, Polly gripped Sid's hand and held it throughout the remainder of the film.

There were several other beds in the ward, each one concealed behind ugly rubber curtains. Cries of distress were coming from some of the beds and Margaret herself was evidently in considerable discomfort. Her bed took up its allotted space but one curtain was left undrawn for the benefit of the camera.

Polly had already identified totally with Margaret, who was about her own age. She could almost feel the pain that the latter was suffering, and was biting her lip in exactly the same way. The camera panned across to the clock on the wall and the scene faded to establish a passage of time. When Margaret was next seen she was in the next stage of labour, and the narrator spoke about the contractions which she was now having.

A nurse was timing the contractions with a watch, when a doctor arrived to examine Margaret. He nodded to the nurse, who released the catch on the wheels of the bed. Polly was now quite alarmed on Margaret's behalf, and so engrossed in watching the film that she did not realise what Sid's reactions were.

Margaret was now in a delivery room, unable to stifle some of the cries of pain. If this was a normal childbirth, Polly wondered, what might she herself expect if there were any complications? Margaret was lying on what looked like a steel table, covered by a thick rubber mattress. It was much higher than a bed to prevent the midwives from having to bend.

What upset Polly was the total lack of privacy surrounding the whole childbirth. Apart from the doctor, midwife and nurse present, there were two pupil-midwives, simply watching. It struck Polly as such a humiliating situation, having to undergo that most personal experience in the company of so many dispassionate observers. Her self-respect was wounded and she could not understand why Margaret herself was so unconcerned by those around her.

Then the baby's head became visible in the darkness of the birth canal and Polly forgot all about her misgivings, becoming completely absorbed in what she saw on the screen. The film omitted no detail, condensing time yet somehow maintaining the impression of a continuous process. Polly felt a sense of triumph when the baby's head finally emerged, and there was audible reaction from the other mothers-to-be who were watching.

After a short interval, a fresh contraction eased out the front shoulder and then the other. The head turned as the baby altered its position and then, after some more pushing, it suddenly surged forward and free of the uterus. As Polly watched the metal clips being put on the umbilical cord to act as tourniquets, she felt the most profound sense of relief and achievement. The cord was cut, the baby wrapped in a warm towel and Margaret was allowed to hold her daughter for the first time. The expression of sheer joy on her face brought tears to Polly.

When the lights went on again, it was clear that the film had made a deep impression on most of the people present, reassuring some, frightening others. Polly turned to see that Sid was quite ashen. During the brief question time which followed, he said nothing and Polly was glad to get him outside into the fresh air. What had been for her an inspiring film had left him harrowed. It was only when they were well away from the hospital that Sid spoke.

'Is it *really* like that, love?'

'Yes.'

'I'm glad I'm not a woman,' he confided.

On the journey home, Polly kept off the subject of the film out of consideration for him. She was both pleased and disappointed that it had cured him of any desire to be present at the birth of their own child. Reflecting on certain sequences in the film, she made comparisons with what her mother had told her and was deeply grateful that she would be having her baby in the maternity wing of the hospital.

Though preoccupied by what they had seen, Polly was still very much aware of the task which was awaiting them. However delicate he might be feeling, Sid could not be let off the hook. When they arrived back in Ambridge, she took him by the arm and walked him in the direction of Honeysuckle Cottage.

The criss-cross patterns on the thatched roof came into view, and she soon spotted Walter Gabriel behind the mixed hedge of hawthorn and honeysuckle which ran along three sides of the garden. He was working on some kind of woodcarving, using a variety of chisels with care and precision. He tipped his battered old straw hat when he saw them and invited them into the garden.

Polly did not want to delay matters and when Sid ignored the elbow with which she nudged him, she prompted him more openly.

'Sid's got something to tell you, Mr Gabriel.'

'Man to man, is it?' chuckled the old man. 'You put yer 'ands over yer ears then, Polly.'

'Go on, Sid,' urged Polly, as he shifted his feet. 'All right, then . . .'

This threat of someone else telling him the tale jerked Sid into action. He blurted out the whole thing at speed and then stepped backwards, as if expecting a violent reaction. Polly added her own apologies but Walter's laugh had already started deep down inside him and he soon began to give it full vent.

'There you are – he thinks it's a great joke!' argued Sid, greatly cheered.

'I do!' roared the old man, leaning against the wall of the cottage for support, and undoing a few buttons on his waistcoat. 'I most certainly do!'

Polly joined them in their laughter, though she was not quite sure why. It was minutes before Walter recovered enough to speak.

'So it's you and young Tony what I got to thank for sending me Cecily,' taking out a crumpled letter from his pocket.

'Who?' asked Polly.

'Miss Cecily Pilgrim,' read the other, squinting at the paper. 'Says here that she'll be on my doorstep at eight this Saturday. How's that for a delivery service?'

Polly realised that he had every intention of letting the visit go ahead as planned, and she was annoyed when Sid encouraged him to do just this. Her sympathies were immediately transferred to the woman who had been assigned to the questionable pleasure of spending an evening with Walter Gabriel.

'You don't mean you're going through with it?' she enquired.

''Course I am. Best bib and tucker, red rose in my lapel

and a gob of that after-shave pong that our Nelson give me last Christmas. I'll give her the works, don't you worry.'

'But you can't,' pleaded Polly. 'It's unfair on her.'

'Not at all. She's a-coming special to see me, in't she? Let Miss Pilgrim make her journey to Ambridge. I'll be her Mecca!'

This time Polly did not join in their laughter.

Chapter Fourteen

From the time when she had been a child visiting her grandparents there, Lilian had always loved tea on the lawn at Brookfield. As she reclined now in a deck-chair, she felt that it was the perfect way to celebrate the first Sunday in June. It was an afternoon for sun hats and summer dresses, for lazing, for chatting, for watching the children play; it was a time for letting the day saunter along at its own lethargic pace and for enjoying the simple pleasure of being with and among one's family.

Shula was helping her mother to pass round the tea things, scolding her brother, Kenton, for sampling the cake before it had been offered to the guests. Lilian's own mother was sitting by the rockery with Jennifer, while her father had dropped off to sleep under the protective cover of an old trilby which he had pulled down over his face. Closest to Lilian, and talking as ever about farming, were her uncle and her grandfather. Snatches of the conversation drifted her way and caused her to take more notice than she had been doing.

'Another job?' Philip Archer said, incredulous.

'Aye, down Hampshire way,' grunted Dan.

'Is he serious about it?'

'Must be. Bad business, Phil. I couldn't persuade him.'

'I'm not sure that I could, Dad.'

'Keep it under your hat, though, won't you?'

'Of course . . . ah, tea time.'

Philip went to help his wife and daughter while Dan came to sit next to Lilian, passing a hand across his brow as he did so.

'Real scorcher, love.'

'Yes . . . where's Gran?'

'Elizabeth dragged her off to take a turn at pushing the swing. She'll be here directly. Doris can hear tea being poured at a hundred paces.'

Right on cue, his wife came round the angle of the privet hedge and smiled at the sight of the cups that were being handed round. Lilian took her own cup from Shula and then selected a few sandwiches from the plate which Jill held out to her.

'Pity Ralph couldn't manage to get along this afternoon,' observed her grandfather when they were alone again.

'He had something on, I'm afraid.'

'You'd have thought even a man as busy as he is could spare an hour on a Sunday afternoon.'

'Not *this* Sunday, unfortunately,' replied Lilian.

Though she had passed on Jill's invitation to Ralph, she had in fact asked him not to join the family at Brookfield. For his sake she was allowing everyone to assume that nothing was amiss between them, but she felt that she had to be away from him if she was to resolve all her uncertainties.

'Happy about the Dower House?' asked her grandfather, eating a second sandwich.

'Naturally.'

'I suppose you've been sorting out ideas for carpets and curtains and all the rest of the paraphernalia that you women seem to think make a home.'

'What's he saying now?' asked Jill, settling down on a rug on the grass. 'Is he teasing you, Lilian?'

'We were talking about putting her house in order,' he explained.

'Literally or metaphorically?'

Lilian laughed but her aunt's remark had been a lot nearer the truth than she would ever suspect.

'When do we get a chance to look over the house?' resumed Jill.

'Aye, Doris was asking the same thing. Amazing how nosey women are, isn't it?' observed Dan, stealing another sandwich from the plate that was being carried past. 'Now me, I couldn't care if I never got inside the Dower House. As long as it was pretty soon.'

'You'll *all* be invited,' promised Lilian, 'just as soon as we get the place straight.'

'I don't think we'll ever get Brookfield straight,' confessed Jill.

'Go on, say it,' teased her father-in-law. 'Me and Doris left it in such a terrible state, you don't know where to start.'

'I certainly wouldn't know where to start with the Dower House. Do you, Lilian? Be frank.'

'I've had some ideas,' said Lilian, quietly.

She found it strange that she could talk quite easily about the Dower House as a thing in itself. It was something she now thought of as her own and she had spent many hours making plans for it, seeing it as something separate from Ralph. Uneasy when questioned about the marriage, she yet wanted the pleasure of discussing something which could only be hers as result of that marriage.

'Have you set a date yet?' asked Jill.

'We thought vaguely about September.'

'News to me that Ralph Bellamy thinks about anything vaguely,' opined Dan. 'That fella's always been so damn exact about everything he wants and does . . . uh, no offence meant, Lilian.'

At this point, David and Elizabeth came running back towards the family group and demanded tea. Jill got up to see to her youngest children, throwing a warning over her shoulder as she went.

'It's no rest-cure being a farmer's wife, Lilian. Mark my words.'

While her grandfather speculated about the chances of beginning haymaking in the coming week, Lilian weighed the phrase which she had just heard. It had never occurred to her before that, if she married Ralph, she would become, technically, a farmer's wife. Thinking about the other farmers' wives whom she knew, she could not find one on whom she could pattern herself.

Her grandmother had been a farmer's wife for almost half a century, running a house, bringing up a family, adapting her routine entirely to suit her husband's working life. Yet Doris Archer had taken no really practical part in the farming at Brookfield. Jill had followed suit in being a farmer's wife who worked in the home rather than on the land, though she had other strings to her bow as well, being an active spokeswoman in local affairs.

Lilian would not be this type of farmer's wife, welcoming the husband home at the end of the day with a meal and a ready ear for his troubles. Unlike her grandmother, she would never know what it was to sew a cow gown or cook on a range or bottle-feed a lamb in her kitchen. Unlike her aunt, she would never have to wait patiently to be the mistress of her own farmhouse or help with the accounts.

If she married Ralph – and she was at least ready to consider the possibility again – she would be a farmer's wife of a kind almost unique in the area. She would have unequalled social prestige and would not need, unless she chose, to take the slightest interest in the way that her husband ran the estate. It was in thinking about this type of farmer's wife – a woman with position, wealth and relative freedom – that she saw the positive attraction of the role for someone like Sarah Latham.

'Got you alone at last!' said Jennifer, sitting on the rug at her feet.

Lilian was surprised to see that her grandfather had moved away to play a game of French cricket with the children, but was glad of the opportunity of a quiet moment with her sister. Since Jennifer had moved to live in the flat over her husband's Borchester book shop, Lilian did not see nearly enough of her.

'I'm thrilled by your news, Jennifer. When is it due?'

'Towards the end of December, we think.'

'You and Roger ought to know,' pointed out Lilian. 'December. The same time as Polly Perks.'

'I gather that she let the cat out of the bag rather early on. We wanted to keep it to ourselves as long as possible.'

'Then you haven't done very well!' laughed the other.

'It's to be kept in the family, please,' requested Jennifer.

'Not if you've told Roger's mother. She'll have hired a van with a loud-hailer by now and be telling the whole of the county.'

Jennifer agreed. She made no secret about the great difficulties she had with her mother-in-law, an imperious lady who had never considered Jennifer good enough to marry her son. Lilian sympathised with her sister and suggested a few violent remedies. As she was listening to Jennifer, she again felt a sensation which had gripped her on a few occasions when she had been with Polly Perks. She wanted – and the sensation became stronger with each minute – to have a baby, to become a mother.

'Have you seen Tony recently?' she asked Jennifer, trying to shake off her thoughts of motherhood.

'Not for ages. What's he up to these days?'

'A lot of no good, as far as the girls around here are concerned,' said Lilian, raising an eyebrow. 'But I just don't think he's as happy as he was in his work.'

'Easy to see why, Lilian. Just look in the mirror. His big sister will have the whiphand over him at last.'

'That'll be the day!'

The sisters began to compare memories of their attempts to control their younger brother over the years, and had to admit that both of them had failed. As a child, Tony had always had a will of his own and Lilian recalled dozens of incidents when he had defied them out of sheer determination to have his own way.

'You know what they say about kids,' remarked Jennifer, wryly. 'The balance of power between them stays exactly the same when they grow up.'

'I don't believe that at all. I mean, look at us. I just don't pull your pigtails any longer or try to pour ink over your dolls' dresses. Do you remember that ink business?'

'Do I! It's engraved on my heart, Lilian. And though there isn't the same outright aggression between us, I daresay we do the same thing to each other in other ways.'

'What a cynical idea!'

'No, I think it's just being realistic. As Grandad Archer always says, adults are only children writ large. There's a lot in that.'

Lilian had to concede that her relationship with Tony had not altered all that much, and it made her realise how unpleasant it must seem to him that she might become his employer's wife. No wonder he was actually thinking of changing his job, and no wonder her grandfather and uncle were so alarmed at this prospect. She felt the pull of divided loyalties yet again, believing that she was directly responsible for bringing so much anxiety to her family over Tony's future, and, at the same time, experiencing twinges on Ralph's behalf. Tony would be letting him down if he resigned and she was suddenly very angry with her brother, not pausing to remember that she had in fact called the marriage off.

A child's voice broke into her thoughts.

'Oh, Adam, not again!' moaned Jennifer, reading her young son's face from force of habit.

'I had a naxydent, Mummy,' he admitted, sheepishly.

'Now that's one thing children *do* grow out of,' said Lilian.

'Thank goodness! Come on, then, darling. Let's go and get you cleaned up, shall we?'

'Haven't you trained Roger to do that sort of thing?'

'You're joking! Can you imagine Ralph ever taking his turn?'

Lilian's next question was spoken involuntarily.

'Jennifer, what do you *think* of Ralph?'

'Does it matter? Anyway, I can't leave Adam like this . . .'

'Please. I'd like to know. We haven't really had time to

talk about him. I mean, I know that he's not exactly your type.'

'*I* wouldn't marry him, if that's what you're asking. But then I'd never get the opportunity. I don't dislike him, exactly. I haven't got any really strong personal feelings either way, except that he's a bit formal, a bit county. The truth is that I resent him for what he is rather than who he is. Pure prejudice. I'll get over it.'

'He's very different from Lester,' confided Lilian, sadly.

'I should have thought that was the best thing in his favour . . . and now I really must get this little boy cleaned up. Off we go, Adam.'

What had been an offhand remark by Jennifer set her sister's mind racing and made her see Ralph in a new light altogether. Maybe she had been wrong to see him in terms of a replacement for Lester and to measure the two men against each other. The two marriages would be totally different in every way, marking two separate stages in her life instead of being things which overlapped and competed.

Without being aware of it, her sister had helped in another way as well, simply by reminding Lilian, that Jennifer had entered upon marriage with far less in her favour. Even in the most broad-minded community, an unmarried mother is at a great disadvantage and Ambridge was far from broad-minded. Lilian would never forgive some of the poisonous comments made in the village about her sister, and she knew the extent of the silent disapproval which had to be withstood on all sides. Marriage to Roger Travers-Macy had brought many benefits, but his mother would always be on hand to draw attention to Jennifer's mistake and to point out that she had opposed the marriage from the start.

Considering her sister's situation, Lilian felt rather ashamed of making such heavy weather over her own decision. On one hand, she was asking too much of a potential husband, needing him to measure up to all kinds of impossible standards; on the other hand, she was perhaps expecting too little, not giving Ralph the benefit of the doubt.

Shula came up and dragged her off to make up a foursome in a game of open-air badminton, and she spent a happy, if breathless, hour trying to gauge the flight of the shuttlecock in the slight wind. A superior knowledge of the rules and a better understanding with her partner helped Lilian, with Shula, to beat Kenton and his father without difficulty. The children had the energy to play on together while the grown-ups sought the welcome of deck-chairs and the reward of a cool drink.

'We shall have to be off, I'm afraid,' sighed her mother, walking over to her. 'Although I think I'll leave your father here.'

'Would you like me to come with you, Mum?' offered Lilian.

'No reason why you should have to live under the tyranny of opening time as well,' smiled the other. 'We shall miss you at the Bull when you're married, you know.'

'But I'll still come and help,' Lilian blurted out, bringing a startled look to her mother's face by the obvious sincerity of her remark.

'We'll see,' nodded her mother. 'I had hoped Tony might call in this afternoon. Jill did invite him.'

'Perhaps he's playing cricket.'

'There's no game today or Phil would have been involved.'

Lilian knew that Tony's absence was linked with his thoughts about moving away from Ambridge. The last place he would want to be at the moment was in the middle of an Archer family gathering at Brookfield, forcibly reminded of all the things he might be turning his back upon. She could not tell her mother this and sought for another excuse which would appease her, and make her less worried about the fact that her son had not spent very much time with her of late.

'I think the explanation is emotional, Mum.'

'How do you mean?'

'Michelle. Tony was very cut up about her.'

'But she isn't here this afternoon.'

'Tony wasn't to know that. He probably feared she'd be handing round the jam tarts. I don't think he was ever really serious about her, but it certainly put his nose out of joint when she upped and got engaged.'

'Serves him right, if you ask me!'

'I daresay he'll recover. Or find plenty of willing volunteers to *help* him recover.'

'Your father was just the same, Lilian. I happened to be the lucky one who caught him when he was finally thinking of mending his ways.'

Lilian decided to walk back to the Bull with her mother and they thanked Philip and Jill for the afternoon before waving their farewells to everyone else. Jack Archer was left sleeping in his chair.

Days passed and she began to want to see Ralph again, if only to tell him that she had still not come round to the idea of marriage. She could not account for the urge which she felt to be with him and tried at first to fight it, afraid that he might make the wrong assumptions if she sought him out too eagerly. They had agreed not to meet until the weekend, but what she had envisaged as a period of rest from him had turned into an intolerable wait, made the more irksome by the nagging memory of Sarah Latham.

The confrontation with Sarah had aroused a jealousy in her that she had not imagined possible. Though still uncertain about her own position in regard to Ralph, she was utterly convinced that she did not want Sarah to be his wife and to become mistress of the Dower House. Yet she sensed that this was an alternative she might be forcing him towards, however reluctant he might at one time have been.

It was Ralph's habit in summer months to ride out for an hour in the early evening and so she elected to be in the saddle around the same time, cantering towards Ambridge Court in the hopes of a meeting with him. Riding had been the first and strongest bond between them and it might be salutary to remind themselves of the fact, if only because it was something which set her strictly apart from Sarah. Sarah's complete lack of interest in the array of riding trophies at the cottage had revealed her as no horsewoman.

Haymaking had begun in earnest and Lilian passed fields where the grass had been cut and lay in the sun drying and bleaching. In one field she saw a tractor at work, moving steadily around the perimeter, its own drone muffled to some extent by the loud, stabbing rhythm of the baling machine which it dragged behind it and which was scooping up the loose grass voraciously. Slowly and methodically, it pushed the bales out on to a sled attached to the rear and at intervals the driver operated a trip-switch which allowed the collected bales to tumble out into a heap in the field.

At the far end of the field a few men were already pitching bales on to a trailer, where they were being stacked by a young woman who wore gloves as a protection against the sharp baler twine. As the men speared the bales, then lifted and tossed them in one fluid movement, Lilian reflected that she was watching something which had been going on for centuries on this land. The scene filled her with a sense of tradition and caused her to think again about the implications of being a farmer's wife.

The tractor pulled up the gradient in her direction, leaving fresh bales in its wake, and she noticed that the driver was wearing what at first appeared to be large earmuffs. It was only when he got closer that she recognised them as headphones and realised that he was listening to a transistor radio as he worked, eliminating the roar of the machines in favour of the siren call of pop music. Her musings about the timelessness of haymaking were rudely interrupted and she turned to canter away.

As she did so, she saw another horse in the distance, the grey which Ralph always rode. But it was not heading towards her any more. Seeing her move away from the gate on Red Knight, Ralph deliberately tugged the grey around and trotted off towards the copse to the left. There could be no doubt that he was avoiding her and it left Lilian hurt and puzzled. Perhaps his feelings about her were beginning to change at last in the face of her shifting attitudes towards him.

Chapter Fifteen

A week which had begun with such welcoming sunshine ended with a series of vengeful thunderstorms. In common with the other farmers around Ambridge, Ralph fell back on the time-honoured agricultural pastime of cursing the English weather. Those bales of hay which had been left stacked in his fields were thoroughly soaked, and his freshly cut grass was drenched. His farmworkers, who had started the week stripped to the waist, finished it in oilskins and hats. Ralph could do nothing but watch and wait and pray.

The frustrations which the weather caused him, however, were mild when he compared them with the doubts which Lilian had inflicted upon him. After all the energy he had put into it, the acquisition of the Brigadier's estate gave him no real pleasure or lift. He had been nowhere near the Dower House since he had become its owner, and he had left the task of making the rounds of his new tenants to Sinclair, his farm manager. Ralph had not even touched the aerial photographs which Stephen Wiley had passed over to him.

Everything turned on Lilian's decision, and he had come to accept that that decision would be to call the wedding off. When they finally met at the end of the week, he was convinced, she would tell him that she was going to make the decision public. He imagined all the people who would gloat over the information that he had been jilted, that he had won a house but lost a wife.

It was this certainty that she could not possibly wish to go ahead with the marriage that had made him avoid her when they had met while out riding. He wanted to postpone the actual blow as long as he could, even though he knew that this would not lessen its impact.

The rain had finally died away by Saturday evening, but he saw no happy portent in this improvement in the weather. He delayed leaving the house until the very last moment, aware that this was the first time ever that he had been unwilling to meet Lilian. Almost as if by design, his car was in need of petrol and it gave him the excuse to buy another small delay at the garage.

As the attendant was filling the petrol tank of the Scimitar, he got out to stretch his legs and was just in time to see a most remarkable sight. Waddling towards him, wearing what must once have been, thirty odd years ago, a best suit, was Walter Gabriel. His boots had been polished as assiduously as his face, and he had even borrowed a tie from someone. In one hand, the old man carried an ancient umbrella which he used as a walking stick, while on the other arm he escorted a small, simpering woman.

'Evening, Mr Bellamy, sir,' called out Walter, delighted to be recognised. 'Oh, I don't believe you've had the pleasure. . . .'

'Uh, no, I'm afraid not.'

'Allow us to present our friend, Cissy Pilgrim.'

'Cecily,' she corrected with a simper.

'Cissy when us is on our own!' cackled Walter.

'How do you do, Miss . . . uh, Pilgrim? You're not from these parts, I gather?'

'Felpersham, Mr um . . .'

'I'm really making a pig's ear of these here introductions,' sighed the old man. 'Cissy . . . um, Cecily, this is Mr Ralph Bellamy, what's took over the Brigadier's estate, whom I was filling you in about last time.'

'Ah yes,' smiled the woman, showing a set of false teeth with a rather startling gap between them. 'You're the young man about to be wed.'

She accompanied this comment with a squeeze of Walter's arm and he responded with a throaty chuckle.

Though stung by the reference to the wedding, Ralph was nevertheless amused that a woman who was not much more than five years older than himself should call him a young man.

'We'm off on our stroll, if you'll excuse us,' said Walter.

'Nice to have met you,' nodded Cecily, vigorously.

'Come on, then, Cissy. We can't chew the fat here all night. You looks like one of them nodding dogs what they shoves in the back of cars.'

She stopped nodding, looked politely offended for a second, then gave a shrill laugh. The couple proceeded on their way along the road, leaving Ralph to ponder on what he had seen. It struck him that the difference in ages between Walter and Cecily must be roughly that between himself and Lilian and, absurdly enough, this thought actually reassured him.

Lilian came out of the cottage as soon as he drew up in his car.

He got out and went round to the other side of the car to open the door for her, apologising for his lateness.

'Where would you like to go?' he asked, climbing behind the driving wheel.

'If you wouldn't mind, to the Bull. I had tea there this afternoon and rather stupidly left my handbag there.'

'The Bull it is, then!' he said, switching on the ignition.

As the car found itself a place in the crowded car park at the public house, she showed consideration for his feelings.

'You stay here,' she suggested, putting her hand on his long enough for him to see that she was wearing his engagement ring once more.

'No, I don't mind,' he volunteered, getting out. 'We might as well have a drink while we're here.'

She was surprised at this but did not oppose the idea.

As soon as they entered the bar, they became the focus of attention and he noted that many of the faces which turned towards them bore no smiles of welcome for him. There was a deal of muttered resentment, a puzzled watchfulness, a ribald joke or two, and a general feeling that Ralph was, in effect, intruding. This was the first time that he had been seen in the village since the purchase of the Brigadier's estate and he was at once acutely aware of how isolated his new position had made him.

Lilian disappeared in search of her handbag and he went to order some drinks. Though free at the time, Nora Salt made no move to serve him, pretending instead that she was busy arranging some glasses on the shelf. For a man who prided himself on his ability to get served quickly by barmaids, it was an irritating situation. Nora was quite boldly ignoring him and this fact was not lost on some of the regulars in the bar. Their comments provoked him into his more usual manner.

'Are you paid to serve customers or not?' he enquired, sharply.

'Oh sorry,' she mumbled, and took his order.

By the time he was paying for the drinks, Lilian had returned and sensed the atmosphere between barmaid and customer.

'What's wrong, Nora?' she wondered.

'Ask your fiancé,' replied the other woman, just keeping within the bounds of civility.

'If it's about the cottage, I have no wish to discuss the matter now,' he snapped. 'You've obviously been told what my plans are.'

'We certainly have!' began Nora, flaring up. Then she remembered where she was and held back what she was going to say.

'What *is* going on?' demanded Lilian, annoyed on Ralph's behalf.

'Nothing, darling. Let it pass,' decided Ralph.

'Easy enough for *you* to say that,' chuntered Nora, under her breath.

She felt the full force of a glare from Lilian and was immediately sorry for the way she had behaved. She stammered an apology, evidently upset that she had spoken out of turn. A customer further down the bar wanted service and the incident came to a close.

'Understandable, I suppose,' explained Ralph. 'It's that cottage she and her husband live in.'

'Of course. Part of the Brigadier's estate.'

'Not any more,' he reminded her. 'Unlike him, I can't afford to let people live on my land at a peppercorn rent. I've had to warn them that they'll be getting a notice to quit.'

Lilian looked quite rattled for a moment, but said nothing. He could see that she was feeling as self-conscious as he was, standing at the bar with so many eyes upon them. He finished his drink with a gulp and she followed suit, but they were not going to be allowed to leave just yet. Tony had just come into the bar and made straight for them.

'A Royal Visit, eh!' he said.

'Don't be cheeky,' warned his sister. 'Anyway, we're just going.'

'Have I got something my best friend ought to tell me about?' asked Tony. 'Let me buy you a noggin at least.'

'Actually, we do have to get on, Tony,' remarked Ralph.

'One for the road. Come on. I haven't had chance to drink to you making the Brigadier's land your very own.'

'Tony!' retorted Lilian, not caring for the tone of his comment. 'You should be glad to be working for someone like Ralph! I think you're mad to try and find another . . .'

Her voice trailed away as she realised that she had said too much, and Ralph pressed her to finish, noticing how uncomfortable Tony had suddenly become.

'Forget I ever said anything,' urged Lilian, trying to retrieve her blunder.

'Look, I think I'll nip into the bar and say hello to Mum,' said Tony, trying to steal away.

'We'll have a chat about it on Monday,' offered his employer. 'If you want to, that is.'

Tony swallowed hard, then embarrassment gave way to sarcasm.

'Have a lovely evening, won't you?' he sneered at his sister and walked away at speed.

The first requirement was to get well away from Ambridge so that its pressures would not be so apparent. Ralph drove for half an hour along country roads, not really paying much attention to where he was going. At length he turned the car on to a grass verge not far from a small stream. Both of them stared through the windscreen for a while until she broke the silence.

'Thank you.'

'For what?'

'Not talking about Tony at all.'

'What is there to say? Anyway, the battle is between me and him.'

'Not entirely.'

'It doesn't seem to be my evening, does it?' he complained, with a grin. 'First, Nora. Now, Tony. You'll be next, I daresay.'

'Possibly,' she said, still looking ahead.

'Would you like to walk for a bit, Lilian?'

'Please. . . .'

They followed the stream until it vanished underground a hundred yards or so away. Like a child, he felt the urge to throw stones into the water and she did the same until a competition was taking place, both of them trying to sink a twig which was floating along.

The game relieved many of the tensions between them and they were soon running alongside the stream, laughing and shouting to spoil each other's aim. After several wide misses, he managed to score a direct hit on the twig and sent it below the water. His celebration of victory was short-lived, however, because the twig bobbed back to the surface. He made more frantic efforts to bomb it with stones, but it was she who finally succeeded, dropping an enormous stone on top of the twig from point-blank range.

Some of the water splashed up on to his trouser leg and he grinned as he threatened to exact revenge, lifting an even larger stone to throw into the stream. She ran further downstream before crossing to the other side on a slippery log and finding a place of safety well away from the water. Abandoning his stone, he clambered on to the log and went after her, losing his footing and being forced to jump into the water.

The shock and the annoyance was forgotten at the sheer entertainment value of his leap from the log, and both of them stood and laughed for many minutes. When he stepped out on to the bank, his shoes and bottoms of his trousers were absolutely sodden.

'You're lucky it was so shallow,' she pointed out.

'I didn't plan to go wading,' he admitted, slipping a shoe off and emptying out water.

'I'm sorry. It was my fault.'

'Rubbish. I was too clumsy. Wet feet never hurt anyone,' he said, bravely. 'Anyway, I'm bound to dry off eventually.'

'We could build a camp fire,' she suggested, jokingly.

'I'd rather head for the car, if you don't mind.'

He replaced the shoe then squelched back in the direction of the car, joining her as she sniggered at the noise he was making.

'Let me drive,' she volunteered.

'I'll manage.'

'But you can't, Ralph. Not with shoes like that.'

'I'll take them off.'

'That's plain ridiculous!' she laughed.

'Then I'll have to learn to live with your ridicule,' he countered, slipping off his shoes and socks.

He was determined not to let her drive him, fearing that he would lose the initiative if this happened. Instead, he put up with the discomfort of driving in bare feet, stubbing his toe on the accelerator at one point and wincing at another when he had to brake rather sharply. What made up for all this was the fact that he felt no loss of dignity in front of her, that the situation, absurd as it was, brought them closer together than they had been for weeks.

'I bumped into Walter Gabriel on my way to Hollowtree,' he began, smiling as he recalled the episode.

'He and Miss Pilgrim have been the talk of the village all week.'

'Oh – then it's not news to you?'

'Hardly. Granny Perkins is up in arms about it. Not that she has any claims on Walter, as she goes out of her way to assure you. But she feels that they have an "understanding". Or did, until Miss Pilgrim rolled on to the scene.'

'Where did she come from?' he asked. 'How did they come to meet?'

'Sid Perks is at the back of it. Aided and abetted by Tony. They wrote off to one of these Computer Dating places and gave Walter's name.'

'And Miss Pilgrim came through the post next day, addressed to Honeysuckle Cottage?'

'Under plain cover!'

'Have you met the lady?'

'No, but I'm about the only person in Ambridge who hasn't. They were seen out together last Saturday evening. Then again on Tuesday evening.'

'And again tonight. Things really do seem to be moving. Perhaps it's a whirlwind romance.'

'What's she like, Ralph?'

He described her as well as he could, commenting on her smartness, her age and her evident delight at being with Walter.

'Then off they went, arm in arm, like Darby and Joan.'

'No wonder Granny Perkins has taken the hump!'

'Miss Pilgrim seems to be making all the running, though. If she's come to Ambridge three times . . . why doesn't he go to Felpersham?'

'Because he loves to stir up gossip and there's no better place to do that than in Ambridge. He's loving every moment of it.'

'You never know. There might be a wedding in the village, after all.'

She fell silent and he wished that he had not said anything. He began to feel more self-conscious about driving in bare feet, and accelerated in order to get home quicker. He was glad when he turned the Scimitar into his drive and pulled up on the forecourt outside the house. He groped around for his shoes and socks and put them back on to walk across the gravel path.

'Why did you avoid me on Wednesday,' she asked, involuntarily.

'I didn't see you,' he lied.

'Why did you ride off?' she persisted.

All the doubts and anxieties which had been plaguing him came back in a great surge, and he felt the need to postpone once again. 'Let's go inside, Lilian.'

'All right, but I want an answer,' she warned, following him.

He showed her into the drawing room, poured her a drink then excused himself to go and change. When he returned in a pair of light grey slacks and canvas shoes, she was kneeling on the floor, studying the aerial photographs of the Brigadier's estate and trying to piece them together like a gigantic jigsaw.

'I hope you didn't mind.'

'Of course not,' he said. 'Another drink?'

She nodded and went on moving the photographs about. He came to help her and they spent some time before they had arranged everything in a semblance of order.

'So that's how it looks to the birds,' she mused.

'Yes, how does it look to you?'

She got up and moved away, mildly bewildered. He went after her, deciding that it was time to know the worst.

'Now don't start that game again, please!'

'What game?' she said, wheeling on him.

'The one called I Need Time To Think It Over. How much longer do you want, for God's sake!'

'There's no need to shout,' she retorted, roused.

'It's about the only thing left for me to do, Lilian. You've kept me suspended in mid-air for weeks now. One way or the other, I've got to know.'

'It's not as simple as that.'

'Okay, if you've got reservations, chuck them at me. But don't just bottle them up and take them off into a corner.'

Her temper was up now and all trace of embarrassment had disappeared. She came right up to him and looked him full in the face.

'First – why did you turn your back on me the other day?'

'That was . . . a mistake.'

'It was so belittling, Ralph!' she complained, bitterly.

'And what about some of the things that I've had to put up with?' he demanded, finding in anger a means to speak frankly at last.

'Such as?' she challenged.

'Such as having my proposal of marriage hawked around every last member of your damn family! Such as being kept in the dark about the fact that Tony wants to quit his job! Such as finding you, alone at night in your cottage, with – '

'I *explained* about Nelson,' she interrupted quickly, flustered by the heat of Ralph's attack. 'He was . . . making a bit of a nuisance of himself, that's all.'

'Then why invite him in?' he argued.

'He sort of invited himself in. It was very awkward. He does *own* Hollowtree Flats, after all.'

'And what rights does that give him over you?' he pressed.

Lilian blushed and lowered her head for an instant, convincing him that he was right to suspect that something was going on.

'So that's why you had his roses in a vase?' he concluded. 'That's why he sent them in the first place.'

'No! It isn't like that!' she yelled.

He took her by the shoulders and pulled her close, ignoring her protests.

'What does Nelson mean to you, Lilian?' he asked, deliberately.

'I might ask the same question of you about Sarah Latham,' she retaliated, causing him to release her.

'Ah, well, that's different,' he pointed out, 'I tried to stop her coming to Ambridge. I did my best to prevent her from bothering you.'

'I can see why!' she sneered.

'Sarah is an old friend,' he blustered, thrown back on the defensive. 'Nothing more.'

'Come off it. A woman like her doesn't drive all this way unless there's something in it for her. And it was easy to see what that something was.'

She pointed towards the photographs all over the floor and this prompted him to explain that Sarah had a lot of good qualities and that he respected her judgement in a lot of things.

'I think she's an out-and-out bitch,' pronounced Lilian, simply.

'But she isn't like that, as a rule,' he argued. 'It was just a . . . a rather unfortunate situation.'

He walked back to the photographs and began to pick them up, hoping that he could talk more easily while he was a little distance from her. The mention of Sarah had knocked him off balance and he found himself talking about how they had first met at a party in London.

'I found her lively, intelligent – '

'For Heaven's sake, you don't have to give a potted version of your sex life! If Sarah belonged to your past, then I wouldn't have the slightest interest in her. You're only human, when all's said and done.'

'Thank you for that concession, anyway.'

'Seriously, Ralph. I mean, I never expected you to be pure and untouched. No woman in her right mind would ask that of a man . . . well . . .'

'Of my age?' he suggested sardonically.

'The point is that Sarah won't *stay* in the past. She wants her stake in the future and she'll fight tooth and nail to get it.'

'That's more than I can say for you,' he snapped. 'At least Sarah is able to make up her mind.'

'Then she's prepared to settle for a lot less than I am!' she said, scornfully, turning on her heel.

Dropping the photographs, he ran into the hall after her and got between her and the front door. Now that she had started, he wanted her to go on, to explain exactly why she was turning him down.

'Explain that last remark,' he invited.

'What's the point?' she sighed. 'Just let me go.'

After a pause, he stood away from the door, indicating that she was free to leave. She ran her tongue around her lips thoughtfully, wandered around the hall for a moment, then came to face him again, speaking in low, accusing tones.

'I'm sorry, but I don't like your idea of what a wife ought to be. I am not going to be part of the scenery at the Dower House for anybody.'

'It isn't like that,' he whispered.

'Be honest, Ralph,' she urged. 'What do you really want in a wife? Someone who'll give you a son, make all the right social noises when your friends come round, and generally keep out of your way. Since that's all that's on offer, Sarah will do the job very well.'

'I don't quite follow . . .' he murmured, genuinely confused.

'You wouldn't even let me go to the estate agent with you. It was supposed to be *our* house, but I wasn't allowed anywhere near the actual buying of the property.'

'I didn't want to bother you,' he protested. 'It was such a tedious business.'

'All the more reason why you should have let me give a spot of moral support. You excluded me completely. As far as I was concerned, the buying and selling of the Dower House was something that took place at the other end of my telephone.'

'I thought that it was the best way to go about it,' he maintained.

'From your point of view, it was,' she declared, passionately. 'But how do you think I felt? And it wasn't only the house. Almost every decision we should have taken together was taken by you.'

'That's just not true, Lilian.'

'You didn't even let me choose my own engagement ring,' she reminded him. 'Yes, I daresay that you took a lot of trouble over it and spent a fair amount of money on it, but . . . it would have been nice to go along to the jeweller's with you and choose for myself.'

'We'll change the ring,' he said, brusquely. 'You can have another.'

'It's too late now.'

'I can't think of any other occasion when I . . . well, took all the decisions on my own.'

'You're so used to doing it that you don't even notice, Ralph. Look at tonight, for instance, when we were by that stream.'

'I rather enjoyed that,' he remembered, wistfully.

'So did I. And when you got your feet wet and laughed, I thought that you were improving. Then you turn round and say I can't drive the car.'

'Ah, yes . . . the insurance . . .'

'No, it's something much nearer home. Sheer pride. You just wouldn't let a woman take over, would you? Admit it.'

His inclined head was admission enough and her passion subsided. He looked up, expected her to walk out of the house, pausing only to return the ring. Instead, she went back into the drawing room, calling him after her. She gathered up the photographs from the floor, counted them out into two equal piles and then kissed him softly on the lips before speaking.

'Let's try again. Together.'

They began to place the photographs in position on the floor again.

Chapter Sixteen

When the police first telephoned her with the news, the shock was so great that it caused a threatened miscarriage. Polly was rushed to bed, the doctor was summoned at speed, and the long, anxious wait began. For a few days it was touch and go, and she had the sympathies of the whole village. Then, miraculously, the danger passed and the baby was safe. Sid, who had run the shop on his own during the crisis, expressed his relief by rushing round to the Bull that evening and buying a bottle of champagne.

'I'm not up to drinking that,' said Polly, sadly.

'You will be, love. We'll keep it by us until the right time comes.'

'Why did he do it, Sid?' she asked, her face clouding again at the memory of it. 'Why? That's what I can't understand.'

'Forget your old man, Poll Doll. You know what the sawbones said – more rest and less worry.'

'How can I help worrying?'

'The police will soon pick him up,' he reassured her.

'They haven't got anywhere so far. Do you suppose he might have – '

'I don't suppose anything, love. Now, relax. Let Sidney take the strain. Any more of those frown lines and I'll cut your lollipop ration.'

'It's Mum that I'm concerned about,' she said.

'She had her chance to move in here with us. But would she?' Sid rolled his eyes in a way that he reserved especially for discussions about his mother-in-law. 'Would she? Like hell, she would.'

'But what if Dad comes back to – '

'We'll meet that problem as and when it arises,' he asserted. 'Now, give your parents the push for a while. We've got enough on our plate with you, me and young Martin John Perks in there.'

'Lucy Anne Perks,' she corrected him.

'It's going to be a boy, I tell you!'

'Yes, I know,' she smiled, anticipating his words. 'There's a virile, male streak in your family.'

'Of which I am the living proof. It's one of the perks of being a Perks.'

'Oh Sid!' she exclaimed, flinching into the pillows. 'That's the worst joke I've heard all week.'

'Give me time, love. I can sink fathoms lower than that.'

It was a tonic to see him back in this mood again and she felt much happier. She was still frightened that her father had absconded from the hospital in order to come back to Ambridge, but she knew that she could face even this contingency with Sid beside her. Throughout the crisis he had been consideration itself and she determined to repay him by not brooding about her father.

The next day found her sitting in a chair in the shop, serving in the post office section, thanking all the people who had given her books and magazines and fruit while she was laid up. Mrs Perkins, mistaking the threatened miscarriage as an indication of Polly's delicacy, thought that she needed 'building up' and brought a large pot of broth and told Sid that he must heat it up for her. Since they were now in the middle of a warm July, the prospect of hot broth did not appeal to Polly but she thanked Mrs Perkins, as she paid over the old lady's pension.

'We'll have it for tea tonight,' she promised.

'*We?*' said the other woman, outraged. 'I'm not letting you waste my broth on a great, hulking brute like him.'

'It is my day for compliments!' observed Sid, grinning over the top of the tinned vegetable shelf.

'You wants looking after, Polly,' argued Mrs Perkins. 'Hot broth and plenty of milk. That's what I allus recommends.'

'I bet that's not what you'd recommend for the Casanova of Honeysuckle Cottage!' giggled Sid.

Polly shot him a look, but the damage had already been done.

'I don't know of anyone what lives in that cottage,' announced Mrs Perkins with dignity, and she swept out of the shop.

'What a stupid thing to say, Sid Perks!'

'Sorry,' he bleated, so overcome with remorse that he dislodged six tins of carrots. 'Tell you what. *I'll* have that broth. As a penance.'

Mrs Perkins was not the only person in the village who disapproved of Walter Gabriel's romance. One or two of the older residents thought that there was an element of scandal in his behaviour, and Mrs Mead was heard to say that she thought the whole episode was indecent. Tact made Polly agree with her mother, but in fact she was rather touched by the way that the relationship between Walter and Miss Pilgrim had developed. When she and Sid were invited to tea at Honeysuckle Cottage on Sunday, therefore, she was delighted to accept that invitation.

'We could take that bottle of champagne along,' she suggested.

'Steady on!' warned Sid, with mock horror. 'Neither of 'em are spring chickens. It might put the finish on the pair of 'em. Walter and this Miss Peagreen.'

'Pilgrim,' emphasised Polly.

'As yes. Pilgrim – as in Progress. I'll remember that this afternoon.'

'I hope so. And please, Sid, no jokes.'

'What! That's like saying to Niagara Falls – and please, no water.'

Polly went to the mirror as she put her summer hat on, ready for church. Sid was still in his pyjamas, flipping through the Sunday papers and searching for items for his chuckle-board. The suggestion that he might go to church with them for a change made him recoil in disgust, putting the newspaper over his head. She went off on her own to collect her mother for Morning Service.

To an unusually large congregation, David Latimer preached a sermon on the need for more tolerance in the modern world. As he presented his case with a kind of modest authority, Polly was moved to compare him with her father. Both were men with profoundly Christian beliefs and with an intense religious fervour; but whereas the Vicar of Ambridge had disciplined that fervour and put it to greatest effect, Frank Mead was its victim and was forced into extremes. In the one man's hands, Christian teachings became things of comfort, while in the other's they became wildly disturbing.

As she left the church, Polly was the centre of a lot of sympathetic comment. Ralph Bellamy and Lilian Nicholson were among the first to tell her how glad they were that she had recovered, and the Tregorrans made equally kind remarks. Jill Archer asked if the doctor had said what had caused the trouble, but Polly evaded the question. Like her mother, she was not willing to disclose the news about her father.

It was only while she and Mrs Mead were strolling back through the village that Polly had her first clue to the reason why her father had absconded. Her mother, who had seemed about to tell her something for the last few days, finally came out with it.

'I wrote to him, you see,' she admitted.

'Dad? When was this?'

'Last week. Saturday. He'd have got the letter on Monday.'

That was the morning when Frank Mead had disappeared from the hospital, and Polly saw the connection at once.

'What did you *say,* Mum?' she asked, but her mother was already in distress. Polly waited till they had reached the bungalow before repeating her question.

'I told him about the baby.'

Polly's stunned reaction made her mother break into a series of apologies.

'He had a right to be told,' she kept repeating. 'Your father had a right.'

Seeing that no purpose could be served by arguing with her mother, Polly pressed her once again to move in with them at the shop.

'Until it's all . . . blown over,' she added.

'This is my home, Polly,' said the other, proudly. 'As I've told you before, I'm only keeping it for him.'

'But if Dad comes here and starts – '

'I'm not afraid of him. He's still my husband. I want him to come.'

Polly accepted that she would never persuade her mother to leave the house for reasons of safety. Notwithstanding what had happened in the past, Mrs Mead could not agree that her husband's mental state might make him highly dangerous.

When Sid heard about the letter from Mrs Mead, the irony of the situation was not lost on him. He pointed out that, in telling her husband about the baby, his mother-in-law had indirectly caused the miscarriage. It was yet another item to be placed on the mental crime sheet which he kept scrupulously up to date on Mrs Mead.

'If you ask me, your mum would be better off in there with him!'

'Sid!'

'She's off her chump half the time, Poll Doll.'

'That an awful thing to say and you ought to be ashamed!'

Instant remorse showed on his face again, and she changed the subject to the tea party that afternoon instead. Sid came to life again, speculating about the friendship between Walter and Miss Pilgrim and wondering if he ought to offer his services as best man.

'After all, I was their Cupid, so to speak.'

'You as Cupid!' she smirked. 'Now I've heard everything.'

'Okay, so I haven't got his bow and arrow,' he conceded, 'but you must admit I have the same rosy, little bum.'

He struck a posture on one leg, firing an imaginary arrow. She gave him a shove and pushed him over.

'It'll be time to go soon, Cupid. You'd better shave.'

'I have shaved, love,' he protested, running a finger over his chin. 'It's only this bit on my stiff upper lip that I haven't touched. I'm growing a moustache.'

'Sid, no!'

'Why not? I thought it might be rather fetching.'

'That's a matter of opinion,' she said, worried. 'Some faces don't suit moustaches and yours is one of them.'

'Whose face is it!' he demanded. 'If I want to grow a moustache, a beard, a set of mutton-chops or a row of runner beans on my clock, then I'll do just that.'

'All right,' she muttered, controlling her irritation.

'It'll win you round, Poll Doll. I promise. It's not one of them wispy, Clark Gable jobs, nor one of those long Charlie Chan efforts that fall into your grub. No, this would be something altogether different. A Che Guevara moustache.'

Polly was alarmed at the idea and wanted to oppose it outright. But she knew that her husband's ideas were best left to grow and perish. When bullied out of something, he never let her forget it and she was still being reminded by him about decisions she had stopped him making years before. She would just have to look the other way and let him get on with it.

When Walter Gabriel had first invited them to tea, he had talked about serving it in the garden. In the event, the wind moved the tea party indoors to the tiny living room. Sid and Polly had assumed that they would be the only guests, but they arrived to find Dan and Doris Archer already there, discussing home-made wine with Miss Pilgrim. The presence of six people in a room already cluttered with furniture made any kind of movement virtually impossible. Polly sat down in the rocking chair to which Walter directed her and accepted that she was stuck there for the afternoon. The host, meanwhile, perched himself on a wooden settle beside Miss Pilgrim.

The oak beams and whitewashed walls and stone-flagged floor reminded Polly of the cottage in Penny Hassett where she had been born, but she was not allowed to reflect on the similarities for long.

'I understand that there's going to be a special event in your family, Polly,' said Miss Pilgrim, hands clasped tightly together.

'That's right,' explained Sid, 'I'm going to take a bath at long last.'

'Have you forgotten what I told you!' scolded Polly.

'Husbands always let you down, Polly,' remarked Doris, indulgently. 'It's second nature to them.'

'Now, then. None of that kind of talk, please,' ordered Walter. 'You'll have Cissy thinking the state of holy matrimony ain't all it's cracked up to be.'

'I think I'll serve tea now!' decided Miss Pilgrim, rather fluttered by Walter's words. 'No, you stay here, Walter. I can manage.'

She picked her way between furniture and legs and went into the kitchen at the back of the cottage. Polly noted the fond look that Walter sent after her, as well as the familiar way with which she moved about his cottage. She began to get a definite sense of them as a couple, which was clearly what her host had intended.

'She's a grand girl, you know,' confided Walter in a loud whisper. 'A real jewel of her sex – uh, if you'll pardon my language.'

'Cecily lives in Felpersham, I gather,' observed Dan.

'Yes,' sighed Walter, scratching at an ear. 'Such a long way for her to come to Ambridge.'

'Only about fifteen miles,' commented Sid. 'Get her a compass and a pair of running shoes.'

'You could always visit *her,*' said Doris, ever practical.

Walter shook his head soulfully, then put a finger to his lips to still the conversation as Miss Pilgrim came in with a tray of tea. Polly admired the skill with which the woman poured and handed round the tea in such cramped conditions, and she saw the evident pleasure that the latter was taking in being the hostess. When Miss Pilgrim went back into the kitchen, Walter resumed in a thick undertone.

'It's her mother, the daft old badger. Real martinet, she is. Treats Cissy like she's still a slip of a girl . . . which she is, of course, in some respects.'

'Have you met her mother?' asked Polly.

'I don't want to shake hands with the devil,' he shuddered. 'No, they lives in this Council flat, you see . . . Cissy and this old harridan . . .'

Polly was keen to hear more but Miss Pilgrim reappeared with another tray. Whatever shortcomings she had in other ways, Miss Pilgrim had no faults as a pastrycook. She had baked a whole selection of delicious tarts, pies and cakes and everyone was soon congratulating her. Both Polly and Doris asked for some of the recipes and she took this as an enormous compliment, simpering on the settle.

'I been trying to get Cissy to use some of my old Granny's recipes,' declared Walter, dropping crumbs down the front of his shirt.

'Some of those ought to be banned by law,' said Dan, who remembered Granny Gabriel from his youth. 'It was either kill or cure with her.'

'Did she have any recipes for aphrodisiacs?' asked Sid, avoiding Polly's warning glare.

'Dozens!' shouted Walter, with an evil cackle. 'They worked, too. I tried one on Betsy Eggott at the Church Outing to Gloucester. Blow me, if she doesn't charge straight up to the vicar and ask him if he'd care to –'

'More tea, Walter?' interrupted Miss Pilgrim gently.

Polly was sorry to be robbed of the end of the anecdote, but was amused by the way that Walter immediately apologised for telling such a story. He was genuinely upset that he had forgotten himself so far as to recall some of the seedier moments in his past. It was a tamed and relatively domesticated Walter Gabriel who spent the rest of the afternoon with his guests, talking about various items of village news.

As she sat enjoying the company and the conversation, Polly began to realise why they had been invited. It was not simply that Walter wanted to repay Sid for – however unwittingly – introducing him to Miss Pilgrim; he was trying to impress her by letting her meet a young married couple along with Ambridge's oldest married couple. Polly was gratified that she and Sid were considered to be an advertisement for marriage, and this helped her to forgive some of the jokes which Sid was contributing as if by nervous reflex.

'Shall we be seeing you at the Fete next Saturday?' enquired Doris.

'I hope so,' replied Miss Pilgrim. 'I do so love these country customs. We have nothing like it in Felpersham, you know. Industrial towns have very little character.'

'What about you two?' asked Dan. 'I suppose you'll have to keep the shop open part of the afternoon.'

'We'll get along to the Fete at some stage,' promised Polly. 'We enjoyed it so much last year.'

'We'll be there,' guaranteed Sid, then, receiving the hint from Polly, he added, 'Can I do the washing-up or something?'

But Miss Pilgrim waved away all offers of help, insisting sweetly that she would take care of everything. Dan and Doris were the first to make departure noises because they wanted to get to Evensong. Walter went out to the front gate with them and Sid sidled after him in the hopes of learning a little more about aphrodisiacs. Polly was left alone with Miss Pilgrim, who seemed to value the opportunity of a confidential word.

She beckoned Polly into the kitchen and closed the door after them.

'I know it only started out in fun, but I'm grateful to your dear husband, Polly.'

'Oh . . . good.'

'You don't know how many disappointments I've had to bear. Walter is the fourteenth, you see.'

'Fourteenth? You mean, you've tried this Computer Dating place before?'

Polly was amazed at the stamina of a woman who could

arrange dates with fourteen men whom she had never met.

'No. I've tried a different organisation each time. Lonely Hearts Clubs, Introduction Agencies, Marriage Bureaux. It was only in desperation that I turned to the Computer and it's been my salvation.'

'I'm glad to hear it,' said Polly, still rather taken aback. 'Um, have you been at this sort of thing long? Writing to places, that is.'

Miss Pilgrim studied Polly's face for a moment and the latter felt that she was being assessed for her trustworthiness. Whatever standards the older woman applied, Polly appeared to measure up to them.

'Six years. It's been a hard road,' sighed Miss Pilgrim. 'Men are so dishonest when they fill in forms.'

'I can imagine,' said Polly, recalling the sight of Sid and Tony giggling over the form which they had completed.

'One is bound to lose faith at times.'

She drew Polly nearer with a gesture and then explained how Walter had restored her faith considerably. Unlike his thirteen predecessors, he had been Honesty personified. Hearing her description of Walter, Polly found it difficult to relate it to the man whom she knew.

'And he's such a charming eccentric, Polly.'

'In what way?'

'Living in this tumbledown old place when he could afford a much bigger house. That's eccentricity, surely?'

'Uh . . . yes, I suppose so,' she said, baffled.

'Since he owns those flats at Hollowtree,' argued Miss Pilgrim, 'you'd have thought he'd move in there.'

Polly at once suspected what had happened and felt deeply sorry for her. Walter had been claiming for himself property which in fact belonged to Nelson. Without realising it, this veteran of blind dates was being wooed by a man who was pretending to be his own son. Polly's first impulse was to tell her the truth, but she had already had personal experience of the power of shock. Besides, she was not certain that Miss Pilgrim would accept her word, so totally taken in was she by Walter.

The men came back into the cottage, their laughter announcing that they had been through all the recipes for aphrodisiacs and discussed all the possible consequences. Feeling that she did not want to be a party to Walter's deception, Polly went back into the living room and made excuses rather unceremoniously. She and Sid were soon outside the house, she relieved and he puzzled.

'What's up, Poll Doll? Has old Cissy got the bubonic plague or something?'

'She's got a far worse disease and his name is Walter Gabriel.'

Polly should have known better than to expect Sid to see it from the woman's point of view, but she told him the tale nevertheless. He guffawed loudly and Polly took him to task about his part in it all.

'If you hadn't played that childish practical joke, a lonely woman would have been spared a lot of aggravation.'

'She's not aggravated,' Sid protested. 'She's loving every moment.'

'Sid, she's bound to find out.'

'Sure – *after* the marriage. What wife doesn't learn that hubby isn't all he made out he was? Anyway, I don't think Walter's taken her for a ride. He's dead sincere about wheeling the old duck up the aisle. Okay, he's a lying old devil, but he's been smitten.'

'You'll be smitten in a minute!' she warned, feeling aggrieved on the woman's behalf. 'Fourteen men in a row. All washouts.'

'If she can bag another one, she'll be able to field a full rugby team,' laughed Sid. 'Yes, the Pilgrim XV. I can see 'em now: pale pink hoops, lace collars and cuffs and a bleeding heart as a monogram.'

Though they were still standing outside Walter's cottage Polly really laid into Sid, telling him that she found his sense of humour callous and disgusting. Only when she paused for breath did she realise that Miss Pilgrim was watching them through the window, smiling benignly like a maiden aunt watching a nephew and niece at play. Polly grabbed Sid by the arm and dragged him off towards the shop.

In spite of the harsh things she was saying about him as they walked along, she was very glad of his supporting arm when they saw the police car waiting for them. This time the message was delivered personally, by a young constable from the Borchester Division.

'A man's body has been recovered from the canal, Mrs Perks. He fits the description that we have of your father. I'm afraid that we shall need someone to come along for indentification purposes.'

Chapter Seventeen

According to the organisers, the forthcoming Ambridge Fete was going to be bigger and better than ever. In addition to the special attractions of a Police Motorcycle Display, Morris dancing and an Intrepid Ascent in a Balloon, the garish posters promised a Fancy Dress Parade, Races, Side-shows, a W.I. Produce Stall and a visit from the Hollerton Brass Band (conductor: Ernest Stapley). Since the afternoon would be rounded off with the crowning of the Fete Queen and a Grand Tug-of-War Contest, the organisers felt that their claims were not altogether unjustified. It was going to be a Fete with more to see, more to do, and much, much more to remember.

The invasion started quietly in the middle of the week when a tent was erected on the village green. More tents and marquees and stalls and fencing poles and ropes and equipment followed, and by Saturday the green had disappeared beneath the invaders. The weather was unco-operative at first, but by noon the clouds had drifted away and patches of blue sky looked down on the acres of canvas and good intentions.

Lilian was determined that her mother would not miss any more of the Fete than was necessary and volunteered to help behind the bar. She put up with the bitter asides of Nora, who was still outraged because she and Greg had been given notice to quit. She ignored the various jokes about Ralph, who had been elected to crown the Fete Queen. She was going to enjoy the Fete and make sure that her mother was there to enjoy it as well.

'Thank you, love,' said her mother, when the doors were finally bolted after the last customer.

'Did you manage to grab a sausage roll earlier on, Mum?'

'Three, if we're counting,' admitted Peggy Archer.

'Then what are we waiting for? Let's go!'

'Not so fast.'

Her mother's expression told her that there was something which took precedence over the Fete. They moved to one of the tables in the bar and sat down.

'I'm glad you sorted things out, Lilian.'

'What do you mean, Mum?'

'I'm not blind,' said her mother. 'But I am glad that . . . you're happier in your mind about it now.'

Lilian nodded, rather put out that she had not kept her doubts as completely to herself as she had thought.

'Nobody else noticed, if that's what you're worrying about,' reassured her mother. 'But they haven't had as much practice looking for the signs.'

'That's something, anyway.'

'The thing is, you see . . .' began Peggy, then had to take a handkerchief out from her apron pocket. 'The thing is . . .'

Lilian offered a hand which her mother took and held gratefully, finding the gesture helped her to speak what she had spent weeks brooding about.

'Your father is not a well man. They don't quite know what's wrong with him, but . . .' Her shrug completed the sentence. 'So that means I have to look elsewhere for what the women's magazines call my 'emotional fulfilment'. Fancy a person of my age talking about something like that,' she smiled, wiping another tear away.

'What you're trying to say is that . . . you're tending to live more through us than through Dad. Very sensibly.'

'It's not that I don't love him or care for him, Lilian. God knows I do and always have done!' she said passionately, then her voice dropped to a whisper. 'Only there's a limit. There's a point at which I've got to stop letting him drag me down . . . does that make sense?'

'A lot of sense, Mum.'

'That's why I've got so much pleasure out of Jennifer's

baby. And out of you and Ralph. That's why what you do is so much more important than it used to be.'

'I see,' teased Lilian, softly. 'You never really bothered about us before.'

'You know what I mean, Lilian. I've been dreadfully anxious about you, hoping that it would all work out, not daring to mention it to anyone else. But now . . .'

Lilian squeezed her mother's hand again, and then leaned across to kiss her on the forehead. The two women got up and walked towards the door, having achieved a new understanding in the brief minutes they had just spent together. Lilian felt that she had been given a privileged insight into her mother's character and was quite moved.

'I do hope Tony won't leave Ambridge!'

'What has he said to you, Mum?'

'Very little. Except that you told Ralph about it and that they had a blazing row.'

'I should think so, too,' argued Lilian, roused on Ralph's behalf. 'What kind of employer would let someone like Tony walk out on him without a by-your-leave. Ralph had every reason to take a crack at him.'

'But Ralph wasn't supposed to know.'

Lilian reddened, still guilty about the fact that it was she who had blurted out the information. Her indiscretion had led to a series of arguments throughout the Archer family.

'Your grandfather is terribly upset about it. He'd set his heart on seeing Tony working at Brookfield.'

'Perhaps he'll come back. Perhaps he won't get the job in the first place. Perhaps he won't accept it if he does, Mum.'

'I don't want *him* to leave me as well,' whispered her mother.

'Look, do you want to go to this Fete?' demanded Lilian, trying to jolt her mother into a happier frame of mind by her brisk tone.

'Of course I do,' said the other, cheering instantly. 'Lead on.'

'It could be worse, Mum. Tony might be going up in that

balloon they've got tethered out there. Then where would he finish up?'

'Heavens!' exclaimed her mother, laughing.

'Somewhere in that direction, I suppose. . . .'

Taking account of the fact that many of the people who supported it worked on the land, the Ambridge Village Fete was always held at the end of July to coincide with the traditional break between haymaking and harvesting. Attendance was usually very high with people coming in from all of the surrounding villages. Again, it was a favourite day for people who had left Ambridge to return and meet old friends.

When Lilian and her mother approached the village green, the noise of a dozen rasping exhausts told them that the Police Motorcycle Display was in progress. The riders were performing feats which would have meant certain death – or, at the very least, arrest – on an ordinary road. Lilian watched enthralled as they roared across each other's path, missing by inches the machines that went immediately before and after them. At the end of the Display, the applause was generous and well deserved. The Borchester Police had got the Fete off to an exhilarating start.

Peggy Archer soon spotted her sister-in-law, Christine, at the W.I. stall and went off to chat and buy some marmalade. The crowd was so thick at this point that her mother had gone before Lilian had really noticed. Many familar faces bobbed up all round, including one she had not expected to see.

Nelson Gabriel was making his way towards her with some urgency, pushing, twisting and elbowing through the crowd. She felt a mild surge of fear and instinctively looked around for Ralph. The memory of her last encounter with Nelson was still fresh in her mind and she was still wary of meeting him. As it was, she had no escape since he was now only yards away. She steeled herself to be polite but distant with him, thanking him for the roses he had sent but making it quite clear that she wanted no further presents from him.

He smiled as he came right up to her and stayed long enough to pull a face of mock dismay at the size of the crowd. Then he carried on making a way through to the edge of the green, where Lilian saw him break into a trot. It was the second time she had seen Nelson make a hasty departure from Ambridge and she wondered what had caused it.

The Morris dancers began their performance in the main ring and most people drifted off to watch them. As the crowd thinned, Lilian caught sight of someone else who was planning a departure from Ambridge. Tony was looking around in search of somebody.

'Who have you lost?' she asked.

'Oh . . . it doesn't matter.'

'Give me three guesses. Tessa Latimer, Tessa Latimer or Tessa Latimer.'

He grinned rather sheepishly and confessed that he was hoping to bump into the Vicar's daughter, who had come home for the Fete.

'How's she getting on with the Social Science Course of hers?' asked Lilian.

'I haven't a clue,' he protested. 'All I've seen of her so far is the top of her head at the Motorcycle Display. The world and his wife seem to be here this afternoon.'

'If I spot her first,' promised Lilian, 'I'll send up a distress flare.'

'If I spot her first, Tessa will need to send up the flare.'

Lilian was pleased to find her brother in such high spirits and decided to take advantage of his good mood to press home a point. But her intentions were written all too boldly in her eyes and he had time to read them and hold up a warning hand.

'Don't say it, Lilian. Please.'

'It's what everyone else will say,' she argued, earnestly. 'You're mad! Giving up your job at the very moment when Ralph is expanding his enterprise.'

'You're a woman,' he said, dismissively. 'You wouldn't understand.'

'I'm not the only one,' she came back, forcefully. 'Have you thought how deeply you'll be hurting Mum and Grandad Archer and Uncle Phil and . . .'

'If you're so worried about the feelings of the family, why the hell are you marrying Ralph Bellamy!'

The rejoinder took the wind out of her sails completely and she could say nothing as Tony nodded a farewell and then went off to resume his search. Now that she herself had come to know and appreciate Ralph so much better she was hurt by the reminder that so many people were still critical or envious or simply afraid of him. All her reservations about him had by no means been dispelled, but she had found him surprisingly willing to compromise and to consider her opinions.

She felt that she wanted to be near him and she remembered that, amongst his other duties, he had been asked to judge the Fancy Dress Competition. Making her way towards the main ring, she could hear the sound of the Morris dancers entertaining the crowd, who were responding with laughter and outbursts of applause. Over the heads of the audience, she could see an occasional glimpse of white as the dancers came into vision. A friendly voice told her what she wanted to know.

'Ralph is on the far side,' smiled John Tregorran.

'It's at times like this that I wish I was taller,' she admitted.

'Height is a disadvantage in a village with so many old cottages,' he assured her from personal experience. 'If you're not cracking your skull every five minutes, then you're developing curvature of the spine instead.'

'That's better than a crick in the neck,' she opined, giving up her attempts to see something of the dancing.

'Would you like a running commentary?' he offered.

'No thanks. I'll work my way round, I think.'

'Remind Ralph that we're still in business,' he grinned, stroking his beard. 'Borchester Antiques,' he added, when she looked puzzled. 'We had hoped you might need the odd piece to fill up a corner in the Dower House.'

'Oh yes, we shall. You'll be seeing us, don't worry.'

She moved off to make her way around to the other side of the ring, pleased that she could now talk about the Dower House without any embarrassment. It was going to be her home, after all, and she could enjoy starting to furnish it.

The dancing had finished by the time she reached Ralph and the Fancy Dress Parade got under way at once. He seemed relieved to see her and took her into the ring with him, consulting her at every point about the costumes which the children were wearing. As the competitors paraded around in a wide circle, Lilian could not help but reflect on the way that television programmes had made their impact on even the most isolated villages in the area. She counted three Daleks, two Mr Spocks of Star Trek fame, and no end of refugees from the Magic Roundabout. To her astonishment Ralph identified all the television characters with ease, even the ones that she had doubts about.

At her prompting, Ralph adjudged that history had made a clean sweep of the prizes. He placed a five-year old Henry VIII first, a budding Cleopatra from Waterley Cross second, and then divided the third prize between a dashing Robin Hood, a striking Boadicea, and a fearsome Jack the Ripper, who had the family bread-knife between his teeth. All the other competitors were given consolation prizes of packets of sweets, so that honour was satisfied all round.

'I still think that Dixon of Dock Green should have been in the first three,' said Ralph, as the children dispersed happily.

'Then why didn't you put him there?' she asked.

'I always listen to my advisers,' he winked, and then escorted her out of the ring. 'I don't know about you, but I'm ready for some refreshments.'

'Have you seen the queue?' she asked.

'You don't think I'm doing all this judging for nothing, do you?' he grinned and led her to a tent nearby. 'This is reserved for organisers and special guests.'

'Which do I qualify as?' she asked.

It was cool inside the tent, which had a selection of sandwiches and cakes laid out on trestle tables. A few people were drinking tea at the far end and they smiled as Ralph and Lilian entered.

'Looks as if it's self-service,' noted Lilian, picking up the large teapot to pour out two cups.

They helped themselves to some biscuits, then moved back to the entrance where the tent flap had been fastened back and they could look out on the festivities. She felt strangely protected now that she was by his side and did not mind the many curious glances which they were attracting.

'Nelson is here,' he suddenly announced.

'Is he?' she asked, pretending that it was news to her. 'I wonder why *he's* come back to Ambridge?'

'The Prodigal Son,' he observed, with some irony.

He paused and she sensed that he was waiting for a comment. But she was no more willing to talk about Nelson than she had been on previous occasions, and nibbled at her biscuit instead.

'He was with his father and that funny little woman,' he continued, obviously having watched Nelson with interest. 'I got the impression that he was being introduced to her for the first time.'

'Is Miss Pilgrim here as well?'

'Very much so. Walter is conducting her round as if he'd laid on the Fete solely for her benefit.'

Lilian began to wonder if all the rumours which she had heard about the couple were in fact true. If they did have any serious intentions of getting married, then Nelson's presence could be explained. He had been invited home to meet his future step-mother though, judging by the speed with which he left the village green earlier, he had not been all that impressed by the lady from Felpersham.

Thoughts about Nelson led her, as if in retaliation, to mention the person who represented a weak spot in Ralph.

'I had a 'phone call from Sarah this morning,' she said, casually.

'Oh?' he replied, anything but pleased.

'She's going to be in Birmingham one day next week. Something to do with one of those charities she organises. She's invited us both to have lunch with her.'

'That's out of the question,' he snapped, then spoke more calmly. 'I mean, I don't think I can manage it. I'm snowed under with work.'

'Would you mind if I went?' she asked, having no intention of doing so but keen to know his view.

'I leave that to you, darling,' he said, with a trace of asperity. 'But don't imagine that it's pure accident that Sarah has cropped up again.'

Before she could ask him what he meant, they were joined by others who were putting in for repairs at the Refreshment Tent. They chatted with the newcomers for a few minutes then went back out into the main body of the Fete.

Stalls and sideshows were doing good business and Lilian was delighted to learn that Ralph was not above chancing his arm. He tried, though without success, to win her a coconut, to throw a ping-pong ball into a white enamel bucket, and to stick three consecutive darts in the pock-marked face of the Queen of Spades.

At one time or another, Lilian saw all the members of her family enjoying themselves in their different ways. The one notable absentee was her father, and it was Jennifer who explained that the excitement had been too much for him and that he had slipped back to the Bull. This news cast a shadow over the afternoon for Lilian, but she said nothing to Ralph.

The ringing of a bell announced that it was time for the balloon to make its Intrepid Ascent, and everyone began to make for the main ring once again. All afternoon the multicoloured balloon had been creaking as it tugged at its moorings in the light wind, and it was now given its freedom. Lilian admired the courage of the two balloonists, who had dressed in Victorian costume for the occasion, and who were hoping to fly to France.

'I couldn't do it,' she confessed.

'You never know,' said Ralph. 'As a matter of fact, I've been thinking of taking up gliding. We could start together, if you like.'

'I don't know about that.'

Under the martial baton of Ernest Stapley, the Hollerton Brass Band started to work through its repertoire.

'The Crusader!' said Ralph, enthusiastically.

'What?'

'This march. I love Sousa. Let's get closer.'

'You go, Ralph. It's not really my kind of music.'

'Fair enough. Why don't I meet you in a while at the judging of the Fete Queen?'

'Right.'

He walked off towards the makeshift bandstand which had been set up near the village pump, and she turned her attentions back to the balloon. It was climbing steadily now and drifting away to the south-east. She imagained that the balloonists would have roughly the same view of the Brigadier's estate as the camera which had taken the aerial photographs. She was still staring up into the sky when a hand fell on her arm.

'We meet again.'

'Nelson!'

'I'm sorry I couldn't stop earlier, but I had somewhere to go. Just as well, as it turned out.'

'I don't follow.'

'You will. But first I have to go and take part in a little rescue operation. Have you seen my father anywhere?'

'He was over by the main Refreshment Tent. Yes, they're still there,' she said, pointing, glad of an excuse to get rid of him. 'With Sid and Polly.'

'Excuse me.'

Nelson walked away purposefully and she watched the scene that followed. Walter and Miss Pilgrim seemed to be chatting amiably with Sid and Polly. A remark must have been made about Sid's attempt to grow a moustache because he lifted a hand to cover his face. The next moment Nelson reached the group and said something to Miss Pilgrim.

Lilian did not know what his words were but their effect was immediate and dramatic. Miss Pilgrim burst into tears, Walter put a consoling arm around her and Sid and Polly backed away in sheer amazement. Nelson spoke again and his father waved a fist at him and yelled something back. Miss Pilgrim had now taken a lace handkerchief out of her bag and was dabbing at her eyes.

In spite of his father's anger, Nelson held his ground and said his piece once more. This time it produced different results. Lilian watched in astonishment as Miss Pilgrim shrugged off Walter's arm, went up to Nelson with a glare of defiance, and slapped him hard across the face. She spoke a few words to Walter, who seemed thunderstruck, then moved away briskly.

As the organisers had promised, it was a Fete that was going to be full of surprises.

Chapter Eighteen

Not even the drama at the Fete that afternoon could take Polly's mind off it for long. As she lay in bed, trying to read her magazine, she kept thinking about him over and over again. Sid came in from the bathroom, whistling snatches from a pop song. He diagnosed her complaint at a glance and came to sit on the end of the bed.

'You've got to try and forget it, love. Or it'll drag the pair of us down.'

'I know, Sid. I just keep remembering what happened. Having to go to that place in Borchester with Mum. Having to look at the dead body and see if – '

'Stop going on about it, Poll Doll!' he ordered. 'It's not as if it was your old man.'

'That's what I worry about. When the policeman first told us about it, I half-wished it was Dad.'

'It might be better for the poor so-and-so if it had been,' he sighed. 'Still, that doesn't mean you have to pace the bedroom every night. Now – shove it out of your mind. Serve it an eviction notice – like Ralph Bellamy did to Nora. Clear out or else!'

She nodded and he began to take his things off before draping them over the chair. Another aspect of her anxiety came to her.

'It was that bit about him in the newspaper – '

'They had to shove that in, Poll Doll. There is a . . . well, a slight danger that he might do it again.'

'Dad's not a criminal!'

'He was involved in those fires. The public's got to be warned. Just in case. It's . . . routine.'

'But it means that everyone knows.'

'Has anyone in the village breathed a syllable about it to you?'

'Well, no . . .'

'There you are, then! Put more trust in your friends. Put more trust in the British policeman. And put more trust in your loving hubby.'

She threw aside her magazine, sat up in bed and gazed at him fondly. Then she had an uncontrollable fit of the giggles.

'What's up now, for Pete's sake!' he asked, offended.

'You – standing there all starkers. You look like something out of that documentary we saw on telly. About the aborigines.'

'Thank you!' he said, grabbing his pyjamas and clambering into them. 'Like an abo, indeed! That is the right old accolade!'

He got into bed, switched out the lamp and snuggled under the sheets. Polly tried to apologise and, when he ignored her, she tickled him into submission. As they lay there together in the dark, she asked him the same question she had asked him every night for a week.

'Sid – will you shave it off tomorrow?'

'Go to sleep!'

'The day after, then?'

'Just shove off to the dear old Land of Nod, will you!' he suggested, snoring noisily to hammer home his point. 'Anyway, I can't shave it off. I've grown rather attached to my moustache.'

The Walter Gabriel saga kept the village buzzing for days. As star witnesses at the Fete, Sid and Polly were called upon time and again to explain to customers what had taken place. At first Polly let Sid do all the talking, but his version began to move so completely away from the truth that she took over the task of reporter herself.

Her problem was that she still had no idea which side she was on, and whether she should feel sorry for Walter or for

Miss Pilgrim. On the following Thursday afternoon, as she was leaving the shop to visit her mother, she was given a chance to make up her mind. Walter himself intercepted her, and she could see from the old sparkle in his eye that he had got over the incident completely.

'Just wanted to apollergise for dragging you and Sid into it.'

'It was Sid's fault in the first place, if everybody had their own, Mr Gabriel.'

'I don't hold it agin him. I'm glad it all happened.'

'Glad!' she exclaimed.

'You got to be philersoffical, Polly, and put these things down to the enriching of your experience.' He wheezed merrily for a moment. 'Doh! We had some grand fun while it lasted!'

'But you agree with what your son did?'

'Oh yes! Our Nelson saved me from a fate worse than Betsy Eggott, and she were like death on wheels, even with that haffrodizzyac inside her! No, from now on, it'll always be Mrs P. before Miss P.'

Like Walter, Polly had refused to believe some of the charges which had been levelled at Miss Pilgrim. She had not been able to understand why Nelson Gabriel had gone to such trouble to check up on the woman. Her curiosity was finally satisfied.

'It were the five hundred that put our Nelson on to it.'

'Five hundred? Pounds, you mean?'

'Guineas, ackshully, even though there ain't such things. But that was what Cissy asked me for. It all sounded so good. With five hundred she could stick that old bag of a mother into a private nursing home for the rest of her natural. Then we'd have no bother about her interfering with the marriage. Between me and Cissy, that is.'

'No wonder she never let you visit her in Felpersham,' noted Polly. 'It was just as well your son thought to drive over there.'

'And what does our Nelson find at the address I was give?

Cissy's 'ubby. Mr Pilgrim, or whatever his real name is.' He enjoyed the memory for a moment, sucking at his teeth. 'It were a fair old racket, you got to admit that.'

'I think it was disgraceful,' she said, hurt that she had been taken in so easily by Miss Pilgrim. 'She made it all seem so plausible. You were the fourteenth, she reckoned. From out of the Lonely Hearts Clubs and so on.'

'Then she ain't done too badly if she lifted five hundred off the other thirteen,' he pointed out, admiringly. 'As our Nelson said, she'd spin her yarn, get her lolly, then do a moonlight flit with her fella.'

'Aren't you going to tell the police? I mean . . . well, it's a kind of fraud.'

'I know,' he sighed. 'And by rights, I should own up. But I couldn't help pretending I owned all that property. Did you see her clock when Nelson told her I wasn't worth a bladder and had asked him for the five hundred on the quiet?'

Polly joined him in seeing the whole thing in a more comical light. She had forgotten that he had in fact led Miss Pilgrim up the garden path. As she recalled the woman's last, vicious words, she realised that being tricked by Walter was punishment enough.

When she went on to the bungalow, she repeated the story to her mother, who was scandalised by the whole thing. Mrs Mead insisted on seeing Walter as the injured party and said that it was their duty to be especially kind to him. Polly knew that her mother had always had a soft spot for Walter, having cleaned his cottage for him at one time. Thinking back on that period, she remembered who had stopped her mother from carrying on with that job.

'Was Dad like it before you were married?' she wondered. 'Cranky about religion and so on?'

'Your father was always a good man. With very strict ideas.'

'I'll say! Remember that time I tried to work at the Bull? You'd have thought it was a brothel or something!'

'He was entitled to his views about drink,' said her mother, coaxing Benjy back into his cage. 'It was just that he . . . took them too far.'

'I know, Mum,' consoled Polly, softly. 'But he's much better off where they can look after him properly. You must accept that.'

'When we went with the police on Monday . . . I *knew* it couldn't be him,' said the other, with quiet triumph. 'Not your father. Not in a canal, like that, poor soul. No, he'll come back.'

'We mustn't think that – '

'I think of nothing else, Polly. He's got to come back. I want him here. I want him home again.'

The Country Park was noticeably quieter that evening and Sid made jokes about the birds going on strike for higher crumbs. Polly was not really listening and only gave a token smile when he picked up a stick and demonstrated some golf strokes in mime. The talk with her mother had alarmed her almost as much as the visit which they had both had to make to the police morgue.

On the lawn in front of Grey Gables, they found Tom Forrest putting down some poison by a series of mole runs. He waved to them as they walked past, then saw something in the ground and moved with speed and decision. Digging the heel of his boot into a mole run, the gamekeeper bent down to grab the surfacing mole by the tail and swung it hard against his toecap to smash its head.

Sid laughed and made a joke of it, but the incident upset Polly greatly and she was forced to turn away. It seemed to her to be part and parcel of a world in which casual aggression was the norm, and in which the very gentlest of men – Tom, Sid, her father – were capable of such unthinking violence. She was glad when they went into the building, finding its coolness a tonic.

Jack Woolley was in a fiery mood, sitting behind his desk and banging it for emphasis from time to time. They listened as he complained about the opposition which some of his plans for the Country Park were meeting. Polly was surprised when he singled out Dan Archer and John Tregorran as 'rabble-rousers', and she reflected that these, too, were both unusually gentle people.

'Right,' said Jack Woolley, relaxing, 'I've had my beef about the Ambridge Protection Society. Now we can get down to it.'

His eye fell on Sid's moustache and he blinked.

'Uh, is that third eyebrow supposed to be a moustache, Sid?'

'It's not fully grown yet,' protested its owner.

'Are you in *favour* of this, Polly?'

Before Polly could answer, Sid reminded them that they had not come there to discuss his moustache.

'Too true, Sid. And if a man wants to disfigure himself, that's his own affair!'

'Now, look here, Mr Woolley – '

'Putting that aside, let's get on with the real reason I asked you around here this evening. Polly, off you go.'

'I've got the accounts here,' she said, putting them on his desk.

'Accounts? We can look at those later. First things first, girl. Tell me everything – and I mean *everything* – about Walter Gabriel and his bit of knitting. Come on. I'm all agog.'

Handicapped by Sid's habit of providing a series of verbal lantern slides, she went through the story once more, much to Jack Woolley's amusement. The latter chuckled throughout and slapped his thigh when she recalled Miss Pilgrim's final words.

'More power to her elbow, I say! Any woman who lets Walter Gabriel woo her has earned five hundred quid.'

'Payment for Services Rendered!'

'Sid!'

'She was an honest villain, anyway,' observed the other man, with feeling. 'A quick killing and then she would have been off. That's a damn sight better than the kind that marry you first and make a long, slow killing afterwards.'

After this brief insight into his private life, Jack Woolley turned his attention to the shop accounts. For an hour all three of them sat around the desk and went through the figures.

Though it was quite late, she decided to wash her hair. Sid was watching an old film on television and trying to work out the plot aloud. She was still in the bathroom when she heard the knocking on the door and she knew at once that something was wrong. By the time she had slipped back into her blouse and wrapped a towel around her hair, Sid had returned with her mother. Mrs Mead was trembling and frightened.

'It's your father.'

'You stay here with your mum,' decided Sid. 'I'll go.'

'No, I want to be there as well,' insisted the older woman.

Polly found a headscarf, tied it in position, then helped her mother down the stairs. She could see that something had terrified her mother, though the latter would not explain what. They walked quickly towards the bungalow, Sid keeping slightly in front of the women.

The door was ajar when they arrived and Sid inched it open carefully before going into the silent bungalow. He reappeared almost at once and tried to wave them both away, but Polly was determined to know the worst. She pushed past Sid and went straight to the living room.

Sitting in the middle of the floor was her father, his head in his hands. She looked around with horror at the overturned furniture, the smashed television set, the torn curtains, the cracked mirror and pictures, the scattered papers and the twisted cage. The room which her mother had kept so clean and tidy had been utterly wrecked. Even the light fittings had been wrenched out.

'It was that bottle,' said her mother, standing behind her. 'The sherry I bought when I heard about the baby. Your father saw the bottle.'

The large reddish stain on one wall and the pile of jagged glass nearby explained the fate of the sherry bottle. Polly felt a great rage building up inside her on her mother's behalf, and she walked over to the figure on the floor.

'Why did you have to come back?'

'Leave it to me, Poll,' advised Sid, stepping between her and her father.

Frank Mead looked up and seemed pleasantly surprised to see them. His suit was crumpled and filthy, and he had a rough beard. His appearance and his imploring look took away Polly's anger.

'You should have told me about the baby, Polly.'

'I know, Dad.'

'You should have told me. I'll be its grandfather.'

'Yes, of course you will, Mr Mead. Now why don't you and I go for a little walk?'

Sid's suggestion made the older man get up very suddenly, and Polly backed away. But her father's temper subsided at once and he glanced around the room sadly.

'I'm sorry. I'm very sorry.'

'This way, Mr Mead.'

Sid took him by the arm and guided him towards the door. He remembered something and turned to his daughter.

'What are you going to call the baby, Polly?'

'Uh, well . . . we haven't quite decided . . .'

'Martin John, if it's a boy. Lucy Anne, if it's a girl,' said Sid, humouring his father-in-law.

'Lucy Judith, actually. We changed our minds.'

'When was this, Poll?'

'A few days ago. We preferred Judith to Anne.'

'News to me . . .'

'You remember, Sid. I said that I wanted to think again about . . .'

Her voice tailed away as she realised that it was hardly the place to argue about the choice of the baby's names. Yet the interchange had somehow eased the tension, and it seemed to satisfy her father.

'Lucy Judith. I like that.'

As he turned to go out with Sid, Mrs Mead stepped forward to embrace him but Polly restrained her. The men left and the front door was heard shutting. The women hugged each other, and Polly comforted her mother as well as she was able. Then they started to clean up the mess and salvage some of the ornaments. When Benjy crawled out from beneath the sofa, it seemed like a signal of hope to both of them.

They had already made some impact on the room when Sid came back. He had taken Mr Mead to the police house at the edge of the village, and a car was being sent from Borchester to pick up the wanted man. Sid pitched in straight away and moved some of the heavier furniture. Then he concentrated on bending the hamster's cage back into shape. It was well past midnight before they had restored some order to the room.

No matter how much they pressed her, Mrs Mead refused to go back to spend the night with them. Polly suggested an alternative.

'We'll stay here, if you like.'

'There's no need, Polly. I'm all right now.'

'Are you quite sure, Mrs M? Just say the word.'

'I think I'd rather be on my own.'

She showed them to the door and thanked them again for all their help. Now that her husband had gone, she seemed to have forgiven him for all the damage and upset he had caused. All she could think about was seeing him again.

'I shall visit him from now on. Regular.'

'That's up to you, Mum.'

'Someone has to. If you and Sid had spared him an afternoon at the hospital, this might never have happened.'

Polly had to bite back her reply. She was hurt by the remark but felt that it contained a grain of truth. She was grateful when Sid took her arm and walked her back home.

When she undid the scarf for the first time in front of the mirror, she recoiled from the sight of her hair which had dried in the most peculiar shape. For once Sid was not on hand with a joke. He came up behind her and kissed her on the neck.

'I need your advice, Poll Doll.'

'Advice?'

'Would you be terribly upset if I shave this blooming thing off in the morning?'

She turned and held him very tight.

Chapter Nineteen

It was one of the older and more gracious hotels in the city, and he found her sitting in a high-backed basket chair between potted palms. He knew at once that it was a mistake to have come.

'I'm sorry I'm late.'

'I'd rather given you up, actually. Trouble parking the car?'

'No . . . I came by train.'

'Where's Lilian?'

'I don't know about you, but I'm ready for a drink.'

'You said that Lilian would be with you. I've reserved a table for three.'

'Ah, the Lounge Bar is that way. Shall we?'

A double scotch soon revived him and he forgot all about the stuffy train journey. The atmosphere in the bar was cool and intimate, which was a welcome change from what he had had to endure all week. Sarah was drinking pink gin and talking about the reason for her being in the Midlands again. Ralph decided that it was time to speak directly.

'Let's be honest, Sarah. You didn't *have* to come. It was simple curiosity which fetched you out of London.'

'That, too . . . uh, you still haven't told me where – '

'Lilian couldn't come. There's trouble at home. Her father.'

This was only partly true but it seemed to convince Sarah. She wanted to know all about the wedding plans and the house.

'Do you mind if we give that a miss for a while,' he sighed. 'I've been arguing about nothing else all week. "Should we have the reception here – or there – or in another place?" It's been driving me quietly round the bend.'

'So that's why you're here. Running for cover.'

'You could call it that,' he admitted. 'We've spent three evenings on the trot showing members of the Archer clan round the Dower House.'

'But you do it so nicely,' she reminded him.

'Frankly, the sheer weight of numbers got me down.'

'That won't happen today.'

They finished their drinks then went through into the dining room, where they were shown to a table in the window. While they were looking at the menu, the waiter cleared away the third place setting. Sarah asked Ralph to order for her and he sensed that she was beginning to use her technique of subtle flattery. It made him speak harshly.

'I ought to be furious with you!'

'You were, as I recall.'

'I still haven't forgiven you, Sarah.'

'But I wrote and apologised. To you and to Lilian . . . if you showed her my letter, that is? I was hoping you'd both let me make it up to you by treating you to lunch.'

'That's not what you had in mind and you know it!'

'You didn't *have* to come here, you know,' she smiled.

He felt that he was at a disadvantage already and knew that she had the skill to exploit the fact. The entrée was served and occupied them for a few minutes.

'How are things down on the farm?'

'Don't patronise.'

'I was being serious. I've taken a real interest in farming since I visited you. Read books and everything. I suppose you'll be getting ready to harvest your spring barley.'

'And what are you hoping to harvest?'

She laughed and was pleased when the wine arrived. Ralph tasted it, nodded to the waiter, then watched him pour.

'I've been offered a job, Ralph.'

'Oh?'

'As a full-time organiser for a national charity. They want

me to stop being an amateur do-gooder and become a professional helper.'

'Are you going to take the job?'

'Probably. I've got to do something.'

It gave him a new slant on Sarah, and made him regret some of the things he had been thinking about her motives. They talked for some time about the job and he could see that she was seriously considering it, even though it would involve a lot of travelling around the country.

'When do you have to let them know?'

'Pretty soon. That's why I was keen to see you first of all. When and if I take the job, I'll be hard put to it to find time for lunches with old friends.'

'All the more reason why we should make the most of this lunch,' he argued.

He enjoyed the meal and felt glad that he had come now. Sarah was not trying to run down Lilian or to influence him in any way. What she was asking for was his advice. He told her to try the job at least, and she agreed.

'That's one problem out of the way,' she sighed.

'Have you got any more?'

'Hundreds . . . but I didn't come all this way to cry on your shoulder.'

'Feel free.'

She shook her head and told him that she would cope one way or another. He pressed her for details but she said it would spoil the lunch.

'Where are you going for your honeymoon?'

'Oh . . . uh, Venice.'

'How gorgeous! Lilian must be thrilled.'

'Yes, I think so.'

'Does she know you're here now?' asked Sarah, unexpectedly.

'No.'

The admission was involuntary and it changed their attitude towards each other at once. While she grew more confident, he began to feel thrown back on the defensive. The waiter brought the bill and he tried to pay it, but she would not hear of it. They went through into the lounge but it proved to be rather full.

'Let's go for a walk instead,' she suggested.

'Here?'

'It's not all shops and office-blocks. They must have parks or something. We could take a taxi.'

'My train goes at – '

'Plenty of time yet. I'll just get my handbag and a coat . . .'

Before he could resist, she had led him into the lift. The attendant pulled the gate across and the lift ascended noisily but smoothly. They walked along thick carpet until they came to her room.

'Don't hover about out there, Ralph. Come on in.'

'Oh . . . for a moment, then.'

'Take a seat. I might as well repair the ravages,' she said, peering into the mirror on the dressing table and reaching for her make-up.

Watching her from behind, he began to feel the old affection for her stirring again. It was this which had made him come alone today, the chance to see her one more time. On the train he had told himself that he was simply enjoying a well-earned break from Ambridge at the end of a hectic week. Now that he was with Sarah, his true motives began to assert themselves.

'Tell me about these problems of yours?' he invited, sitting on the edge of the bed.

'They'd only bore you. Why should you be interested in me?'

'You know quite well why.'

She looked at him in the mirror, then swivelled round on the seat to face him, holding out her hands towards him. He was in a quandary now, beset by guilt and apprehension yet wanting to get up and take her hands.

He found himself crossing the room to help her up from the seat. His hands ran along her shoulders, and then through her hair. Sarah was careful to make him realise that he was making the decisions.

'What about that walk?'

'Forget that.'

'There's your train.'

'I can take a later one.'

'In that case, I've got time to tell you about those problems.'

'I'd like that,' he said, leading her across to the bed.

They sat down together and he tried to kiss her, but she stopped him with a raised eyebrow.

'That's my first problem, Ralph.'

'Sarah – '

'No, I'm not trying to stop it. Not any more. You're obviously so anxious to marry *somebody,* it might just as well be her. What I want to know is . . . where will it leave me? Afterwards?'

It happened so quickly that he was not sure what made him do it. He pushed her back on the bed and began kissing her and fondling her. She kicked off her shoes and wriggled up the bed, trying to help him off with his coat. It proved to be too difficult and so he knelt up to remove his coat, looking down at her. The pause and the triumph in her smile were enough to make him change his mind and step off the bed.

'Where are you going!'

'I should take that job, if I were you,' he suggested straightening his tie. 'It might keep you out of mischief.'

'Ralph, please . . .'

This time the extended hands had no power to entice him. He had made his choice and was absolutely certain that it was the right one. Her face hardened and she got up off the bed to challenge him.

'You don't want *me,* Sarah. You just want to get back at Lilian. You want to hurt her through me.'

'Do you blame me?' she sneered.

'No, I blame myself. For letting you think you could get away with it. Goodbye.'

'I won't expect an invitation to the wedding!'

'No, I shouldn't . . . oh, thank you for the lunch, by the way.'

She turned her back on him and walked away. He let himself out, went into the corridor and hurried towards the staircase.

It was still only late afternoon when the train pulled into Hollerton Junction. Having found his car, he drove swiftly towards Ambridge, wondering why he had ever felt the urge to have a break away from it. The sight of the church spire in the distance reassured him, and he had an urge to walk through the village itself and to draw strength from it.

He parked the car near the green, waved to some people walking past, then began to stroll down towards the church. Walter Gabriel was in the garden of Honeysuckle Cottage, working away at his wood carving. When Ralph hailed him, he waved a chisel in acknowledgement.

'How's the love life, Walter?'

'Ask Mrs P.,' called out the other.

'Lilian tells me that you and Mrs Perkins are on speaking terms again.'

'Well, I has to get my constipation from somewhere. And Mrs P. has been a wonder at that kind o' thing. Molly-coddling me like I was snatched back from the jaws of death.'

'She might have something there!'

'A treasure, that's what her is. Underneath all that huff and puff and blow yer house down, she'm a treasure. The furriners has a word for her. '*Simpetigo.*'

'Sounds like a skin disease,' laughed Ralph. 'Don't you mean *simpatico*?'

'Either will do, Mr Bellamy, depending on whether you likes to be understood or scratched! Any rate, the point is this. I learned the error of my ways. From now on I'll chase after the local talent. East and West, the girls of Ambridge stays the best. You must have found that.'

Walter went back to his piece of wood, which appeared to

be some kind of animal in the making. Ralph left him to his task, and walked on down to the Village Stores. Though he had no need of anything, he went on in. Sid was stacking boxes on a shelf and listening to a cricket commentary on the radio. Polly was adding up the money in the till.

'Just caught you in time, by the look of it.'

'With minutes to spare, Mr Bellamy,' said Polly. 'What can I get you?'

He bought a packet of small cigars, and then noticed the chuckleboard. Prominently displayed were a series of post cards.

'Seaside humour,' explained Sid, crossing to the board. 'This one is from Jethro Larkin and his missus – not that the lady on the card is his missus, mind.'

'I should hope not!' said Polly. 'Sid, I'm not sure those cards should be up there.'

'It's all good clean fun, Poll Doll.'

'I don't think it does any harm,' agreed Ralph. 'This kind of thing is only a safety-valve.'

'The very word, Mr Bellamy,' thanked Sid.

Ralph paid for the cigars, slipped them into his pocket and then remembered something.

'I was sorry to hear about your father, Polly.'

'Yes,' she muttered, bowing her head.

'That's all been sorted out,' explained Sid, quickly. 'It came to a head last night and . . . well, it's all over now.'

'Good,' said Ralph, seeing that they did not wish to talk about the subject. 'Well, I suppose I ought to let you shut up shop. Just one thing. . . .'

He went back to the chuckleboard and had a last laugh at some of the items and the post cards.

'I need a safety-valve, just like everyone else,' he chuckled.

When it had first been arranged at such short notice, the party at Brookfield had not appealed to Ralph at all. The prospect of an Archer family gathering filled him with misgivings and reminded him that he had been anything but accepted by all the members of Lilian's family. Yet now that they were actually on their way to Brookfield he began to look forward to the occasion, grateful of the opportunity to commit himself to the Archers.

Since it was, in effect, a belated engagement party for them, he had expected a rather formal affair with speeches and toasts. But it turned out to be quite the reverse and he was soon blossoming in the relaxed, informal atmosphere. There had been a time when he might have felt stifled by the cosiness of it all, but now he welcomed it.

Though the younger children had been put to bed, Shula and Kenton had been allowed to stay up for the party and were making themselves useful by passing round bowls of peanuts. Michelle was serving drinks and Ralph was amused to note that Tony never strayed far away from her.

It was the first time that he had met the whole Archer family together and he was surprised that he had no sense of being an outsider. Everyone seemed to be making an effort on his behalf and he was especially grateful to find Dan so affable.

'I bet you're tickled pink about Tony,' said the old man.

'Tony?'

'Wake up, Ralph!' suggested Philip, smacking him between the shoulder blades. 'Tony. Your dairy specialist. You're pleased he's staying on, surely?'

'Look at the fella,' chuckled Dan. 'Anyone would think it's the first he's heard about it.'

'To be honest, it is,' confessed Ralph and all three burst out laughing.

'He's decided to give you another chance,' remarked Philip.

'There must be more to it than that, Phil.'

'My guess is that it's laziness that's keeping him here,' observed Dan, with a wink. 'If he goes to fresh pastures, he's got to start building up his stockpile of girlfriends all over again.'

'When is he going to get himself married?' asked Ralph.

'When they can find a shotgun big enough,' said Dan.

They laughed again at Tony's expense and watched him trying to persuade Michelle to sit beside him on the window seat. She kept pointing dramatically at the engagement ring she was wearing, but he was not to be shaken off and kept pleading his case. Ralph was delighted that he was not going to lose Tony after all, and he believed that he knew what had changed the latter's mind. Excusing himself, he went straight to the kitchen.

Peggy was alone, dabbing at her eyes with a tissue which she put away as soon as he appeared.

'I thought I saw you slip in here,' he said.

'Something in my eye. I'm ready to come back in again now, Ralph.'

'There's no rush,' he smiled. 'Mrs Archer . . .'

'Now that's one thing I won't have. Call me Peggy, please.'

'Very well. Peggy . . . I'm terribly sorry about what's happened.'

'Don't be, Ralph. It's something I've resigned myself to all along. It's a relief, in some ways. Jack will be better off in that Clinic. It's a thing that had to come sooner or later.'

'Pity it couldn't have come just a bit later.'

'Yes. He'd have loved to have stayed for the wedding. He still might get back. Who knows? Scotland isn't all that far away. And if he's well enough . . .'

Ralph could see that she knew her husband would not be well enough. They had almost certainly seen the last of Jack Archer in Ambridge.

'I just wanted to say . . . well, if it does get lonely for you at the Bull. . . .'

'With all those customers to serve?' she laughed, nervously.

'You know what I mean, Peggy. If it does, you'll always be welcome to move into the Dower House.'

She was overcome for a moment and took out the tissue from her sleeve. Then she crossed to Ralph and kissed him on the cheek.

'Come on, you two!' called Jill, head round the door. 'Everyone else has started eating. There'll be none left.'

The head disappeared and the door swung to. He offered his arm to Peggy with mock gallantry.

'May I?'

'Yes, please. I can take a lot of this sort of thing!'

Through the remainder of the party, he had little chance to speak to Lilian who was being monopolised by the ladies. On the few occasions when he got within earshot she was being questioned about the inevitable topics. Jennifer was asking her about bridesmaids' dresses, Doris was making suggestions for the hymns for the service, Jill was issuing warnings about certain photographers.

Ralph himself spent most of the time discussing his plans for the estate, and was pleased that both Dan and Philip felt able to make helpful comments. Tony joined them at one point, having given up his somewhat inhibited pursuit of Michelle.

'I daresay you've heard by now.'

'Yes, it's trickled through to me at last, Tony. But then, I'm only your employer. I'm the last to be told.'

'Sorry about that, Ralph.'

'I was only joking. But you and I must work out a better system of communications.'

'Teach the lad semaphore,' said Dan.

'His arms are never free for long enough,' argued Philip, with a grin at the others. 'They're usually wrapped around his latest in the back row of the cinema.'

'I'm entitled to have my fling!' Tony retorted. 'You all had yours, didn't you?'

'That would be telling!' said Dan. 'Besides, I fancy that Doris is listening.'

'Well, I sowed my share of wild outs, if truth be told,' confided Philip. 'I daresay that Ralph would admit the same.'

Michelle spared him the embarrassment of having to answer. At that moment, she backed into the kitchen with a tray of empty glasses and Tony hared after her. Noises from the other side of the door confirmed that it was simply not his night.

Towards midnight people began to drift away and eventually Ralph and Lilian were the only guests left. They thanked their hosts and made their way out to the car.

'Can I drive please?' asked Lilian.

'No, darling, I'll . . .' He paused, remembering. 'Yes, certainly. Here are the keys.'

'Now, that's what I call real luxury,' decided Jill. 'To be driven home by a ravishing *chauffeuse*.'

'Do you mean that you can still say words like that, Jill?' complained her husband. 'You obviously haven't had enough to drink.'

He waved his farewells and took Jill back into the house. Lilian and Ralph got into the car and sat there for a moment.

'Hello, stranger,' he said.

'Hello. Nice to see you again.' She kissed him on the lips.

'What was that for?'

'You know quite well. For talking to Mum.'

'It was the least I could do, Lilian.'

She switched on the ignition and let the engine run, making no attempt to drive the car. He wondered why she was waiting until she turned to him and smiled.

'How was Sarah?'

'Um . . . well . . . actually . . .'

'I had a feeling you'd go in the end.'

'Lilian, all that happened – '

'You don't have to explain, Ralph. You're not on trial. As long as everything was . . . cleared up.'

'It was. I can promise you that.'

'Then that's all that matters,' she said putting the car into first gear and releasing the brake.

'How did you guess?'

'Easy. I'm learning to know you.'

'Then I'll have to watch myself,' he said. 'I love you, Lilian.'

'So you should. Come on, I'll take you home.'

He told her how much he had enjoyed the party and how friendly everyone had been to him. He was in the middle of recounting what he had seen of Tony's misadventures with Michelle when he noticed where they were.

'I thought you were taking me home?'

'I am.'

She swung on the steering-wheel and went down the long drive, the headlights picking out the main features of the house. The car squeaked to a halt in front of the main entrance and she switched off the ignition.

'You've got the keys, haven't you?'

'Well, yes . . .'

'And there's no one else here?'

'Not as far as I know.'

They got out of the car, locked it and went into the Dower House together.

CHAPTER TWENTY

SUNSHINE GILDED the Church of St Stephen on the day of the wedding and made it a perfect setting for the occasion. By the time the first guests had begun to arrive, a small but vocal crowd of well-wishers had gathered at the lych-gate. Polly and her mother joined the crowd in time to see Dan and Doris Archer getting out of a large black sedan. There was a flurry of admiring comment all round, which Dan acknowledged with a cheerful wave of his topper.

Polly was struck once again by what a fine couple they made. Dan looked really distinguished in his grey morning suit, but it was Doris's outfit which impressed her most. She was wearing a smart ginger brown suit, with matching dark-brown hat, gloves, handbag and shoes. An orange bow at the neck added the final touch, and Polly could not help wondering if she would ever look as fine when she reached that age.

'I loved her corsage,' said Mrs Mead, as the couple went up the path towards the church.

'I think they look marvellous, Mum. Both of them.'

'Where's the groom, then? He hasn't come yet.'

'There's no rush. He'll be here on time. Can you imagine someone like Mr Bellamy being late?'

'No. He knows how to do things proper.'

'And so does the Archer family. Everything will go off like clockwork. There won't be a single hitch.'

Downing a glass of scotch at Ambridge Court, Ralph would not have been able to endorse Polly's remarks. A major hitch had already developed and thrown him into a frenzied last-minute panic. He had awoken that morning to learn that he was without a best man for the ceremony. Owing to engine trouble, the plane bringing his nephew home for the wedding had been forced to land at an airport in southern France. There was no way that his nephew could arrive in time.

After a frantic round of telephone calls, Ralph had finally solved the problem. Jack Woolley had agreed to deputise, and Ralph was leaning on him heavily.

'Are you sure I look all right, Jack?'

'Almost as good as I do, so stop worrying.'

'I'm having trouble with this tie . . .'

'Leave it to me,' said the other, adjusting it. 'There. Spot on.'

'I can't thank you enough for stepping into the breach.'

'Delighted. Must have been a bit of a job for you. Finding someone in Ambridge who wasn't an Archer!'

Ralph poured them both another drink, then paced the room. Now that the day had actually come, he was feeling tense and nervous. Jack Woolley's sense of humour was no help.

'I wonder what Sarah is thinking right now!'

'For God's sake, Jack!'

'Oh, yes . . . sorry. . . . Water under the whatsit and all that . . .'

The sound of the car drawing up outside prompted both of them to drain their drinks. Ralph made a final dash to the mirror to check his tie, and when he turned round his best man was holding the door open for him.

'Cheer up, Ralph. It's a marriage, not a hanging ceremony.'

If Ralph was worrying about his own appearance, Lilian was more concerned with the general appearance of the wedding group. She was waiting at the cottage with Tony, fearing that she had made a grave mistake. With her father unable to attend, she had had to find someone else to give her away in church, and her own choice had been her grandfather. But her mother's preference for Tony had made her think again and she had come to see that not only would the responsibility do him good, but that she really wanted her brother.

While she had no qualms about his ability or his readiness, she now worried that it would look rather incongruous if she were given away by someone who was younger than herself and very much younger than the groom.

'I feel like Fred Astaire,' said Tony, still not used to the top hat and tails.

'As long as you don't start tap-dancing down the aisle.'

'It'll take all my strength to stay upright.'

'Nervous?'

'As the proverbial kitten.'

'The car will be here any minute.'

'Then it's too late, isn't it?' he asked, coming up to her.

'Mm?'

'I know what's on your mind, love. Me taking on Dad's job. Ralph doesn't mind me being a shade younger than him – so why should you?'

Lilian was cheered by the remark and shook off her doubts. She walked impatiently around the room, sniffing her bouquet of cream roses.

'I bet the cows would fall about if I turned up to milking in this clobber,' laughed Tony. 'By the way, I mean to say . . . I think you look smashing.'

'Thank you, Tony.'

'What colour do you call that?'

'Café-au-lait.'

'I could do with a cup of that right now,' he confessed. 'Haven't *you* got butterflies as well?

'Not any more.'

'D'you know, I reckon they've blooming well forgotten us!' he exclaimed, crossing to peer out of the window.

Tony looked uncannily like his father at that moment, and,

as she watched him, Lilian knew that she had been right to choose him.

Polly was the first to see the car rounding the bend, and she raised the alarm. There was great anticipatory delight among the crowd, and a cheer went up as the car door opened and Tony helped his sister out. Polly thought that the wedding dress was quite breathtaking and was particularly impressed with the deep lace collar and cuffs. Tony proudly offered his arm to his sister, and escorted her through the lych-gate to where Jennifer, the Matron of Honour, was waiting with the two bridesmaids.

As the little group moved up the path in procession, Polly and her mother followed at a distance. There was a pause while some photographs were taken and then, after the bride had been led in, they were able to slip into the church themselves.

To the traditional organ music, the bride was still making her way down the aisle and there was an audible murmur of welcome from the congregation. Seeing that the majority of guests were on the left-hand side of the nave, Polly guided her mother into a pew on the bridegroom's side. From this position, with so few heads between her and the altar, Polly had an excellent view of the service.

David Latimer was standing at the foot of the altar steps to greet the procession with a warm smile. Ralph and Jack Woolley took up their positions alongside Lilian and Tony, and the marriage service began.

'Dearly beloved, we are gathered together here in the sight of God, and in the face of this congregation, to join together this Man and this Woman in holy Matrimony; which is an honourable estate . . .'

While her mother followed the words carefully in the Prayer Book, Polly tried to imagine what was going through Lilian's mind. She was bound to be remembering her first husband at this moment, and to be suffering some pangs of regret. She was certain to be sad that her father was too ill to be at her wedding. But she was too radiantly happy to be disturbed by such thoughts for long. Polly had seen Lilian's face as she had stepped out of the car, and sensed the sheer joy which the bride was feeling. Whatever doubts Lilian had once had, Polly knew that they had now vanished.

It seemed like no time at all before the vows were being exchanged and the voices of both bride and bridegroom were heard, loud and firm. Guests craned their necks as the best man fumbled in his pocket for the ring and handed it over. Ralph repeated the words after the vicar.

'With this Ring I thee wed, with my body I thee worship, and with all my worldly goods, I thee endow: In the Name of the Father, and of the Son, and of the Holy Ghost. Amen.'

At this point, Polly noticed a few handkerchiefs being taken out in the pews on the other side of the church. Peggy Archer was visibly affected and Dan put a hand on her arm. Polly knew that it must be a wonderful moment for Lilian's mother to see her daughter married again.

When the vicar led the way towards the vestry for the signing of the register, there was a general sigh of relaxation. The organ played quietly, the guests whispered or nodded, and there was an air of contentment all round. Polly turned to find that her mother had tears in her eyes, and she began to understand why she had followed the words of the service so closely.

Philip Archer announced the return of the bride and bridegroom by striking up the chords of the Wedding March on the organ. Polly felt a real thrill as she saw them heading the procession up the aisle. Lilian was so poised and beautiful, Ralph was so elegant and dignified, and both of them were so unashamedly happy. Polly believed, as she had always done, that they were ideally suited.

Ralph had no chance to reflect on such things as he and Lilian stepped out through the main door of the church and into the afternoon sun. During the whole ceremony, he had been in a pleasant daze and even now he was not really aware of what was going on. He remembered being told to smile and move further left and then kiss the bride. He recalled snatches of remarks made as the entire wedding party lined up for the photographs. And he was conscious of leading Lilian towards the waiting car and ducking as Polly and Mrs Mead threw showers of confetti over them.

When he came out of his daze, they were sitting at the head of the table in the Mayfair Suite at Grey Gables and Jack Woolley was discharging one of his functions as best man by reading through a pile of cards and greetings telegrams.

'Best wishes to you both. You deserve each other. Sarah,' read Jack, catching his eye.

Lilian's hand squeezed Ralph's under the table and he smiled his thanks for the understanding which they now shared. Wherever he looked, he was met by grins of congratulation and uplifted glasses, and he sensed that at last he had been fully accepted by the Archer family.

Putting down the telegram from Stephen Wiley, the best man picked up the next, clearly revelling in his role.

'Come back – all is forgiven. Nelson.'

As the laughter echoed, it was Ralph's turn to squeeze Lilian's hand.

Unlike Ralph, Lilian could remember every single detail of the marriage service and of the scenes outside the church immediately afterwards. She had not dreamed she could be so completely happy, and she found the day full of things to cherish and look back on.

Lilian knew that she would never forget the moment when Ralph actually put the ring on her finger, or the joy she had seen in her mother's eyes, or the pride that Tony had shown. She would always remember the kind words, and the sincere good wishes, and the carved horse from Walter Gabriel, and the cutting of the cake, and the telephone call from her father, and the photographs on the lawn, and the way that her whole family, from the oldest down to the youngest, had rallied around her and shared her delight in the day.

But most of all, she would remember the moment when

Ralph had stood up at the reception to make his speech on their behalf and had begun with the words. 'My wife and I . . .'

Lilian Bellamy *was* his wife, she wanted to be his wife, and she knew that she would always be his wife.